T0316469

THE BIG BOOK
OF SUBMISSION

THE BIG BOOK
OF SUBMISSION

69 KINKY TALES

EDITED BY
RACHEL KRAMER BUSSEL

Published in the United States by Cleis Press, Inc., 2246 Sixth Street, Berkeley, California 94710.

Printed in the United States.
Cover design: Scott Idleman/Blink
Cover photograph: Fuse/Getty Images
Text design: Frank Wiedemann

First Edition.
10 9 8 7 6 5 4 3 2 1

Trade paper ISBN: 978-1-62778-037-7
E-book ISBN: 978-1-62778-054-4

Contents

INTRODUCTION: THE MANY MEANINGS OF SUBMISSION

S ubmission means so many different things to different people, which is why I'm delighted to present to you sixty-nine varieties of serving, spanking, obeying, taunting, teasing, worshipping and more. These very short stories offer a glimpse into the mindset of those who live to serve, who desire to be bound or spanked or told what to do—or perhaps all three. They get off on giving themselves over to the men and women who control them, whether in the bedroom or the world beyond.

When the narrator of Corrine Arundo's "Unanchored" is ordered to masturbate, the "submissive vixen" shares some of the magic of the command: "I love the words, like sharp pokes into my cerebral cortex, tricking me into forgetting everything else but this moment." In many of these stories, a pet phrase or command is enough to trigger the submissive's desire.

What many of these submissives want is to be seen, acknowledged, known and valued precisely for their eagerness to give every part of themselves over to another person. "I want to never be able to hide from you," Joy Faolán writes in "I Want to Feel You," which perfectly encapsulates the way the tops in these stories exhibit their mastery from the inside out.

You'll find so much here, from naughty professors to sadistic former students to sex clubs, art galleries, photo shoots and more. Wherever the setting, the submission exhibited in these stories runs deep, far below the surface of the recipients' tender skin, far louder than their cries of pleasure (and pain). Whether you read one story a day or devour them all at once, I hope these quick and dirty stories turn you on to new authors and new naughty possibilities.

Rachel Kramer Bussel

I WANT TO FEEL YOU

Joy Faolán

I *want to feel you.*

Not just physically. I don't just want to feel your cock inside my cunt or your hand in my hair or your breath hot upon the shell of my ear as you whisper to me. I do want those things, but I want *more* than those things. What I want is deeper and bigger than us both.

I want to feel your power from across the room. I want to know, when I feel your eyes digging into the back of my head and your gaze chasing me through the crowds and finding me despite my attempts to hide from you, that I've become the object of your desire. I do not want to feel that I am someone you have to convince of something. I don't want you to "hit" on me. I don't want you to walk up to me and charm me or tell me jokes or offer to buy me a drink. It's not that I don't enjoy that sort of behavior. I take it as a compliment when men do this to me, but you and I both know that there is something much better, much more *powerful,* to be had. I want you to pursue me. I want you to hunt me down and make me your own. I want to know that you are convinced that you own me long before I even decide if I *want* you. I want to be your *prey.*

I want to feel you.

I want to know, as I walk out of the party that night, that your eyes are following me to my car. I want to feel uneasy about it. I want to have doubts and fears, but I want the *knowledge,* deep inside of me, that I will belong to you, eventually, because you want me to. Because you've decided. Out of all the other things in that room, I want to be the thing that you've chosen to be yours.

It won't be a courtship. I don't want you to *ask* me on a date. I want you to *tell* me where I'll meet you, when, and how I will be dressed. I want to feel you inside my head. I want to be confused that you know *so much about me* when I've told you nothing. I don't want to understand that it's because you've been watching me for months. I don't want to know that it's because you made up your mind that I was yours long before I knew you even existed. Not yet.

I want to feel you.

I want to feel you taking me over, your tendrils curling through my soul and wrapping themselves around every intimate fiber of my being. I want you to know everything about me. I want you to study my face as we sit in silence. I want you to watch in amusement as I squirm in my chair, uncomfortable in the quiet and wanting nothing more than for you to say something. I want you to watch my mannerisms when I am nervous, happy, fearful, sad, anxious and every other emotion. I want to never be able to hide from you.

I want you to systematically hunt me down, emotionally and mentally, and trap me in your cage. I want you to own me in ways that I will never fully understand. And I want it to be because *you* decided that you own me. I want it to be because you wanted me so much that it did not matter whether or not I wanted you. I want to be your *obsession*.

I want to feel you.

NAUGHTY PROF

Louisa Bacio

You say I've been a "bad girl" and ask if I want to be punished. If only you knew how naughty I've been.

Left my dirty clothes on the floor, forgot to change the empty paper-towel roll and smart-mouthed you. On purpose.

I can take what you can give me, and more. You know my limits, and how to stretch them, as you stretch me—wide.

We met in college, like many couples. Except you were the returning student, and I the professor. Every time you came to my office hours, you called me "prof," with a slight turn-up of your lip and a semi-mocking tone. Should I have known then how quickly you'd get me to lift my skirt, bend over the desk and let you spank me?

On the first day of the fall semester, you sat in the last row, chair tilted back, leaning against the wall, arms crossed over your chest. While the rest of the students were the expected age, late teens to early twenties, at twenty-nine, you were only a few years younger than me. Among the lanky boys in the class, you stood out as a man, with broad shoulders and a self-confidence that unnerved me.

I tried to ignore the stare of your blue eyes, the curl of blond hair that refused to stay off your forehead. How I wanted to twist it. And each week, you moved one row closer, until midterms, which brought you to the front. As I lectured, each time I passed, the scent of your cologne filled my senses.

I'd never had a teacher-student relationship. It was a barrier I wouldn't break. On the day of the final, you borrowed my textbook. One by one, everyone finished, turned in their tests and left, until only you and I remained in the room. You stood, stretching your arms upward, your blue T-shirt lifting to expose a taut belly covered with a soft curling of hair. I tried to look away—to look occupied with something else—but you caught me, and smiled. By your saunter to the front, I could see you knew your power.

Already, you controlled me. I just didn't know it yet. I hadn't surrendered my will.

As you handed over the book, your fingers grazed mine. "You know, Ms. Yvette, I really enjoyed your class. It's a shame I won't *have* you again. I'm graduating." Your voice lifted at "have," offering a double meaning.

Heat flushed up my chest, and my cheeks. "Thank you, Scott. It's been my pleasure."

"Not yet."

The moment you walked out the door, I lifted the book to my face and inhaled your alluring scent. You'd left a mark on my property. It wouldn't be the last.

I flipped through the pages, stopping on a blue Post-It note stuck on *titillating*.

Friday, 7 p.m. Coffee shop on Grand. Wear your black skirt, nothing underneath.

My hands shook. Could I? Would I? The message didn't ask. It demanded.

Anticipation tingled through my sex, and I grew wet. I've never dated someone so forward. Although I'd harbored fantasies of submission and giving up control, no one had ever followed through. I'd hinted with my last boyfriend, but he never took the bait. Did something in me call out to you?

The days passed slowly, until Friday evening finally arrived. I dressed, sliding up the skirt, putting on my panties, removing them, then putting them on again. It wasn't even a date, was it? I didn't plan on sleeping with you on our first date. How would you know if I wore them or not? I stuffed a pair in my purse, and right before getting out of the car, slipped them back on.

You stood outside the restaurant, in the shadows, leaning against the wall. "Hey prof, over here." I moved toward you, and the minute I was within reach, you slid your hand over my ass, pulling me against the hard ridge of your cock. Your mouth pressed against mine, taking what you wanted. If anyone had seen us, they'd have pegged us for longtime lovers.

Trailing small bites along my neck and chin until reaching my ear, you said, "Such a naughty girl, not listening to me." To make sure I knew what you meant, you snapped the elastic of my underwear on the curve of my ass. "Now I'll have to punish you so you listen next time."

A warm heat rushed between my thighs. No matter how much I tried to fool myself, I became fully aware of your intentions. You guided me toward the back alley, a hand on my elbow. Darkness blanketed my sight. When we reached the farthest depths, you pushed me against the brick wall.

"Hands up high, and spread your legs wide. I want your ass out." You punctuated each order with a slap to my inner thighs, forcing them apart. Your fingers flicked over my core, feeling the slickness. "I'm not going to do anything you don't want. Do you agree to this?"

My voice stuck in my throat. My mind told me to say no and get the hell out of here. There was still time to stop whatever was about to happen. But I didn't want that.

"Yes."

Without another comment, you reached under my skirt, gripped both sides of my panties and ripped them off. "In the future, you will listen to what I say, correct?"

"Yes."

"Good. Now for your lesson." You stuffed my own panties in my mouth to silence my screams, and folded my skirt up, tucking it into my waistband and leaving me exposed. The unfamiliar texture on my tongue distracted me, until the first smack hit my bare ass. Instinctively, my hips pivoted forward, and you held me steady.

You continued to spank me barehanded. One cheek, and then the other, until my flesh burned and you moved lower to the curve of my ass and upper thighs. Tears spilled down my face as I lost count.

"Hush," you said, your fingers soothing over the soreness. You pushed your fingers into my aching sex and rubbed my clit with your thumb. I moaned against the gag, and pushed my ass against you. "You took it like such a good girl, and now you get your reward."

I heard the sound of a zipper going down, then the foil of a condom wrapper. Your thick, hard cock nudged against my pussy, and you dove into me, to the hilt. My knees rubbed against the wall from the force, and I steadied myself for the fucking I was about to receive. One hand slipped under my bra to tweak my straining nipple, while the other massaged my clit. Already on edge, I shattered, my body convulsing in climax. You pumped into me until you came, biting me on the shoulder.

"You're mine now."

A week later, I moved into your condo.

* * *

Here we are three years later, and I'm still not trained. As you open the front door, you take a look around. Your gaze lands on me lying on the couch, watching cartoons, my feet propped on the armrest.

"Have you been a good girl?"

"No."

Oh, baby.

STRIP

Medea Mor

S trip."

The command came suddenly, his voice waking her from her reverie.

They were in his car, on their way home from a family get-together. They'd just entered the snowy lane that served as a back entrance to their sleepy town. They'd be home in less than ten minutes.

"Excuse me, Sir?" she asked, not sure whether she'd heard him correctly.

"Strip," he repeated.

She obeyed, as she always did when he gave her that order. A titillating bolt of anticipation shot through her as she unfastened her seat belt, but taking off her long winter coat in the narrow passenger seat proved to be a harder task than she'd anticipated. She nearly hit Sir in the head as she pulled her right arm from her sleeve, causing him to swerve. No sooner had she succeeded in peeling off the coat than the next challenge presented itself in the form of her sexy black minidress. She heard him chuckle beside her as she struggled with the long zipper and clumsily wiggled from side to side to wrench the tight garment down over her hips. She was glad he'd told her not to wear any underwear that day; two items fewer to struggle out of made her assignment just a little less cumbersome.

"The boots, too, Sir?" she asked a little tentatively when she had folded her coat and dress and put them on the backseat.

He shook his head. "Leave the boots on, girl." He continued driving, a mysterious smile playing on his lips.

She sank back into her seat, wondering what he had in mind for her. Was he going to let her sit naked next to him to display her to the world, showing off his devoted toy in all her glory? Or was he going to pull over to the side of the road, slide his seat backward and fuck her while she rode him, the snow-laden trees the only witnesses to her moans and his groping hands? Or was he finally going to make good on his promise to fuck her over the hood of his car? That would be a chilly experience, she suspected, what with the car having been outside in midwinter temperatures for hours. However, she trusted Sir implicitly, and if having her on the hood of his car was what he wanted, she'd comply. What was more, she'd probably enjoy it. She couldn't deny that the thought of being taken on his car sent a small thrill through her, raising goose bumps on the back of her neck. When she looked down, she could see her nipples poke forward, hardening at the thought of his hands on her body and the cold bite of the steel below her.

They drove in silence for two more miles before he suddenly pulled over to the side of the road. "Out," he commanded.

She stared at him, dumbfounded. "Out, Sir?"

"You heard me, girl. Get out of the car." To her dismay, he showed no intention of getting out himself. His seat belt remained resolutely fastened and the engine kept running.

"But…but it's at least five miles to our home, Sir," she protested. "And it's freezing." *And I'll probably catch pneumonia and die, all because of this whim of yours. That is, if I don't die of embarrassment first.*

He shot her his sternest look. "I believe I gave you an order, girl."

That humbled her. "Yes, Sir," she mumbled contritely. The last thing she saw before she turned away to open her door was his smile, an odd mixture of triumph, curiosity and anticipation.

She got out of the car, a little nervous but strangely turned on by the thrill of not knowing what was in store for her. From the corner of her eye, she saw Sir give her an encouraging smile as she slammed the door shut behind her. Then, to her acute horror, he drove off—

slowly, very slowly, but unmistakably increasing the distance between himself and herself.

She stood rooted to her spot for a second, too petrified to move. As the cold wind howled around her and snowflakes melted on her breasts, she followed the car with her eyes, scarcely able to believe that he'd leave her like this in the middle of winter. She breathed a sigh of relief when the car came to a halt about one hundred feet down the road.

She stepped forward, hearing the molten snow splash under the high heels of her boots. The road was slippery, and she had to watch her step in order to avoid slipping.

When she was nearly within touching distance of the car, she caught Sir's eye in the rearview mirror. He was smiling at her, teasing her, challenging her. She smiled back, not really understanding the nature of the challenge, but determined to rise to it, anyway.

He revved the engine. Slowly, ever so slowly, the car pulled away from her again, leaving her to the company of the wind and the snowflakes.

She understood the challenge then. He was watching her in his rearview mirror, avidly following her every move, her every facial expression. She'd better give him a good show.

Straightening herself and pulling her shoulders backward, she took a deep breath, allowing the crisp winter air to pervade her lungs. As she began to walk, she relished the cold wind lashing her skin and making it tingle. Each time a snowdrop alighted on her arms, she felt a thrill she had not experienced since childhood—a joy once cherished but forgotten, a throwback to a time when she'd been innocent, before she'd met *him*.

Suddenly, she began to enjoy the challenge. As she put one foot in front of the other, exulting in her nudity, the cold and the opportunity to show off for Sir, she felt her hips sway from side to side, and the sexiness of the move sent a pulse of pleasure coursing through her, resonating deep in her pussy.

He'd pull away from her again when she reached the car. She knew it in her bones, but the thought didn't faze her, because at some point he'd stop and reward her for putting on such a good show. She knew *that* in her bones, as well, and the thought made her pussy pulse with excitement.

Focusing her eyes on the tiny rearview mirror she could see in the distance, she gave him her most seductive smile. Then she took another step forward, and another, swaying her hips in a way he'd once told her drove him wild.

Onward, ever onward. Toward him and toward her reward.

TRAINING MY DOM

Tilly Hunter

He started it. We'd flirted by text for weeks. Filthy texts: *I want to feel your hard cock deep in my throat, I'm going to lick your pussy until you scream...*

Tell me where your imagination's been today, I wrote during a quiet moment at work.

I thought about some handcuffs, came the reply. His mind was obviously not on office business either.

I asked for clarification: *For you or for me?*

I was thinking of using them on you xx.

Halle-fucking-lujah.

I'd wondered how to suggest that he might like to tie my wrists to the bedposts. He'd shown promise, pinning me down at the elbows with his arms and holding my hands. He was strong. We'd messed about, me trying to escape his grip, glad I couldn't, breathless by the time he pushed my legs apart with his own and shoved his cock inside me. But actual bondage...I didn't want to send him running for the hills. We had a definite spark, obvious from the moment mutual friends introduced us, and I really thought we could have a future together. He'd even mastered how I like my tea. Strong and sweet.

But I couldn't go on letting him think vanilla sex was enough. He had the potential to give me what I needed, but I agonized over how to coax it out of him. Jeez, the man didn't even watch porn on his laptop, let alone the sites I was drawn to late at night. He thought vanilla was just a flavor of ice cream.

I think that's a very good idea, I replied. Later, over a glass of wine, I confessed, "Actually, Sam, I've been wondering how to ask you to tie me up. I love it when you hold me down and fuck me hard."

He hadn't thought through the implications of one pair of handcuffs, the fact that with my arms locked in metal behind me it would be difficult for me to lie on my back for sex. And he seemed uncomfortable with the idea of making me do anything. Even after he cuffed me and I got to my suddenly weak knees and tongued his cock into my mouth, instead of grabbing a fistful of hair and fucking my face, he helped me to my feet, sat me on the edge of the bed and licked my pussy. He finally relocked the cuffs at the front and used a scarf to tie them to the top of the bed, then fucked me into mindless incoherence. It was a start.

After the cuffs, we bought a gag. And I showed him

the blindfold I owned. The ropes. The nipple clamps. All this stuff I was familiar with. But not Sam. Sam didn't know that if you're gagged facedown, drool is going to pour out of you onto whatever is beneath—his pillow, the carpet, bathroom tiles. Sam didn't know that the shape of my nose meant I always had a sliver of vision under the bottom of the blindfold, unless he tied something over the top to press my eyes closed. And Sam didn't know that the initial bite of the clamps was just the start. That eventually the nipples would numb only for fresh pain to flood in with the returning blood on their removal.

These things I taught him. Slave training in reverse.

Now, we'd booked a dirty weekend in a cozy cabin, miles from civilization, for our first anniversary. Sam really came into his own as a dom. And yet he was still Sam. Tender, considerate and far more romantic than me. I hadn't even noted the date we'd first met, but a couple of months ago he'd asked, "Would you like to go away for our anniversary?"

"Sure. When is that exactly?"

So there we were, isolated in the middle of nowhere. Where no one could hear me scream, as he put it. I was standing naked on a hard slate floor beneath the mezzanine bedroom, arms high up my back in a box tie, rope wrapping them tight against my torso. More rope strung up from there to the bars of the balcony above, pulling me onto my toes. Ball gag, silk blindfold and silver bar nipple clamps screwed tight—and then screwed some more.

I'd taught him to let me squirm before moving in for the action. That night, he left me until I was a whimpering, drooling mess, then he swung me to face the wall and spanked me. He'd perfected a ruthless, swatting action. He aimed right for the most tender spot he knew—not the meat of my butt but to the side, near my hip. I danced for him, hopping from one foot to the other, squealing around the gag, until I thought I could bear no more. I swung myself back, pressing my ass into the cool wood paneling for protection. He had other ideas. He tugged on my nipple clamps until I winced. Until I danced away and exposed my ass again.

It turned into a game. I heard him chuckle about it. I'd turn my front to him and he'd abuse my nipples. I'd turn my back to him and he'd beat my ass. I was screaming, "No, no, no," through the gag, but never once wanted to use the safe signal, a decisive shake of the head accompanied by three low grunts. He left me no time to analyze, no willpower to resist. When he reached between my legs and rubbed my clit, I came in seconds.

He half-carried me to bed and held me while I fell asleep. The next day we walked in the woods, hand in hand. Lunch in a country café followed by tea and cake. Sensible footwear and shower-resistant fabrics. Admiring a view, enjoying a moment of sunshine between clouds. Simple pleasures. Normal holiday activities. Damp throbbing in my cunt the whole time, kept frustratingly strong by his gentle hand on my ass, his tongue darting between my lips, his strong chest pressed against my tender nipples through clothing. Normal couple activities.

"I've got an anniversary present for you," he told me as we arrived back at the cabin. It was beautifully wrapped in burgundy paper with gold bows. He was thoughtful in everything. I opened it carefully, not ripping the paper. A collar. An inch-wide leather collar with a traditional buckle. I idly wondered if my trousers' shower resistance worked from the inside. Otherwise I'd be sitting in a puddle.

"Thank you," I murmured. I looked him in the eye and said it louder. "Thank you."

"From now on, when we play, I will put this on you. When we're finished, I will take it off. You do not touch it. Understand?"

"Yes." Oh yes.

"If you want to play, you may ask to wear it. But you must get to your knees, place your hands behind your back and bow your head before saying the words: 'Please, Sir, may I wear my collar?' Understand?"

"Yes." Oh yes. Sam buckled it around my neck and I wore it with pure indulgent joy for the rest of the weekend and the journey home.

DEAR SIR

Kay Jaybee

*D*ear Slut,

    As you were not permitted to speak, your task today is to write a detailed account of how yesterday's events made you feel.

    Sir.

Dear Sir,

    Forgive me Sir, but this was the first time one of your fantasies frightened me.

    It wasn't that it would hurt, or that I'd feel small or neglected. I have faced your ropes, clamps and whips. You've kept me tied in a cupboard, spanked me until my flesh blooms from pink to scarlet, bound and gagged me before playing with my helpless body for hours, and sent me shopping wearing only a short coat, leaving me fearful that I'll accidentally flash my butt or pussy to the world. These humiliations I don't fear.

I confess, Sir, I'm often anxious in the fulfillment of your fantasies; my palms prickle, my pulse races but anticipation makes my clit burn. As I obey you, my thighs become slick with need, and sometimes, Sir, I fear my breasts will swell so much with desire for you that they'll burst from my bra.

Afterward, Sir, when I've done what you've demanded, my sense of achievement is huge. Especially when I'm rewarded with a climax for a task well done. A task completed for you. To make you happy, Sir.

If I haven't performed to your standards, then my palms sweat. My body trembles, and my heart rate triples as, naked and trembling, I excitedly wait to see what I'll have to do to make amends for disappointing you.

This time though…this time I was afraid in a very different way. I couldn't stop thinking this was your way of replacing me. That after seven years, you'd become bored with my service. I've been expecting dismissal since my fortieth birthday, Sir. Every day I think it will be the day you swap me in for a younger model, with less marks of life upon her fresher flesh.

Yesterday the shine in your hazel eyes was as deep as I've ever seen, as you took me by the wrists, pushed me to my knees and instructed me to listen as I sucked your cock. An opportunity had arisen for us to live out one of your long-held fantasies.

I'm always grateful to be allowed to take your length within my mouth, Sir, but as I listened yesterday, goose pimples dotted my arms, and it took more effort than I've ever known not to react negatively to your plan. I could tell by the speed with which you came between my lips that you were more excited by this than your low steady voice was letting on.

You've shared me before. Invited men here, and instructed me to do their bidding as you looked on, your pride in my obedience as intoxicating to me as any of their touches. There have been women here, too. You have carefully placed advertisements for females who have always wanted to be with a woman, but have never dared, have brought strangers to our home to use me in whatever way they want. I love observing you, Sir, as you become voyeur, your strong hand wrapped around your cock, wanking in time to these willing amateurs' laps at my clit.

Yesterday was different. I wonder as I write for you, Sir, if perhaps you saw the uncertain fear in my eyes as I obeyed you. I hope not. Truly, Sir, it never occurred to me not to obey.

We were to visit a younger woman. Much younger. A twenty-year-old. She, you informed me, had let you know in no uncertain terms that she wanted you. You'd initially informed her that you were spoken for, but she hadn't given up. In the end you bluntly told her there was only one circumstance in which she could see you fuck. A circumstance she agreed to.

You gave me one hour to shower and dress in my best underwear, black hold-up stockings, miniskirt, and a black vest top. Then I was to slip on a sweater and boots and wait for you in the car. I was to say nothing. Nothing at all.

I felt sick as you drove, your cock visibly hard beneath the denim of your jeans, your red shirt crumpled, your short hair spiked up, the stubble around your chin making you look every bit as attractive as when I first knelt before you.

Young and mature. That's what you wanted. You would fuck us both at the same time. You would enjoy observing her young skin against mine. Sir, never have I felt so frightened. How could I compete with a woman half my age? I was so conscious of the gray within my hair, the wrinkles that highlight my eyes. Sir, I was convinced I'd enter her home as your Slut, but leave as nothing.

You kissed me as we stood on her doorstep, before placing a finger on my lips. Despite my unease, I felt the frisson of power you engender flow through every fiber of my being, hardening my nipples as it shot on a course that aimed between my legs with ultimate certainty.

The front door opened. She looked at you, Sir, and then at me. Her eyes gave little away except that she was nervous. I hadn't expected that. It was her home, yet you pulled me up the stairs into her flat, leaving her to trail behind us. The way you looked at me, Sir, it was as if your blazing eyes were telling me you'd never wanted me more.

You stripped me faster than ever before. I thought my blood would burst from my veins it was pumping so fast. My competitor's eyes widened as you told her to strip at the same time as you did.

Once naked, oh Sir, it was not her you fell on, but me! Your lips met mine, and your cock buffered against the slight pot of my belly. It was so hard not to make a sound. I remained mute though. This girl wasn't going to take you from me because I'd failed.

Twisting me to look at her, I saw how huge her tits were, how rounded her belly was, and I was desperate for you to let me fall upon her pliant flesh. Thank you, Sir! For you pushed me down, burying my face between her luscious breasts, letting me squeeze and flick her nipples, as you slipped on a condom and slid inside me.

Pushing a finger into her glistening channel, you took us together, your eyes never leaving the line of contrast where our flesh met. Mine light and fit from regular sex, hers softer, pale, plentiful, and deliciously yielding. I could have become lost in her, but only because you were there, Sir, only because you wished it.

It was your eyes that took away my fear, Sir. When you told me to put my finger inside her while you played with her tits, and she filled my palm with juice, yelling out her joy, I knew that this truly was one of your fantasies. This was not about replacing me.

I hope this account pleases you, Sir.
Slut.

PUT YOUR HANDS UP

Sommer Marsden

It's all through the party that I wait. I love the company, our friends and family over to see our new home, but under it all runs a thread of distraction. A steady pounding beat of arousal that catches me in my throat, my chest, between my legs.

He's wearing his pocket watch. The round watch is in the small pocket of his vest, the shiny chain clearly visible. Everyone is commenting on how suave he looks. Garrett smiles and blows it off with a joke. But I can look at that chain and hear him in my head: *Put your hands up…*

I flutter around like a coked-up butterfly, briefly forgetting what's going to happen to talk to someone I love or someone I haven't seen in ages. But then he walks in and I see that chain and my cunt flexes wetly and my mind goes a little fuzzy. His hazel eyes find me, and he grins that grin that turns me to nothing but liquid and hope.

It's already eleven at night and I wonder if these people will ever, ever leave.

Finally, thankfully, they do. When the door snicks shut, Garrett turns to me. "You got yourself pretty wound up about that party."

"I always do," I admit. My voice is just little puffs of air.

"You know I don't like that. You should have more faith in yourself as a hostess."

I look at my feet. I really had worked myself up into a froth. I'd snapped at him and I panicked and at one point even cried that we would not have enough food or booze or guests.

I'd been a mess.

He looks at the watch as if regarding the time. He's not. "Go upstairs, Izzy."

I turn on my heels, my body thrumming with antici-pation. Anticipation of pain. Of pleasure. Of peace. Garrett will take me all the way up so that I can come all the way down.

When I reach the top of the stairs he yells, "Get ready for me."

I don't have to ask. I know exactly what to do.

I take my dress off delicately, then drape it over the back of the armchair by the bed. I roll my hose down, careful to remove my panties and my bra and fold them neatly. Then I sit on the end of the bed with my knees pressed together to wait for him.

He takes his time coming up the steps. Every time his foot strikes the carpet I grow more restless inside, more desperate.

When he enters the room, I stand. My feet are planted dead center on the throw rug. It looks like a big black-and-gray bull's-eye. I curl my toes to the nap and try to remember to breathe. He smiles at me perfunctorily as he walks past me. I hear the whisk of his belt coming out of the loops. His clothing whispers conspiratorially as he takes it off. Then there is a sudden crack of sound and I jump.

The crop is black and blue. Garrett jokes that it's the same colors as the hues it imparts.

"How are you, Izzy?"

Vibrating…

"I'm better."

"Better now that you're alone with me?"

"God, yes," I say, forgetting myself. I blush like we're new lovers. He smiles, running the crop along the back of my thigh so a slow tremble begins at my knees and seems to roll through me like a wave.

"Good. I'm glad. Now let's say we work out all that angst."

The pocket watch is gone, but I know what time it is. I nod and try not to brace myself. It's better if you don't.

"Put your hands up," he says. I see that his cock is hard just saying it. This is a matter of will—my will and his.

I put my hands up like I'm under arrest.

He strives to make me break. I strive to persevere. In the end, everyone wins. I like my pleasure with a pain appetizer. Garrett likes to watch my face as I struggle and either surrender or succeed. I am rewarded when I win, and rewarded when I lose.

The crop slides up the back of my thigh, whisks pleasantly along my bottom, drags lazily along my lower back. I don't know—not at all—where he will strike. The urge to brace myself is nearly overwhelming.

The first strike—much like a snake—comes along my flank. I must not put my hands down. Not until he says that he is done. The natural urge is to cover yourself when hit. I must resist that urge.

The second and third blows crisscross each other and my arms begin to shake. My pussy clenches, hot and greedy. I chew my bottom lip to focus. He taps the crop against my pounding clit—gently, but enough to make me quiver. I cry out but keep my fucking hands up.

The crop bites at the top of my thighs, the swell of my ass, the crack between my cheeks. It snaps at my legs and my calves and I tremble, sweating just a bit on my upper lip. But I keep my arms up as my anxiety ratchets higher but then begins a swift descent. I am finding my peace, my Zen.

Four more sharp blows and I am sobbing but my hands are up like a good sub and I haven't covered myself against his blows. I've kept myself open to him.

"Good girl," he growls and drops the crop. "I'm very pleased."

So pleased that he grabs my aching upper arms and spins me to the wall. He plants my hands against the cool plaster and knocks my legs wide apart. A single finger is inserted into me and he flexes it. I shudder and sob and he laughs softly.

"Do you know how wet you are?"

"Yes," I confess.

And then he's in me. Big hands gripping the bell of my hips, his cock nudging me apart before thrusting in again, deeper and deeper it seems with every stroke. I push my forehead to the wall and shut my eyes and let all the worry left in me spiral away. He's here and taking care of me and I won. I was successful. I was a good girl.

Garrett's mouth comes down hot and wet on the back of my neck. The skin prickles and my nipples spike. He's driving into me with quick, brutal thrusts. My womb clenches up, my pussy grows taut. He finds my moisture and spreads it to the plump knot of my clit. In just a few slick swirls, I'm coming. I succeeded, I am allowed.

I climax with a great sob, feeling utterly boneless. Empty of worry or stress or fear. I'm empty but for him. He yanks my hips back against him, presses his teeth to my neck and whispers, "Good girl," once more before coming with a growl. The room grows silent. My hands are still up.

CRUNCHES

Annabeth Leong

Long before I noticed myself getting wet while doing sit-ups for Shira, she attracted me. Her thick librarian glasses seemed incongruous with her brightly colored workout clothes. Considering her abundance of lean muscle, she had a magically generous ass. I wanted her immediately, even more than I wanted to be like her.

The way I am, that meant I also wanted to do as she said, as much and as well as possible. I wanted to hear her call me a good girl.

Sexual fantasies blurred most of our initial consultation. I kept imagining sweat dripping off the ends of her long black hair as she tied me to the suspension training hookups dotting the gym walls and forced me to pull at my restraints until I passed out from the effort. When she asked if I thought she would be a good personal trainer for me, I just stammered.

The first few months, even when I thought she didn't know, my desire got me unprecedented results. It warmed my heart to think about the complimentary notes she could write into my file, about how I was so hardworking, so dedicated and so devoted to our process. I couldn't have cheated on her dietary suggestions any more than I could have slept around behind a beloved girlfriend's back.

The pounds melted off. I did double takes at the elegant shape of my neck in my shadow. Every movement I made, I felt Shira watching, controlling and approving—even when I was alone.

One day, after she'd put me on the adductor machine and had me squeeze my thighs together against heavy resistance, I gave in to the urge that had been building. I rushed home, ripped off my sweats and jumped into the bathtub with my vibrator in hand. I held myself in a half crunch (careful to pretend I had an orange under my chin for proper neck position), and stayed that way until my pulse pounded like a jackhammer and it felt like every drop of blood in my body had gathered just below my tightened abs. I shoved the vibrator deep inside my cunt, switched it to maximum intensity, then clenched every muscle in my body until I came. As I gasped and shuddered, hot water splashing around my shaking thighs, I could have sworn I heard Shira's voice, counting off the spasms.

The next time she squatted near me while I did crunches, the smell of my arousal wafted from my cunt, sharp and undeniable. Her face didn't change, but a few moments later, I scented an answering tang. I moaned softly, but only the burning red of my cheeks acknowledged the sound.

When she emailed my weekly workout instructions later that evening, I couldn't believe my eyes. Crunches and adductors and the locust and the exercise bike—a routine guaranteed to arouse me beyond all reason. I had hidden nothing from her. And at the bottom of the email, an especially odd note: *Remember, you can always stop a session if you feel uncomfortable for any reason—just tell me you need to take a break. I must also formally request you refrain from other workouts of any kind. I don't want you to stimulate your muscles on your own, without my supervision.*

I stared at my computer screen. I don't know how the message would have looked to someone who'd never tried BDSM, but I couldn't mistake Shira's hidden meaning. She'd given me a safeword and an order to refrain from masturbation, all without stepping out of her role as my personal trainer.

I needed to tell her I understood, that I was more than okay with this turn. Biting my lip, I typed, "Shira, you are my one and only exercise mistress." A little cheesy, but clear enough, I hoped.

The week of stimulating exercises combined with no orgasms had me vibrating with need by the time our next appointment came around. Now I could barely breathe whenever Shira's slim fingers adjusted my position. Toward the end of our workout, she ordered me onto the exercise bike, guiding me so far forward my clit mashed flat against the hard, thin seat between my legs.

I wanted to moan, but we scheduled our sessions for right after I got off work, when the gym was packed. People worked out less than two feet away from me in every direction. Shira's hand rested lightly on my shoulder blade, implicitly commanding me to remain in place. "Do you need to take a break?" she whispered.

"God, no." It sounded like the orgasmic plea it was.

Her smile cleared away any remaining confusion. This was sexual. "Did you follow my instructions? You haven't been doing extra workouts, have you?"

"No." I stayed in place, restrained by the pressure of her hand as surely as by a rope harness.

"Good. I can't have you overstimulating yourself."

I wondered if someone overhearing would pick up her naughty meaning.

"I think it's time for crunches," Shira said.

My legs shook as she led me off the exercise bike and over to a mat. I got into position.

"You've gotten strong," she told me. "We need to increase the challenge." She took the largest round, flat weight from a nearby rack and settled it over my chest and belly, flattening my torso.

"I can't—"

"Hug it tight."

I crossed my arms over it.

"Now crunch."

My muscles trembled from the strain of holding up the weight. My nipples rubbed against it. Shira settled near my feet, her hands trailing down the backs of my calves, then holding my ankles in place.

I gasped and panted. My cunt felt tighter than a clenched fist.

Shira looked straight into my eyes and adjusted the weight so the edge rested on my mons. It was so heavy, I felt its pressure squeezing the subterranean part of my clit, where ordinarily only the most powerful vibrations could reach. "Hold that up until you feel every muscle in your body release. Give me your best effort."

I needed her approval even more than I needed an orgasm. I tightened my core and humped that weight for all I was worth, grunting as I did. Still holding one ankle, Shira leaned forward and pressed the weight harder against my body, increasing the tension inside me without touching my clit directly.

I came with a whimper, falling flat on the mat with sweat pouring into my eyes. Shira removed the weight immediately, replacing it on the rack and returning with water in a small paper cup. "Good girl," she said, and my entire body thrilled to the words I had longed for. "How are you?"

I smiled as much as I could manage through the lingering burn in my abs. "I think we need to schedule more sessions. Maybe three times a week?"

She clucked her tongue, her eyes devious behind the slight fog on her glasses' lenses. "You'll have to come to my home office if you want to work out that often."

BUTCH UNBOUND

Salome Wilde

I caught myself holding my breath again. I was spread, impossibly wide, in every sense of the word. No one before Lakeisha had ever been able to do this to me, had ever wanted to. I felt the burning in my lungs that meant I would have to give in, take another ragged breath that would communicate my submission better than any pleading or safeword. Lakeisha was opening me, owning me, and I craved her control with every inch of my bound, aching flesh.

"My baby's pretty pussy needs fucking, doesn't it?" she mocked, tugging my pubic hair.

I squeezed my eyes shut as my hands balled into fists, straining against the cuffs that were locked behind my head.

Lakeisha yanked.

I yelped, a sound so wrong I'd never regain my reputation if anyone other than Lakeisha ever heard it.

"Tell me, baby," she cooed, as if she hadn't nearly brought tears to my eyes with that merciless grip. She was teasing me now, fingertips trailing through the thatch she'd threatened to shave on more than one occasion.

I bit my lip, desperate not to yield to her manipulation. I was no one's "baby." My cunt was no "pussy," pretty or otherwise. I longed to wrench my ankles free and slam my legs together, trapping her hand with the dark, thick, muscular thighs I showed to no one but my Lakeisha-girl.

She threaded her fingers deeper and squeezed. When she pulled up, I hissed through my teeth. "Bitch."

Lakeisha laughed. "That's right, baby," she answered, voice sweet and rich as only my vicious black femme could make it. "I'm a bitch." She released and patted me gently, condescendingly. "But right now? You're *my* bitch." She shoved two fingers into me, hard.

"Fuck!" I hated this just as much as I needed it. Even though I knew it was coming. Even though I hadn't given in to the taunting this time. Even though I was bigger, stronger, rougher. None of it did me a bit of good. My cunt was hers because I wanted it to be. I was her bitch and then some. I twisted in the bonds, and she laughed more fully as she climbed over me and shoved her sweet, shaved pussy in my face as she added a third finger and pumped me.

"Shit," I gasped. "Lakeisha...shit!" Any other complaint was smothered with dark, wet flesh, ground across and over my mouth. Her weight on me meant I couldn't even get my tongue in to taste her. I had to take whatever she gave, however she chose to give it. I could barely breathe, barely see the round, honey-brown ass rocking back and forth as she took her pleasure from me at both ends. Slowly, I yielded to the rhythm, as I did every time, mind diving into shame as my body rose to glory.

To our friends, I was Lakeisha's Daddy and she was my girl. My arm fit just right around her slim waist, fingertips tucked into the front pocket of her tight jeans. She loved my short natural and I loved the dark curls that rippled over her shoulders. She made me flex for her, and I made her come for me.

The first times we'd fucked, it was just as it should've been: I gave and she took. Fingers, strap-on, mouth: I made my baby girl peak and shatter and beg for more. The power was delicious and familiar. But Lakeisha wasn't satisfied with familiar. She loved her Daddy, but she wanted to love Lisa, too. *Lisa.* I wasn't "Lisa" except on my driver's license and at Mama's house for the holidays. Even at my warehouse job, they used my last name.

But New Year's Eve betrayed me. Long before midnight I was drunk as hell, and my girl was too gorgeous in her electric-blue thong to deny. She had me tied up in knots even sailors don't know before I thought about stopping her. By then it was too late for anything but straining and cursing until she broke me… and claimed my heart forever.

I was arching into her thumb as it worked my clit while she rubbed my soaked face raw. I could feel her swell as I fought climax. The butch in me needed her to come first, while the dominant femme in her wasn't going to have it. The fight was terrible and beautiful until I felt her hand at my rib cage, edging along the bottom of the bandages that bound my chest. From beneath her flushed, swollen pussy, I whined.

Lakeisha paused, then slowly climbed off. Her wide brown eyes locked with mine. While one thumb brushed my clit with determined lightness, the other was slipping beneath the elastic of the binding.

Every tensed muscle in my body was screaming *no* as my mouth hung open. Having Lakeisha control me sexually had made love and lovemaking new and miraculous. From oversized anal plugs to devious paddlings— I never balked. But this…was this the ultimate submission my girl needed?

I was terrified. I felt cold sweat breaking out as Lakeisha's first finger over the cloth met her thumb beneath. I imagined her reaching into the night-table drawer to take out the little knife she liked to tease my pussy with and slitting the bindings completely. My small, soft breasts were released—large, dark nipples suddenly hers to lick and bite, pinch and pull…or suckle, becoming my baby in a way I couldn't bear to contemplate. I pulled my mind away as she tugged at the formerly tucked tail of the bandage. Time stopped.

Lakeisha had seen me wrap so many times. She'd even helped me for a week after I'd sprained my wrist. And we'd been naked together plenty, stripping down after a workout or showering together. But we'd never fucked that way. We'd hooked up in the first place because she liked who I was—a bound butch in over-sized shirts, baggy pants, and kicks. Nothing we did in bed would change that, I thought. Clearly, though, there was a part of me she still wanted to expose. My parted lips couldn't form the word *Don't* as my gaze hardened, betraying the truth that while I didn't want limits to my submission, I didn't want this, either.

Lakeisha looked away, and then gave the tiniest of nods as she carefully but firmly tucked the cloth back in. She sighed softly as she lay beside me, wrapping an arm across my chest, her head on my shoulder. My heart was pounding in my ears. "Why did you stop?"

"Hard limit, Daddy," Lakeisha murmured, kissing my collarbone. "Not yours, but mine."

I smiled.

THE PRODIGY

Valerie Alexander

The gray fog of dawn was just beginning to lift over Las Vegas as I left my sleeping boyfriend in bed. Philip looked as pretty as ever in the sheets, his dark-gold hair and rich-boy features turning him into a sleeping Adonis, but I felt no urge to wake him up. Once he'd been my Master, my dom who knew how to degrade and subjugate and thrill me. But over the last week, it had become obvious that our once-hot connection was dead.

We'd come to visit his very rich and very kinky friend in Vegas to rekindle the kind of games we used to play. His friend's enormous villa was dedicated to BDSM, with frequent play parties and an elaborate dungeon. But Philip had been at the casinos every day and drinking every night; he hadn't dominated me once since we got here. I didn't actually care if he ever touched me again, but I was aching for a good hot scene with some beautiful brute.

I was also aching to see Alejandro one more time, but that wouldn't be happening, either.

Alejandro was the nineteen-year-old pool boy. Aloof, tanned and silent, he'd been my secret pleasure on this vacation. His face was moody rather than handsome, his full lips curling into a sneer when the other guests gushed over his bronzed chest and tattooed arms. But the way he flexed his hip to net the leaves out of the pool, letting his pants fall down just enough to show off his rock-hard abs, said he wasn't immune to being admired. Alejandro knew how to package himself: the unattainable boy who was all ink, muscle and attitude.

I hadn't bothered flirting with him. He was way too young to master me the way I needed, despite his lofty arrogance. And besides, I'd heard of other villa guests trying and failing to enjoy an hour of his surly charms. So I made small talk with him while I was tanning and left it at that.

Unfortunately today was Sunday and I figured he didn't come in on the weekends. I wouldn't see him again before leaving tonight. But I tried not to think about that as I walked through the house in my short cotton nightie. All the other guests were sleeping in whatever bedrooms they'd staggered off to hours earlier. One couple was asleep on the sofa, her naked but for her pearls, him naked but for her panties. I stepped outside, my bare feet cold on the patio. Then I heard a familiar noise: the click of the backyard gate.

My heart lifted with joy as Alejandro slipped through. His normal disdainful expression changed to surprise.

"Why are you here on a Sunday?" I asked.

"I come every day," he said. "But I'm supposed to come early on the weekends so I don't disturb the parties."

The way he said *parties* indicated he knew exactly what kind of parties went on here. My cheeks went hot. It was both arousing and humiliating to think of Alejandro knowing the dirty things I liked: being handcuffed, spanked, forced to expose my pussy to interested strangers while Philip grinned.

"So I gotta say, you don't seem like the rest of the freaks who come here," he said, as he began to net the insects and fallen leaves off the surface. "All that weird equipment inside—are you really into that kinky shit?"

Despite the scornful attitude, I sensed a real curiosity in the question. Those dark almond-shaped eyes lifted to mine and my knees went weak. *Get a grip*, I reminded myself. He was fifteen years younger than me, probably vanilla and probably not interested in me that way.

"Answer me," he said. "What's your deal?"

I summoned my courage. "My *deal* is that I like being dominated. I like being tied up, ordered around— mastered."

Alejandro put a chlorine tablet in the pool filter. Then

he walked up to me and pulled my cotton nightie over my head without warning. Instinctively I reached for it but he was faster than I was, and bound it around my wrists.

"Okay then," he said with a smirk. "You've got a new Master now. Follow me."

Feverish thrills soaked my pussy as he led me through the gate to the street. The sky was streaking pale with dawn and I shivered from both the coolness and the excitement at being naked on the sidewalk. The neighborhood of stucco villas was still silent but a dove-blue sky was lightening over the tiled roofs; any early morning dog-walkers would see us.

Alejandro packed up his net and canister of chlorine tablets, then roughly pulled me up into the van. My clit twinged as he shut the doors; I was at his mercy at last.

He yanked me forward and fingered my cunt. "Is this what you like, you little slut?"

"Yes," I muttered. Alejandro wasn't doing too bad for a youngster.

He withdrew his fingers and slapped my clit. "Don't talk."

He sat down on a box and pulled me over his lap, giving my ass a firm smack. Part of me rebelled at this kid who was practically half my age thinking he had the authority to spank me. The other part melted in the delicious humiliation of it.

His hand came down again and again, spanking me with one hand as he rubbed my clit with the other.

"Look at you," he said contemptuously. "You're dying for my cock, aren't you?"

I wiggled desperately on his lap. "Yes, please…"

He slapped my clit again. "I told you not to talk. Now bend over and spread your legs."

He pushed me over the box. The cardboard was cool against my inflamed clit as he forced my legs open and drove his swollen head into me, so rough and demanding that I cried out with excitement. Alejandro responded by holding me down by the nape, a reminder of my powerlessness. Then he began to pump into me in a relentless rhythm, while I twisted ecstatically beneath him.

His narrow hips worked against me, fast and urgent. I hadn't been fucked like this in years, or dominated and held down with such a strong, commanding hand. My pussy swelled with what felt like a slow-motion supernova, exploding and then drenching my thighs. I was still throbbing as Alejandro pulled out of me, turned me around and came on my face, decorating my mouth and cheek with ropes of come.

He stepped back, breathing hard. He looked stunned for just a moment. Then his customary mask came down and he was the aloof pool boy again, remote and disinterested.

"I, uh, I got houses to get to," he said without meeting my eyes.

Being dismissed was the perfect final touch of debasement. Alejandro untied my nightgown from my wrists and I tugged it on before heading back to the gate. My boyfriend Philip was just waking up as I entered our bedroom.

"Who the hell were you with?" he asked, staring, confounded, at my face.

"A prodigy," I answered, and got into the shower.

BEAUTIFUL

Teresa Noelle Roberts

As Alexis led Jane to the chain web in the center of the still-empty dungeon and told her what she planned for the first play party since the surgery, Jane's heart threatened to burst out through her scarred chest. It took all her courage not to safeword or simply start a plain vanilla argument with her girlfriend and domme.

She used to love being on display, an object to be enjoyed by the eyes and roving hands of the other party guests. Loved the eyes on her. Loved Alexis's pride as people admired her sub. When Alexis reclaimed her, she'd been wet and eager to play hard.

But Jane had been beautiful then, her body lean and shapely and unscarred. A credit to her own commitment to fitness and healthy living—which had proved no match for genetics. A credit to Alexis, because at a public party, a sub's good looks reflected on the dominant who was with her or him.

And now Jane wasn't perfect. Not even average, but damaged.

They'd kept playing at home, as much as her body would bear, throughout the long ordeal of treatment and recovery. As long as it was just the two of them, Jane could enjoy entwined pain and pleasure, freedom and restraint. She could trust the desire in Alexis's eyes, because Alexis loved her, as she loved Alexis, in a way that delved below the pretty surface. They'd known that long before cancer made everything in their lives uglier.

But other people were a different story. She'd seen the looks on the street as her hair fell out and her face became gaunt—pity, fear, even disgust, as if her illness should be hidden away so it didn't offend others.

Now she'd be exposing a far more graphic reminder of mortality than a bald head.

Alexis understood Jane's fears without Jane saying anything. "You're gorgeous," Alexis whispered, clasping the cuff around her wrist. "You're strong." Alexis ran her hand along Jane's outstretched arm, tracing the muscles Jane had worked so hard to keep in shape before her surgery, muscles that were no longer as defined as they once were. Jane winced, but the sincerity in her domme's voice cut through her panic. Alexis believed what she was saying. Jane might not, but she trusted Alexis, so she breathed the deep, cleansing breaths she'd mastered during treatment, and tried to accept.

"I want everyone to see you," Alexis said, securing the other arm. "You're so beautiful. So tough." She repeated the litany as she wove rope around Jane's torso and hips, supporting and ornamenting her. At first, Jane remained tense, her naked body cold and rigid as Alexis went through formerly familiar rituals. But as the rope and her beloved's hands moved over her skin, she began to warm. To open up. To her astonishment, arousal flickered deep in her belly—not the pulsing desire she once felt when she was on display, but a softer erotic feeling that was as much from pushing past her fears to please Alexis as it was from bondage, exhibitionism, anticipation of public play, or any of her old triggers.

Alexis bent and kissed the curve of Jane's belly, softer now than it once was. Flabby, even, after so long a time of not being able to work out, though she was thinner than ever. She nudged Jane's legs apart and secured her ankles with another set of cuffs, the wide leather acting as a firm embrace. In the past, Alexis could suspend her completely, letting the bonds and the web itself support her weight. But this time, she was letting Jane have the security of the floor beneath her feet.

It cut that she wasn't fit enough, at the moment, to be fully suspended, that it would put too much strain on her upper body. At the same time, she was grateful to Alexis for not waiting for her to be that fit again, because it might never happen. They'd had to remove muscle to save her life. Feet on the floor, ropes around her, Jane felt how Alexis accepted her changed body, and that helped her to do so. Alexis rocked back on her heels. "Radiant," she breathed. Jane didn't understand what she meant. But when Alexis pressed her face against Jane's pubic mound, Jane surged with desire and no longer cared if she understood.

Then Alexis began to lick and finger her, driving her hard and fast toward orgasm.

In the past, Alexis would leave Jane needy and craving when she was a party decoration, letting the gazes of others push her ever higher without driving her over the edge. She'd let Jane come only with her, and only after the display was over and they were flogging and spanking and fucking.

Never like this.

Never before the party even started. Never on her tongue, a tender intimacy reserved for the privacy of their bedroom. It marked this time as different, a new beginning.

When Jane begged, "Please, may I come?" Alexis intoned, "Yes!" and Jane shattered. No, she had been shattered and she came together on Alexis's tongue, all the shards resolving into someone brighter and braver than she had felt since she'd heard the words *breast cancer* and then *invasive* and *mastectomy*.

Alexis kissed her way up Jane's body, lingering at the scars where her left breast used to be. A protest fluttered on Jane's lips—she'd never let Alexis kiss her there before, not even at home. Here there were other people around, putting the last touches on the setup before the doors opened. Jane knew them all. They were friends, had visited her in the hospital and helped keep Alexis sane during the worst times, but she still felt self-conscious about drawing attention to her scars.

But heat spread from Alexis's lips and tongue right into Jane's heart, and some long-held tension snapped inside of her. Tears streamed down Jane's face, but they were good tears, cathartic tears, and she didn't try to hold them back. "My lovely survivor. So proud of you," Alexis whispered. "I want everyone to see you didn't let cancer win."

"Welcome back, Jane," someone called from across the room.

"Looking great!" someone added.

But as Alexis wrapped the final hemp rope around her, first above and then below her beautiful scars, the mark of a survivor, Jane had eyes and ears only for her domme.

LARIAT

Michelle Augello-Page

I walked into his room wearing high, high heels and an alarming red dress, cinched at the waist with the rope he had left in my bed. The lasso was knotted tightly, loose threads dangling seductively on my thighs. His eyes narrowed. His rope was around my waist.

We'd known each other for a few months, having met through mutual friends, and over the last several weeks, we had been talking on the phone nearly every day. I knew he was interested in me because inevitably, he would turn our conversation toward sex.

"What do you like?"

"Everything."

"Do you like being tied up?"

"Yes."

I had told him that even though I'd explored some

facets of bondage and discipline with previous partners, I had never been with anyone truly into BDSM. I had never had a dominant–submissive relationship. Whips and chains and ropes and straps belonged in some sexual promised land that I never seemed to find.

Even though he had been into BDSM for years, he'd had bad luck in relationships. His girlfriends always thought that his sexual desires were strange, something they had to put up with, a problem that would change over time. He had a collection of toys he couldn't play with, gathering dust. Until he met me, he'd become convinced he would never meet anyone sexually compatible.

By the time we were hanging out regularly, I was still unsure about having sex with him. I didn't want a relationship, and I didn't want casual sex, either. I didn't know what I wanted. But he did—he wanted me.

He told me he wanted to show me his toys. "Check this out," he had said the last time I was at his place, reaching into a nearby bag and handing me a leather cuff.

"What's this?" I asked, turning it over in my hands. The cuff was smooth black leather with a metal belt-like clasp. I was already turned on by the time I gingerly placed it on my wrist and looked at him.

He took my hand and belted the cuff tightly. Then he reached into the bag and took out the other one. Silently, solemnly, he affixed it to my wrist, then held both my hands in his. His eyes were blurry with desire. My heart was beating furiously. He pointed toward the ceiling, where an O-ring gleamed.

"I want to tie you to that and torture the fuck out of you."

I laughed. He helped me take off the cuffs. But later that night, we kissed for the first time. The next time he came over to my place, he brought rope and tied my ankles and wrists together while we had sex. It felt so good to be bound. I loved the feeling of the tight rope confining and securing me, pushing me farther into sensory wonderland. It felt so good to feel his long, rock-hard cock inside me, with his body pressed against mine. He caressed me with a whisper of touch. He tore into me with rough abandon. My body simply responded as tears fell from my eyes. "Oh my god," he said, thrusting deeper, "you were made to be fucked by me."

When we connected it was a thousand synapses firing, flashes of heat lightning, pulses of electromagnetism, sparks igniting motion, fireworks exploding, a brushfire in dry summer. We looked at each other, breathless, fear entwined with desire, knowing that the body never lies. We didn't talk about what it meant.

I walked into his room wearing high, high heels and an alarming red dress, cinched at the waist with the rope he had left in my bed. His eyes narrowed. His rope was around my waist.

He tugged at the lariat, pulling the knot loose.

"Strip," he said.

I removed my clothing as he playfully hit me with the rope.

"Lie on the bed. Facedown."

I did. I trembled with excitement, not knowing what would happen next. I was desperate to fuck him again. My body tingled with anticipation. He worked swiftly, pulling the rope around and through my ankles. Then another rope, around and through my wrists. I felt him pulling and twisting my legs and arms, contorting my body into a bow position, leaving me hog-tied.

I couldn't move. Pain flashed through my body. The stretch in my arms and legs was severe. He didn't touch me. He just looked at me. His face was sensuous and cruel as he circled me. I was helpless, at his mercy. He could do anything he wanted to me. He had me knotted tightly and bound, completely exposed to him.

"Do you really want this? This is how it is with me."

He walked around the bed, holding a crop, never taking his eyes off me. The lashes from the crop stung my skin. He was hurting me. I wanted him to hold me. I wanted him to touch me. Tears sprang to my eyes. Waves of sensation rippled across my skin. Then the lashes felt like little bites, sharp kisses. I realized that he was already touching me. Intensely. I realized that he was already holding me, more securely than I had ever been held in my adult life.

"Yes," I said through my tears. "This is what I've always wanted."

He freed me, released the ropes binding me, then gathered me into his arms as I cried. "You are mine," he said softly, keeping me bound in his close embrace. Then he kissed my tears, pressed his body against my body, and encircled me with his ruthless and protective love.

TOASTED MARSHMALLOWS

Tilly Hunter

I stare at my best friend's cock. I've never seen it before. But from this position—on my knees—I'm getting a close-up view. It's around the same erect length as my own, but a little thicker. Its head is darker.

"I said, suck it." Karen repeats the order. She doesn't like having to repeat an order and I don't like letting her down. I stick my tongue out, shape it around Nathan's head and guide it into my mouth. I'd use my hands, but she's cuffed them behind me—and linked them to my ankle restraints for good measure.

It's such a strange sensation. Like a moleskin cover on a hardback book. Soft skin sliding over rigid, engorged flesh. Of course I've felt the same thing before in my hand. I'm a twenty-seven-year-old guy—I feel my own erections most mornings in the shower. But to have someone else's in my mouth, stretching my lips and pushing my jaw down…well. I suck, running my tongue up the underside. It seems the thing to do. I realize I've never analyzed the precise movements Karen's mouth makes to cause my shaft to stiffen and pulse to climax. She only does it when I've been a good boy and obeyed her satisfactorily. I'm hoping for a reward today, more than the toasted marshmallows she's promised from our backwoods campfire. But if she punishes me instead? I'll still enjoy it.

"You're doing well, sweetie," she says, placing a hand on the back of my head and pushing me on until I cough. Nathan, one of the few old college pals I've kept in touch with, has no choice but to stay in position. He's standing against a maple, arms pinned back around the trunk and more rope wrapping his torso against the rough bark. A thick stick between his teeth, tied in place around the back of his head, gags him. I watched his girlfriend, Rosie, put him in place while I knelt in the leaf mold waiting to be told what to do.

Who'd have thought it? Nathan and I don't discuss sex much. We're more on a beer-and-baseball footing. But it turns out our partners, who became friends through us, do discuss sex—often and in detail. I was a bit annoyed when I found out. Embarrassed. But then Karen persuaded me to come along on this little summer picnic expedition. "You know how much I like being outdoors," she told me. "I love the warmth of the sun on my bare skin."

And I love it when Karen bares her skin. I also love it when she orders me around, ordering me to pleasure her, or to kneel patiently while she pleasures herself with a vibrator. Nathan and I have more in common than we realized, apparently, though Karen tells me he's often deliberately naughty because he likes to get beaten with a riding crop. Me, I can do without pain. Bondage and submission, hell yes, but I'm no masochist. If I really misbehave, she bans me from coming for whatever period she deems right—a few days, a week. Once she made me hold out a whole month. I remember arguing over whether it should be a calendar month or just four weeks, never really expecting to win the argument.

Nathan is moaning around his gag and straining against his ropes, trying to thrust his dick harder into my mouth.

"You boys," Karen laughs. "Put something warm and wet around your cock and you don't care who or what it is. Now, Rosie and I are going to sixty-nine on the picnic blanket. Lee, I want you to keep going until Nathan comes and make sure you swallow it all down like a good little slut. Rosie thinks I should beat you with her riding crop while you suck. I've explained that you're too pathetic a creature to withstand pain, but if you don't swallow every drop I might beat you anyway."

An animalistic growl erupts from the back of my throat. It's pretty much the only sound I'm capable of as I concentrate on overcoming my gag reflex. I can hear

Karen and Rosie moving around behind me and I'm so tempted to turn round to see if she and her friend really are licking each other out. I try to picture it in my mind, but I want to see it for real. Nathan can see what's going on and from his insistent moans and squirming, it seems the view is to his liking. I resist the urge to stop and look, instead trying to see how deep I can take Nathan's dick. The choking sensation sends adrenaline shooting through my pelvis and has my own cock at attention. I'm burying my nose in his pubes and the tickling discomfort and mildly musty smell only make me harder.

I actually start to imagine how a crop landing across my shoulders or my ass might feel. Would it make me cough and splutter as Nathan's thickness stifled my cries of pain? I try to shake the image. I don't like pain. But it won't go away.

Nathan's movements become jerkier. A salt tang seeps over my tongue as his precome oozes. I'm vaguely aware of the feminine noises behind me getting louder. Then my mouth is flooded with liquid, thicker than water but still sliding easily down my throat, so easily I barely register the taste. I suck and slurp, not letting a single drop escape my lips. Christ, I've done it. I've sucked him off. Another man. My best friend. And I don't want to let that cock go.

I rest a moment with it softening on my tongue. I'm not sure if I'm allowed to turn and see Karen and Rosie together. Before I can make up my mind what to do, Karen is there at my side. "Well done, honey," she says,

rubbing my shoulder. "Come and help me make a fire."
I let Nathan's dick slide out and he grunts as it drops
from my lips.

I kneel, my cuffs separated but still hugging my wrists
and ankles, to pile up dry sticks we've collected and coax
them into flame. My gaze is pulled toward Nathan, still
bound to the tree as Rosie beats his chest and the front
of his thighs with her crop. He's pressing his head back
into the bark and his eyes are shut tight. His groans are
somewhere in the gray area between pleasure and pain.
Even when I wrench my eyes away, the sound of the
crop is there, rhythmic, in the background. *Thwack,
thwack, thwack.* It has me wondering.

"You seem very interested in that riding crop,"
Karen says. She's got a marshmallow on a stick above
the fire, its surface browning. "Are you changing your
mind about pain?"

I wish I were gagged. "Maybe. I don't know."

"Perhaps we should borrow it. Have a gentle try." I
don't have to answer as she holds the stick to my lips. I
shape my mouth around the crisp shell and sticky sweetness oozes over my tongue.

THE SHOOT

D. L. King

D o you mind if I touch him?"

I was working on a new body of images illustrating male submission. Yes, I know, it's a recurring theme with me, but I do so like the appearance of the male form restrained and straining. I was looking for subjects between the ages of twenty-one and forty-five with specific characteristics, so I'd sent out a call to dominants in the international community. I explained the project and invited them to send photos if they were interested and willing to come to New York for shooting sessions.

Evidently, my reputation is such that the offer of a free print will coax people from across the globe to travel to my studio. The farthest reply was from a woman in Japan. She was planning a trip and sent the most delightful photo of her plaything. Language barriers often cease to be a problem when sex and art take over. In the photo, Kazuhiro was transformed by his Mistress's intricate rope bondage. If Tatsumi arrived here in time, with Kazuhiro, he would be a lovely addition to the show.

But now, the woman standing in my studio shrugged her shoulders. "You have carte blanche. I've seen your work, that's why we're here."

I ran a fingernail over his nipple and watched it react. "What's his name?"

"Jordan."

Jordan's Mistress was getting a signed print of her choice in payment for today's session—that, and first refusal of the finished prints of her boy before the show opened to the public.

"Very nice, Jordan," I purred. Turning to his Mistress, I asked if she'd brought his shaving things. She said she had and I told her to set them up on the table by the reclining barber chair. While she got everything ready, I directed Jordan to take off his sweatpants and climb into the chair. After fastening his wrists and ankles, I raised the chair to a comfortable height for his Mistress.

The sweats were loose on him but there was still a mark that would show on film so I had a bit of time to kill. All in all, it wasn't too bad; it would have been a much bigger time waster if he'd worn jeans. Of course, I prefer to have boys arrive at my studio naked, but that can only occur in winter. Boots and a coat somehow

seem out of place in the summer. I took my time setting
up the lighting.

A half hour later, we were ready to begin. "Okay,"
I said. "When we communicated, you indicated you
preferred to shave him dry, with talc, but I'd like you to
use shaving cream today. The contrast pops so nicely in
black and white, especially with the steel and mother of
pearl of the straight razor."

As she began to shave Jordan, I started shooting:
close-ups of her black-gloved hand pressing down on the
base of his erection and the razor flashing in the lights,
medium shots of his crotch, half shaved with her black
silk-clad torso as the background, a long shot, including
his face—head back, eyes closed and mouth open. I shot
from a slight angle, just beyond his feet, taking in the
whole scene along with the edges of the black seamless
paper roll, the light stand in the corner behind his head,
and black electrical cords snaking around the floor. The
industrial look can sometimes be the most intimate and
voyeuristic.

I could imagine the finished prints on the gallery
wall. Yes, these pictures would go well with last week's.
Jordan, pale and russet, juxtaposed with the obsidian
and pink of Geoffrey; I would hang them as diptychs.
The two would pair so nicely for the shaving pictures.

I shot fast, as I always do. "All right, if you're finished
with the front of him, let's have him on all fours on the
table."

His Mistress released him from the chair and walked

him over to the low massage table. His cock stood proud and swung from side to side as he walked. Once she had him positioned, I walked over, gently ran my hand down his back and cupped his perfectly rounded ass. Although his breathing sped up a bit, to his credit, Jordan hadn't made a sound since he'd entered my studio.

"Very nice, Jordan, arms in front of you now, on the table," I said as I patted his bottom, giving him the clue to raise it. "That's it, now open your legs for me," I said, gently pushing and prodding him into the position I wanted. I ran my finger up his hard cock and pulled and stretched his balls down in back. An involuntary shudder coursed through his muscles. "Very good, Jordan. Later, Mistress will give you a nice reward," I whispered, as I smoothed my hands down the backs of his thighs. "Won't that be something to look forward to?" I detected a small tensing of his muscles as a drop of precome slipped from the tip of his cock and splashed onto the table, between his legs.

I fastened him to the table with black leather straps just below his knees and elbows, and at his ankles and wrists. It was all about the contrast. With Geoffrey, I'd used white leather straps. What a lovely pair they'd make.

Satisfied, I asked his Mistress to complete the shave with his balls and anus. Using the bristles of the shaving brush to apply the creamy soap, she swirled it again and again over his pulsing opening. Helpless to fight it any longer, he treated us to the music of his lovely, deep moan.

I finished these first shots, impressed with Jordan's composure, and curious to see how he'd do during the strap-on shots. I always like to think ahead during a shoot. My thoughts kept bringing me back to Geoffrey.

Geoffrey's master kept him in excellent shape, as fit as Jordan's Mistress kept him. Perhaps I'd ask to have them brought in together for one more shoot. I could see the close-up of Geoffrey's cock entering Jordan's delicious ass. As I said, it really is all about the contrast.

SUNDAY IN THE ART GALLERY WITH GEORGE

Elizabeth Coldwell

George has been looking at the woman's ass for the last ten minutes. I know it's only rendered as a series of broad charcoal strokes on canvas, but he's studying it as intently as if it were warm, bare flesh. Yes, he may be an ass man, but this is taking it a little far.

I scuff the toe of my black patent T-bar shoe on the wooden floor, trying to attract his attention. We take turns at choosing how we'll spend our Sundays, and as soon as he said he was going to take me to the art gallery I knew I was in for an afternoon of sheer, unrelenting tedium.

"Can we go yet?" I ask, my voice loud enough to make the frumpy, middle-aged woman admiring the reclining nude to our right turn in my direction. Her gaze scans my too-short skirt, my swinging ponytail tied with a childish polka-dot ribbon, and she can't keep her obvious distaste from her expression. Wherever she thinks my place should be, it's certainly not in the hushed confines of an art gallery.

"Be quiet, Mina. We've still the Pre-Raphaelites room to visit."

Oh god, the Pre-Raphaelites. George's favorites. Endless depictions of faux-medieval melodramas and sulky-faced women with lips like bruised fruit.

"Don't wanna see the boring old Pre-Raphs," I whine. "Wanna go for a hot chocolate."

George's patience, which has been steadily wearing thinner since we arrived two hours ago, snaps. He grabs me by the arm. "I've had just about enough of your acting out, young lady. Come with me."

His grip is almost hard enough to bruise as he hauls me out into the corridor, and it sends an excited thrill shooting straight to my pussy. In truth, my panties have been wet almost since we left the house, my mind racing with thoughts of how I'd bring my husband to his breaking point. I catch a glimpse of the frump as he drags me away; I can't tell whether she's shocked or secretly delighted that I appear to be getting what's been coming to me. If only she knew.

Glancing around, George spots a roped-off corridor, with a sign reading STAFF ONLY hanging from it. It's perfect for our needs, and he slips the looped rope off the metal pole that keeps it in place, so we can slip through into a private area. We're breaking all kinds of rules by being here, but that only makes my heart beat a little faster, my pussy flood with sticky juice.

A few feet down the corridor, we come across an alcove with a narrow window set in it. The thick windowsill will make a perfect sitting spot for George; the fact the window only looks out onto the museum's waste bins means we're unlikely to be spotted from outside.

"God, I've been longing to do this to you," my husband breathes as he guides me onto his lap. I wriggle and pout, trying to stop him flipping up my skirt to reveal my white cotton panties, but it's a perfunctory effort. I want him to do this to me, to go further and pull down my panties to bare my bum. Even though there's a possibility some staff member might discover us here, I need the shame of exposure.

Instead, he bunches up the fabric of my underwear in one hand and smoothes the fingers of the other over my naked cheeks. My dominant husband, the avowed ass man, can't resist taking a moment to play with my raised half-moons.

"Oh, Mina," he sighs. "What a wicked little brat you are, embarrassing me in public like that."

"Yes, and you love it, don't you? What else was I going to do, wait till you'd dragged me round the Pre-Raphs?"

Even now, when my punishment is assured, I can't resist annoying him further. It's in my nature, coded into my DNA. I've never been the kind of submissive who complies meekly and sees obedience as the ultimate virtue. I'm a brat, just like George says, and I thrive on pushing and provoking him until he gives me what we both want.

"Oh, Mina, you've really done it now…" That's all the warning I get before he starts to discipline me. His palm cracks against my cheeks, delivering smack after smack. Without any kind of warm-up, there's no gradual introduction to the pain. It's there from the very first swat, raw and intense. But time dictates George do this hard and fast, and already I'm responding. It's hard to stifle the cries that want to burst from my throat, but I do my best, and my muffled moans and kicking heels can't fail to let him know the effect his slaps are having.

With my panties twisted in his fingers, the cotton pulled taut against my cunt, there's a delicious friction on my clit as I wriggle and squirm. George is hard, too; his baggy trousers managed to disguise his excitement as we toured the gallery, but here, the thick rigidity of his cock is all too apparent to me as I writhe on his crotch.

"Are you sorry?" he asks me, as he brings his stinging assault on my bottom to a halt. I wish I could see my cheeks; they're hot and tender, and they must be stained a vivid crimson, but unless he permits me a visit to the ladies' room, I won't have the chance to admire them. And he won't be doing that, not yet; it would give me the perfect opportunity to sneakily relieve my maddening need to come, and that only happens when my Master permits it.

So it'll be a sore, frustrated brat who follows her husband round the Pre-Raphaelites room, all too aware of the throbbing in her ass and the itching in her pussy. But it means the reward for taking my spanking without complaint will be all the sweeter when it finally comes.

George understands my needs so well, just as I do his, and that's why we complement each other perfectly. When I finally get to come, with his cock buried deep in my ass, it will be with a silent thank-you to whoever decreed this willful, bratty submissive should find the man who really knows how to tame her—if only for a little while.

Next weekend, it's my turn to choose our Sunday outing. I think I'll suggest the science museum. I hate going there, and I'll never be able to still my bored fidgeting. George will need to do whatever it takes to see that I do. What fun we'll have…

THE THIRD
PLUG

Nick Mamatas

The third plug wasn't the hardest, as you thought it would be. After two weeks of training, it slides in easily…almost. The first plug felt so big. Now, with Sir's palm warm on your ass, cool lube flowing like a snake down your bottom and the largest plug your man owns wedged tight inside you, you can't help but giggle, and giggle again at the swat you get for giggling.

"Put on some panties," Sir says, his voice close and hollow in your ear. "Those lace boy shorts this time." He usually likes thongs, but they tend to look a little ridiculous on a plugged rear. You wiggle your butt at him and stand up from over the bed. "Yes, Sir," you say and try to saunter to the bureau to get dressed. The plug makes walking a bit hard, but you can feel it flaring out your hips, forcing you to move like a whore, the way the heels Sir has you wear sometimes do.

"How do you feel, slut?" he asks.

"Is this it, Sir?" you ask as you slide on your panties. "It feels…big. It makes me want a cock in there, but—"

"Wait," he says and you know the conversation is over. The schoolgirl skirt and camisole go on next, and then you're out for the day, just another couple, except that you have to very quietly ask permission to give him a kiss on the cheek or leave his presence. He keeps his hand on your ass as you walk around the mall and whenever you sit he slides his hand up your skirt to massage your thighs. You're distracted, squirming in your seat—but not by that. His words were what did that: "You tell me when you understand," he said, after approving the way you put your hair up to show off the back of your neck. "Today, you tell me when you get it, slut." *Get what?*

You're in the food court at the mall, drinking almost comically oversized sodas. Sir's picking at some awful glop he calls "automatic curry." It's so strange—you never go to the mall. Neither does he, ever. He had even printed out directions, which you'd spotted on his bureau when he took the belt to your ass for being five minutes late to his home. Sure, you call him "Sir" and sometimes, when your sweaty back is on wrinkled sheets and you catch a glimpse of gray chest hair, come out with "Daddy"—but he doesn't shop at the mall. You're pretty sure most of the furniture in his apartment came right from the curb, or was there when he moved in. At least he lives by himself, and off-campus, so you put up with the socks—hell, one time you found a sock, along with half an onion and a jar of mayonnaise, and nothing else, in his fridge—for your get-togethers.

Your mind wanders, and really, so does his. He's not looking very dom-like at the moment, eating as he is with a plastic fork out of a Styrofoam clamshell, just like everyone else. You're still feeling somewhat hot—you like showing off your cleavage, though you worry that the flesh over your thighs is forming a visible roll, and your shoulders feel a little fat, too. You wish he'd look up at you. You squirm in the plastic bum-mold of your own chair and slurp from your straw, feel the plug between your thick cheeks and a bit of wet comes back to your thighs. You wish you could run off to the restroom to finger yourself, but dare not ask Sir for permission.

He sees you squirming and looks up. "Do you get it yet?" he asks, with the air of boredom that you always read as a challenge. You fail this time though; you don't get it, whatever *it* may be. You blush and lower your eyes and wonder if he'll let you come tonight.

He takes you onto the T headed back to Harvard Square, where everyone is silent and resting their chins on their chests. You keep your legs open, just a touch, just enough to let every man in the carriage know that you are a whore who is ready to be fucked at any time, throughout the whole ride. Nobody notices, or if they do, there are no leers from the men or scowls from the dowdy old women in their industrial pantsuits.

Sir leans in close and commands you: "Watch them sit. Watch them stand."

Out of the T and back on the street, you feel a bit more cheery. Sir lets you hold his hand for a bit, and after you ask properly, lets you kiss him on the cheek and on the side of his neck. He's standing tall, a dom again, his hand sliding up your arm and cupping your breast while a few of the kids sitting in the pit by the T entrance hoot at you. You watch them closely, making eye contact and smiling, encouraging and inviting them, all for Sir. One drops his monkey-like glare for a second, shocked, and you march on proudly, even as the plug in your ass starts to chafe at the skin.

At the pub, Sir wants a drink and has you pay for it with the notes in your cleavage. He's leaning back, arms draped over the top edge of the booth, enjoying the sharp intake of breath and the stilted "Right!" that the waitress barks as she takes your money. He watches her walk back to the bar, and you stare at her flat bum as well. Then you notice something about the way she moves. About how everyone, men and women both, sit in their stools or lean over the trivia machines. You remember the T; the passengers weren't frowning, they were...satisfied.

Sir sips his beer. "Get it yet, slut?"

"I do, Sir," you say, not caring who might hear you call him Sir.

"Oh yeah? What do you get?"

"I can't stop thinking about it," you tell him. "Whenever I see someone sitting down a little tenderly, or working behind a counter, or walking slowly, I..."

"Go on."

"I just think of them all wearing plugs. Everyone's a dirty little whore wearing an ass plug for his or her Master. The whole town is sex." You lick your lips at the thought of how wonderfully hard you're going to get fucked tonight.

Sir squirms in his seat, almost a little uncomfortable.

OTHERS

Jade A. Waters

On her thirty-fifth birthday, Carley found herself ass-up in the Kink Club.

Jeremy took her here for any big celebration—her birthday or his, a promotion and even the time they made it safely through a pregnancy scare. He was a masterful lover, and though she would love him til death did them part, sometimes things just needed a little extra kick.

At the Kink, Jeremy became a different man. He wasn't her tender, lovemaking husband; here he was a passionate commander. Carley always followed his instructions, losing herself in the orders to touch him, suck him or even spread her lips wide as he fucked her senseless in front of the other attendees. And of course there was the time on his birthday three months ago, when he chose another woman and told Carley if she had any hope of him sticking his cock deep inside her, she better make out with that woman.

And she had.

So before Jeremy had left her here—tenderly caressing her cheek, then slamming his hand against her bottom to demand that she bend until her skirt crept high over her ass and the cold air tickled her damp, hot cunt—she thought the next natural step would be for him to ask her to *really* play with a woman. And while she wasn't much into girls, the way Jeremy would pump her for hours after made compliance an easy option.

But now she waited, wanting to scream in embarrassment and longing, unable to see much at this angle except the legs of couples who stopped to stare, some of them silent, others whispering as her legs quaked beneath her. They wouldn't dare touch her, but as the minutes passed slowly by—an eternity with her nakedness exposed—her sex pulsed for them to do just that. When Jeremy returned, Carley was well on the path to an orgasm built solely out of desperation.

"That's my girl," he whispered. She could feel him staring over her in approval, and she wanted to taste him, feel him—anything to ease her maddening excitement. He thrust one finger into her but drew it out as fast as it had come. "You're already drenched, I see. I love how much you adore an audience. Do you want to feel my touch again?"

"Yes, please." Carley could see between her legs that more people had gathered to watch her lover's movements. She clenched her inner walls tight, aching to know what he plotted, trembling with their eyes on her. "Please, Master."

"In front of you is a surprise, my love. If you treat it as well as you treat me, you will feel me again. Keep your body low and lift only your head—then suck."

Carley quivered at his words, and she raised her head as ordered, expecting to find a naked woman in front of her.

Instead, she found the largest cock she'd ever seen, an uncut rod whose owner waggled it back and forth, nearly brushing himself against her lips. Carley started to lift her head, but Jeremy clapped his hand over her bottom so hard the viewers gasped.

"No."

She whimpered and stared at the cock, its length sheathed in a purple condom and making her blood spike hotter. She'd told Jeremy she had a fantasy of two men at once, but this…

He rubbed her ass again. "I want to see you suck him, Carley. I want you to come while everyone here watches you swallow another man." He leaned close to her ear, sliding his hand over her wetness. "You have an audience of at least twenty. Now keep your hands on your knees and *blow him*."

The stranger groaned.

Carley lifted her lips to the anonymous shaft. It was beautiful—one she would have admired anyway—but to have Jeremy order her to do it made her feel like a slave. She wanted so badly to despise the feeling, but as he dipped his fingers inside her dripping cunt, she cried with longing.

She drew the man into her mouth, letting her lips rub every inch of his tremendous length, until he reached the back of her throat. There were more inches to go, and her eyes watered as she tried to take him farther without using her hands.

"Oh yes," he said. Carley reared back to swallow him again, and Jeremy snapped his hand on her in another smack. This one made contact with her pussy, sending the sweet cupping sound of dry flesh against wetness around the room.

"Fuck him with your throat. Make him come like you do me, and I will shove myself inside of you as a reward. Do you want that, love?"

She moaned, her pussy so wet she knew she must be dribbling over his fingers. Jeremy spanked her and caressed her as she ran her lips along the cock's ridge, and the man wrapped his hands around her head.

"Yes. She loves that. She's so wet, please continue."

He began to pump Carley's throat, making her excitement build. She loved pleasing Jeremy this way, and as the man thrust against her mouth, she countered with a hum that drove him faster. He grunted, tangling his fingers in her hair and fucking her throat. Waves of pleasure began to course through her. She ached to grab him, to use both her hands and mouth to enjoy him more thoroughly, but to do so might stop Jeremy's touch.

"You are so good, sucking this man down!"

"I'm...I'm going to come," the man growled, and Carley heard in his words that he was gritting his teeth, could feel him convulse along her tongue. She arched against Jeremy's hand and slammed her mouth over the stranger.

From behind her, Jeremy said, "Excellent. Carley, you've been so good, it's your turn."

In an instant, he rubbed the head of his rod along her sopping lips. She cried out against the cock in her mouth, and Jeremy slid right inside, burying himself deep. A tear slipped from her eye as the stranger rocked, then bucked hard with a grunt that told her he'd come. And once he did, pulling himself out of her mouth and away with a sigh, the pleasure rolled through her harder than ever before. Jeremy drove himself all the way into her.

"Yes, my love," he moaned. "Come!"

A wail poured from her lips and clapping sounded behind them. The wave swept over her, spreading tingles through her limbs while Jeremy lost himself in the contractions of her pussy. He came with her, grabbing her breasts and folding over her back with a breathy grunt. For several minutes they panted like this, the others in the room cheering, some shrieking their own satiated moans.

Jeremy withdrew his withered shaft, then told Carley to stand. He rubbed his fingers on her tender inner lips while she squirmed. Her cheeks burned red with humiliation, and though she still hadn't seen the owner of the cock she'd swallowed moments before, she felt the heat return.

"Shall we find another, beautiful?" Jeremy asked.

Carley grinned. "Yes, Master."

WITHOUT QUESTION

Lucy Felthouse

I do it without question. Every single thing she asks of me. I relinquish all power, all responsibility. It is wonderfully freeing. It is sublimely beautiful. Just like her.

"Kneel," she barked. I did it. I dropped to my knees before her perfect form. Part of me wanted to look up, to drink in the sight of her standing there, hands on her hips, her body encased in shiny black leather. I knew I wouldn't lift my gaze, though. I couldn't. I have the utmost respect for my Mistress and never want to do anything to displease her. Especially since my Mistress is also my wife.

Ever since I got back from Afghanistan and met her in a restaurant, she's been testing me. Then, it was teasing my cock under the table while she was wearing sharp stilettos, bringing me to the very edge of climax, right there in the restaurant. Now, she occasionally takes over the role of my ex-commanding officer and treats me like some kind of new recruit.

"Now drop and give me twenty. No, scratch that. Make it forty."

It was clichéd, totally unoriginal, but it got me harder than I'd ever been in my life. After so long taking orders without question, it was impossible to change that aspect of my personality, which is why I'm so grateful that Cassie came into my life—permanently—when she did. She took over the role of the Army, directing me here, there and everywhere, helping me to move forward, to adjust to civilian life. Together, we took baby steps, and when I felt able to cope, she scaled back her bossiness and reserved it strictly for the bedroom. Or, you know, anywhere else we had sex. Which was everywhere.

It worked perfectly. Day-to-day life was mine to control, to live. But as soon as we slipped into a scene, I was completely submissive—just the way I liked it. I closed my eyes as the sight of the carpet coming closer, then moving farther away, was in danger of making me feel queasy. I obviously wasn't working hard enough, because a spike-heeled boot settled into the small of my back and pressed down, hard. I hesitated for a millisecond, gathering all the strength I had, and continued with the push-ups. It was more difficult, of course, but it was also much more rewarding. Not to mention arousing. The shards of pain generated by the boot's heel sliced through my body, making my blood pump faster, harder, twisting my pleasure dial up to eleven. Thankfully my boxer shorts were tight enough to keep my cock under control, otherwise it would have gotten in the way as I lowered myself to the carpet.

I concentrated hard on keeping track of how many push-ups I'd done. If I fucked up and miscounted, I would be punished. And as much as I loved the punishments, I loved my Mistress and her delectable body more, and the sooner I satisfied her whims, the sooner she'd let me loose to play with her, pleasure her. Make her come.

"Very good," she eventually said, placing her foot back on the carpet. "You're getting so good at these impromptu fitness tests, Holden. I'll have to think of something different. More challenging." She fixed me with a stern gaze.

"Yes, Mistress. Whatever you say."

"Of course you'll do whatever I fucking say!" Like lightning, her hand left her side and slapped my face, hard. The heat and the humiliation zipped immediately to my groin.

"Please," I murmured. Then louder. "Please!"

"Please what?" she said, putting a finger beneath my chin and yanking my head up. Her eyes flashed. My cock throbbed.

"Please can I...touch you, Mistress?"

Clearly as aroused as I was, her expression softened just a little, and she gave a curt nod. "You may, slave, but only because you've been so good. Don't expect me to let you off this easily all the time."

"I won't, Mistress, I promise."

"Fine. Take off your clothes, then lie on your back. I want to see that stiff cock of yours. And then I'm going to ride it."

I gulped, then hurried to do her bidding. The anticipation, the excitement made me clumsy, and I got my head momentarily stuck in my T-shirt, then turned all thumbs when it came to undoing my jeans and getting them off. Cassie crossed her arms and tapped her foot impatiently. Seconds later I was in the position she'd commanded.

"About damn time, too." She reached down and undid the flap in her leather outfit that gave access to the heaven between her legs. Then she straddled my stomach, her slickness smearing against my abs. It took every bit of willpower I possessed not to grab her and impale her on my cock.

She crawled up my body and positioned herself over my head. "Lick me. When you've made me come, I'll allow your cock inside me."

"Yes, Mistress." Immediately, I lifted my head to reach her and stuck out my tongue. She hadn't given me permission to use my hands, so I folded them behind my neck for support. The first taste of her tangy sweetness was sublime, and I was sure that if I could see my cock, I'd glimpse the precome seeping from its tip. God, how I wanted her.

I pleasured her the best way I knew how. There was no teasing my Mistress—she wouldn't allow it. So I didn't delay. I went straight for her clit, flicking and circling it with my tongue until it swelled, then sucked it into my mouth and pulled until she came.

There was a moment when she stopped being a Mistress, my Mistress, and simply became a woman thrust into oblivion. "Fuck...oh fuck...yes...yes...YES!" She continued to swear and babble nonsense as her pleasure washed over her.

I didn't move a muscle. All I wanted was her hot, tight sheath around my shaft and I wasn't going to do a damn thing to jeopardize that. My good behavior was rewarded. As soon as she recovered sufficiently, Cassie shifted back down my body, grasped my cock in her hand and pointed it at her entrance. Then, without preamble, she dropped down onto it. One second I was out, the next second I was in. My body and brain couldn't quite catch up with what was happening, and were further confused when she began to ride me, fast and furious.

I was helpless. All I could do was lie there, like some kind of sex machine rather than a human being. She was fucking me, but using my cock for her own pleasure. I still didn't know if she was going to allow me to come—she'd said I could get inside her, but not that I'd be allowed to climax.

It was torture and perfection all at once. It didn't matter whether she gave me permission to climax or not.

My Mistress was on me—in more ways than one—and she was happy. And when she was happy, I was happy.

For me, that was heaven.

IN THE DARKNESS

Regina Lafayette

I strain my ears to listen for her. My hands are stretched above my head, wrists held in cuffs anchored to the bed with thick chain. I blink fruitlessly against the blind-fold Nicole has placed on me and let out a frustrated groan.

Dammit, I think. *I don't even know if she's in the room right now.*

My whole body is alert, lying exposed and at her disposal. Suddenly, I feel her swing a leg over to straddle me. The soft touch of her leather crop kisses my neck, the flat tip dragging agonizingly slowly over my breasts and down the center of my belly. With a sure and quick motion she flicks the sensitive flesh of my clit, making me cry out. I tense, unable to see where she's aiming her next blow.

"I love when you tense like that in anticipation," she says, amusement clear in her voice. "Now where shall I hit you?" she asks, and I feel her shift. I think she's putting herself in a better position to wield her crop until I feel her mouth descend onto my cunt.

"Oh fuck," I say, the deliberate strokes of her tongue catching me by surprise. She works over my clit almost lazily, and I grind upward into her mouth, desperately seeking more pressure, more speed, then make a garbled sound of protest as she pulls away and robs me of her perfect tongue, leaving me throbbing and breathless.

"On your belly," she says calmly. Firmly. A small snap of the crop just in case her command wasn't clear enough. Emboldened by frustration, I resist.

"No," I say sulkily. "Make me."

"Oh, honey," she laughs, sounding amused. "Gladly." Before she even finishes speaking the crop strikes the meaty side of my ass, all teasing gone.

"Oh," I gasp as she revisits the spot. Her hand comes next, centered over the small rising welt, mixing the pain of the dull slap with the sharp sting the crop left behind. My hips jerk up reflexively and she takes advantage of the movement to grip me firmly with both of her hands, flipping me over so I'm lying panting on my belly. She runs her hands over the backs of my thighs and ass.

"Beautiful," she says, dropping a kiss on my cheeks.

"Ah," I cry out as the soft feel of her lips suddenly gives way to a bite harsh enough to bring tears to my eyes.

"So pristine and asking to be marked," she finishes.

She pulls my ass roughly up into her, leaving me leaning down into the cuffs, ass and throbbing cunt exposed for her. Flush against her, I feel the outline of her garter belt. *Fuck,* I think. *She knows how much I like that.* She swats at the side of each breast. I feel the tip of the crop underneath me dragging over my belly and across my slick folds before reaching my ass, where she swipes it in a few places, seemingly judging their merit as a target. Swipes give way to swats. Gentle—infuriatingly so—teasing.

"Harder," I beg, too aroused for the torture of these featherlight sensations.

"First defying me, now ordering me around," she says with fire in her voice. "I don't think so." The crop falls swiftly. "You've been a bad girl," she says, increasing the intensity of her blows. I can hear how much she's enjoying this in her voice, and the throbbing arousal of my clit gets worse.

"Aw, this spot is sore, isn't it?" Nicole asks teasingly as she pauses and runs her hand over what must be a nice welt developing. "What a shame," she says, not sounding sorry at all as she brings the crop down with perfect aim on just that spot.

"Oh fuck," I pant, the leather on my sore flesh toeing the brink of too painful, a delicious pain that I want to endure for her.

"I love watching you take this from me," she says appreciatively. "You're nice and pink for me now," she continues. She reaches between my legs to find me soaking.

"Just like I thought," she admonishes. "Bad girl, you enjoyed that too much."

All I can do is whimper. Her hand barely brushes my clit and I grind into it, needing her fingers inside me. But I know I can't ask. I've been bad.

"Bad girl," she says again, followed by a quick and purposeful strike with her crop. After a pause in the blows and with her hand between my legs, the sting of the leather feels exquisitely painful.

"Are you sorry yet?" she asks.

"Yes," I pant. "I am."

Nicole's breath hovers in my ear for a moment and I turn my face to kiss her, wondering if my punishment is over, but then the breath disappears and the leather lashes across my skin.

"That didn't sound sorry enough," she explains.

"I'm sorry. I was a bad girl for disobeying you and enjoying your punishment," I say sincerely, taut with preparation for another blow, but I hear the crop drop softly on the bed. My legs are pushed roughly apart.

"I think you've learned your lesson." Her hand slides to my cunt.

"So wet for me," she says softly as she reaches around me, leaning down to bite the top of my shoulder, hard.

"Oh fuck, yes," I moan as her fingers dance over my still-throbbing clit. She gives a few teasing flicks before settling into a rhythm. I whimper, starting to come apart in her arms as she strokes me.

"Are you going to be a good girl and come for me?"

she asks, sliding two, and then three fingers into me from behind and working them inside in all the right ways that she knows I like.

"Yes, fuck." I lose my words into an unintelligible moan as I throw my head back, hips starting to move against her hand as I feel myself about to come. She stills my hips, holding me firmly in place.

"No," she says firmly as she fucks me relentlessly with her hand. "Be still. No wiggling." Her commanding voice and restraint send me over the edge. I come hard around her fingers, the orgasm pulsing through me as I'm held immobile by her hands and the cuffs.

"Good girl," she says, removing my cuffs and blindfold. I struggle to turn myself around, but she holds me down, gently now, to kiss over the welts teased up by the crop.

"Mm, you're going to have some nice marks tomorrow, babe," she says, pleased. I smile, looking forward to the little reminders. I turn around and pull Nicole to my level, raising myself up to look down at her appreciatively.

"Fuck, you look sexy in a garter belt," I tell her, eyes roaming up her long legs to her naked exposed pussy, topped by the belt's black lace. My hand roams up one thigh, skimming the straps.

"And being tied up looks wonderful on you," she says, pulling me into her and locking her arms firmly around me.

THE TEST

Kristina Wright

D o you trust me?"

It is a question that causes my throat to go dry as you click the lock on the collar around my neck. I'm trembling, overwhelmed with emotions. Excited. Nervous. Terrified.

I do not like anything around my neck, not even a necklace. It was the one thing I would not allow you. Anything else, you could have. Anything else, I would do. But not my neck. Not until now. And you have worked very hard to get to this point. You have earned my devotion. My love.

"Yes."

You nod. You knew it already, but you needed to hear it. So did I.

"Now," you say, "repeat the rules so I know you

understand them."

I swallow hard, conscious of the wide leather band that is almost too tight. Almost.

"You will give me a key, but I am not allowed to use it."

"Yes."

I stare into your eyes, remembering everything you said. "I am not allowed to conceal it under my clothes."

"Go on."

"If someone asks about it, I'm to tell them the truth."

"Which is?"

"I'm a submissive. I am yours."

"Are you?"

I do something I never thought I would ever do in my life. I nod.

"Good," you say. "Will it be difficult?"

I feel like you are studying my every reaction. You are, of course. You're a psychology professor; it's second nature for you to study human behavior. Especially mine.

"No. I think it'll be okay." I swallow again. It's easier this time. "No, I know it'll be okay. I trust you."

The three hardest words for me to say and I say them to you.

"Thank you." You slap my ass hard. "Time to go."

I risk a pout. "I have an hour."

You're silent. Just when I think you're going to say no, you say, "On your knees."

I'm moving before you finish speaking. Eager, hungry, ready to please. It's the collar, in part. The rest is all you. What you do to me. How you make me feel. I should be concentrating on what I'm doing in an hour. Instead, I'm concentrating on the task at hand—getting your pants open, getting your cock in my mouth. Tasting you, sucking you, licking around the head and down the shaft. Milking you with my hands, first one, then the other. Then both, when I can't take it anymore and I'm desperate for your release. You oblige me, three long spurts down the back of my throat, a tug on the collar for good measure. Suddenly, the constriction around my neck is no longer a hindrance; it's a promise.

"Good girl. I'll give you your release when you return."

I knew you would say that. That's what all of this is about. Delayed gratification, the reward after the work. I run my tongue around my lips, reminding myself to reapply my lipstick.

"Thank you. For everything."

Another tug. "Much as I like your long hair, I'm rather enjoying the collar as a means of moving you about."

I can hear the amusement in your voice, and I smile in return as you help me rise.

"As you please, Sir."

You nod. "You please me always. Now get going."

For the first time all day I'm nervous. "Yes, Sir."

You catch me by the chin, tilt my head up to meet your gaze. "You'll do brilliantly. Won't you?"

I smile. "Yes, I will."

"Yes, you will. Good luck."

You kiss me then and the kiss is sweet until the end. You nip me hard and I whimper.

"Think of me," you whisper. "Whenever you get nervous, remember what is waiting for you."

I'm trembling as I slip out the door, another stinging slap on my ass to remind me I'm not wearing underwear beneath my demure gray dress.

I return six hours later, jubilant. You are waiting for me in the bedroom. Naked.

"Undress," you say when you see me in the doorway. "Now."

I don't hesitate. There are a row of buttons down the front of my dress. I start at the top, releasing buttons until I reach my waist, then letting the dress fall. My shoes were kicked off by the door, so now I wear only a plain bra.

"No. Come here," you say when I reach for the hook.

I kneel on the side of the bed and stare at your erection. I'm wet—I can feel it, the heaviness of my desire. You release the clasp of my bra, massaging my breasts as the fabric falls away.

Once, twice, you wrap the bra around my wrists and I don't protest. I want this. I've needed it since I left this morning and now...reward for the work.

You tie me to the headboard; I'm still on my knees,

but now also resting on my elbows, ass in the air.

"How did you do?"

"It went well, I think."

You slap my ass. "Want to rephrase that?"

I squirm. Do I? I would really like a few more slaps like that; the heat ratchets up the level of my arousal. But I'm already hot, already wanting.

"I did well. I was poised, organized, prepared for every question. I never hesitated. You would've been proud."

You give me what I want—each cheek receives a stinging slap. "I *am* proud. I never doubted you."

I tug at the bra restraining me. I prefer more restraint. But I know this is only a prelude to more. The hint of the reward to come.

I'm lost in that thought when you suddenly thrust into me. I cry out in surprised joy.

"I've been waiting for you for hours," you all but growl. "I can't wait any longer."

"Yes, Sir." I'm in full agreement.

"And the collar?" You thrust into me as if to emphasize your point. "Did anyone ask?"

I moan, filled—and fulfilled—by you. "No, but they stared. They were wondering."

"Let them wonder."

"How did you know it would work?" I'm curious, though I'm having a hard time concentrating. "How did you know it would help me?"

You tug the collar again. I arch my neck obligingly.

Anything for you.

"I knew you'd be so focused on the collar, and what they were thinking, that you wouldn't be nervous about your oral boards. You'd be too distracted by me to second-guess your answers."

"I was nervous," I gasp, as you fuck me hard. "I was blushing down to my toes."

"But you weren't nervous about the boards." You slap my thigh, hard. "Were you?"

"No!"

"And soon, there will be two doctors in the house."

History nerd girl that I am, the thought arouses me even more. "Yes!"

"What do you say?"

"Thank you, Sir," I gasp, my orgasm rolling over me in a wave as you put your hand in the small of my back and push me down to the bed. "Thank you."

Your thighs tremble against me as your climax takes hold. Then we're there, together, where we belong, your finger tucked inside the collar, giving it a gentle tug as a reminder. As if I need reminding at all.

PATIENTLY WAITING

Alyssa Morris

Her nostrils fill with the scents of leather and the vanilla candle that she knows is lit on the table. On her knees, leaning over the ottoman next to the couch, her breasts rub on the cold leather as her nipples harden and try to push deeper into the material. The added stimulation is welcome, especially since she has been tightly blindfolded and had earplugs put in. She can't hear anything, and even if she got the blindfold to come off she wouldn't be able to look behind her due to being bound in her current position. Her hands are tied tightly behind her back, forcing her to use her chest to keep herself balanced. She can only imagine how she looks, chocolate skin draped over the smooth cream-colored leather. She waits, the fan blowing above her creating a gentle breeze that caresses her body from the back of her shoulders down to the crack of her plump ass. Her brown dreaded hair is down, just how he likes it, and she can feel some of it tickling the nape of her neck.

For her, being told to wait is one of the hardest commands to follow. She can suck cock on command, get in position for a spanking when asked and be open and ready for a good fuck whenever her Master gets hard. However, waiting is the most painful act. To her it feels like a waste. Why make her wait when she could be being used in some way? She already knows the answer to this question as it floats through her mind. Because it is about submitting to her Master; he knows how to push her limits in just the right way. Some have their limits pushed by pain or extreme behaviors. Not her; when she is waiting her mind races, wondering when he will appear.

As what seem like hours pass before her, she thinks about what might be coming. Will it be a spanking or will her Master be so horny from watching her squirm in anticipation that he won't be able to keep from fucking her? Her mind continues to race. At least when he's behind her with a riding crop or a paddle she knows there is another blow coming, another jolt to her nervous system, but waiting is completely different; she doesn't know where to expect a sensation of pleasure or pain. He's told her that he would test her both physically and mentally. She should have known that when he asked her what her biggest personality defect was and she responded, "I can be so impatient sometimes, I'll work on it though," he would be the one to help her get there. Even though she feels like this is some kind of punishment, she knows it isn't, and trusts him to know when she's reached her limit.

She is starting to fidget and even tries to strain her hearing through the earplugs to see if maybe there's some noise loud enough to let her know what is going to happen next. The effort is futile; he wouldn't do anything to make this easier for her. This is about her learning something about herself and pleasing her Master. As more time goes on, she also knows that she is getting closer to finding out just what he has in store for her today. This thought alone excites her. Her clit is starting to swell, the early stages of wetness forming between her thick lips. She sighs a little, hoping that maybe he will hear and make a move soon. She moves her knees just enough to give her body a small break from the current position.

Moments later, she feels the breeze pick up and knows that he must be there, coming up behind her. Something makes a trail down her spine. She arches her back up to meet it, savoring the touch that she has been waiting so long for. Her earplugs are taken out.

"I watched you the whole time. I saw you squirming and I know how hard it was for you to just wait for me." He slides his finger through her drenched pussy. She loves every second of the sensation and tries to push back, but she feels his finger moving away. He holds his finger up and sees that it is glistening.

"It seems that you like waiting more than I thought," he says, and she knows not to respond for fear of what he might, or might not, do next.

Right after she hears these words leave his mouth, she feels his fingers back between her legs as he rubs on her clit, making it swell even more.

"Hmmm. I see you really like that, Sierra. I like how your body is just calling out for me. I think you're almost ready," he says with a smile in his voice.

She knows exactly what this means; she feels the change in temperature as he pulls his body away from her and goes off somewhere. Whining or speaking will only make it last longer. He left the earplugs out so now she can hear noises, what sounds like metal. All she can do is continue to wait.

BRUNCH

L. C. Spoering

They were sitting at the table when the phone buzzed, and, out of habit, Nina checked the time. It was one hour, almost to the second, since they'd left the apartment, and the bet she'd had with herself had proved right about when the text message would arrive: five minutes to walk to the café, twenty-five minutes to order their coffees and consume them, half an hour to chat between themselves. It was a generous allotment of time in any circumstance, and she wasn't bitter about it, only self-congratulatory that she'd predicted it so accurately.

Lizzie looked up from her book, her expression seemingly indifferent, but Nina could read the fight between anxiousness and excitement in the lines between her eyebrows and the single twitch at the corners of her mouth—to say nothing of the movement under the table, her knees coming together and pressing, hard.

"You finished?" Nina asked sweetly, sliding her papers together between her hands, lifting the stack to push them, in a rather undignified fashion, into her shoulder bag, snapping it closed with one movement of her fingers.

Lizzie was slower to move, her toes turning in toward each other under the table. She shut her book and picked up her pens. The table was scattered with them—ballpoints and highlighters, the trappings of a grad student—in conjunction with her thick and heavy textbook, corners gouged and pages dog-eared. Nina possessed only the papers and her red pen, glasses on her nose and hair in a messy bun giving her the air of a naughty librarian—none of these perceptions, about either of them, was off. Lizzie's hair was short, her face makeup free, her sweater black. They could be book-ends on either side of their educational divide, a before and after.

They rose in unison, bussed their cups and saucers, Nina's fork stained red from her lipstick. The café was bustling, and Nina took the lead toward the back; there was an exit there, but she redirected them to the bathroom, with its flimsy door with only a knob lock, which she pushed in before she even flipped on the light.

The fluorescent bulb was slow to warm, and so the room was greenish, the walls covered in a garish sort of graffiti, left with pen and marker and dug in the walls with fingernails. Nina focused, for just a moment, on a lopsided heart drawn in green next to the paper-towel dispenser before she carefully set her cell phone on the edge of the sink.

"Panties off," she breathed out, her bag sliding off her shoulder and to the floor. They were both wearing skirts, Lizzie's shorter, a stretch of pale skin visible between the hem and the cuffs of her kneesocks.

Lizzie's bag was already on the floor, and she rose up on the toes of her sneakers as her fingers went under her skirt to tug her underwear off—a black lace thong, the same as she always wore, damp in the middle. She blushed as she untangled the garment from her shoes and held it out to Nina, who draped it by the cell phone.

The room was slowly being filled in as the bulb warmed, and Nina could hear the scrape of chairs and feet, the chatter of voices down the narrow hall lending a sort of musicality to the scene, disjointed and distant as it was.

"Skirt up." Her voice didn't waver with the commands, and she kept her eyes on Lizzie's; the student, in turn, seemed unable to tear her own away, even as she flipped up the hem of her skirt and inched it up her thighs, holding it at the waistband.

She was clean shaven, but her cunt was already swollen and purple, an almost startling contrast to the white of her thighs. Her head tipped back against the wall, next to a narcissist's epitaph scrawled in uneven black letters, her eyes following Nina's descent to the floor, like water cascading, one fluid movement, her skirt billowing and pillowing around her knees when she landed.

There was a time allowance—there always was, either by design or by the sheer fact that they were in a busy restaurant during the Saturday brunch rush, and Nina wasted no time pushing Lizzie's thighs apart and forcing the girl to rise up on her toes again to keep level, her ass pushing away from the wall almost automatically. Nina had to giggle, and Lizzie whined at it, her big dark eyes still on the woman on the floor, but already unfocused, fingers kneading at the fabric clutched in her hands.

Nina used only the tip of her tongue first, pressed to that crest at the top of Lizzie's sex, slipping down that little hill to meet the exposed tip of her clit. Lizzie's response was quite instantaneous: a sudden high-pitched whine, quickly choked as she ducked her chin, an effort to keep herself quiet. Her hands were occupied, so she couldn't bite at her palm. Nina flashed her a smile, conspiratorial, and repeated the motion, and again, a teasing, testing flick, back and forth, too much and too little at once.

Lizzie sputtered out something that could have been English, or Swahili, or some long-dead language, pulling her skirt up over her belly as she tipped her pelvis closer to Nina's mouth. Nina let her advance for just a moment, flat of her tongue caressing the girl's clit, slit and smooth inner lips all at once, before she drew back.

"You know what you're supposed to do," she said, eyebrows raised, all teacher with her glasses and patronizing expression.

"Please please *please*," came that pant, without hesitation, the lips on Lizzie's face gone purple, too, with that same rush of blood. She was nodding her head with each syllable, eyes blinking desperately already against the tears pooling along the rims.

Nina's mouth curled in a smile. "There you go." And there was a reward for that, of course, tongue pushing her folds apart, firm this time, lapping along her clit, over her wet pussy, with full intention and attention now.

Lizzie squirmed over Nina, desperation making her pull her skirt higher and higher until it was locked under her breasts, hands pressed to her ribs. She whined and wiggled and pleaded, and, when she came, it was with a squeal, like she'd been pricked with a needle, her body spasming up from the wall before smacking back against it, shaking.

Nina wiped her mouth and got unsteadily to her feet, her own cunt pulsing, neglected. She was dizzy as she reached for the phone and touched the screen so it illuminated, the speakers turned all the way up.

"Good girls." His voice was warm over the line, and the light above the sink finally synced into place, as though waiting for his commentary, just as they were.

Nina rubbed her cheek to her shoulder and Lizzie

fixed her skirt, face flushed. "Thank you." They spoke in unison, like dolls with their cords pulled.

"Come on home, then," he said, and there was the distinct clink of his belt over the line, clear as day. "I miss you."

LOVE AND SALT

Erzabet Bishop

G ood, you're here." Mrs. Coulter smiled and held out her hands for me to hand over my clothes.

I put down my bag and slid my shirt over my head. Not wearing a bra was preferable on Tuesdays. Besides, it saved time. Slipping off my sandals, shorts and panties, I knelt on the ground at her feet and allowed her to add whatever accessories my Mistress had in mind for today's activities.

Mrs. Coulter brushed my hair and gathered it into a ponytail. She slid a blue nylon dog collar around my neck and snapped on the leash.

"Get up."

I lowered my eyes to the floor and did as she bade me. It had been a week since I'd seen my Mistress and my pussy yearned for her touch. Still, I wondered why a nylon collar and not my leather one. Had I done something to upset my Mistress? The thought had me biting my lip in frustration and I almost missed an instruction.

Mrs. Coulter led me into the kitchen and ordered me to sit on the floor. She then tethered me to a new ring that had been placed on the island. Interesting.

"Wait here."

I knelt in Mistress's favorite position, with my knees bent and separated, my shoulders back, thrusting out my breasts for her inspection. I knew from experience that I had better be ready or face a punishment.

"Victoria. How lovely to see you." Mistress entered the kitchen, still in her work clothes. The silver-gray suit and frosted lavender blouse highlighted her waves of dark curls. I longed to feel them against my flesh.

"Yes, Mistress." I lowered my eyes, a smile brightening my face.

"Get up so I can see those beautiful breasts."

I wobbled a little as I stood, keeping my hands behind my back and my breasts thrust out toward her.

"Lovely. Now, remove my clothes." She unhooked my leash, and I hurried to do as she commanded.

I draped her jacket on the top of one of the kitchen chairs. Fingers shaking, I unbuttoned her blouse and let the silken fabric pool under my fingertips as I unfastened the buttons. She slid out her arms and, clad in her bra, bent down and kissed my left breast.

"I have missed you, my girl." Her slate-gray eyes

twinkled with mischief. "Now, hurry."

I moved behind her and slid the zipper down on her skirt. Her bra was easy to unhook, but as I knelt down to remove her shoes and underwear, I paused to kiss her shoe.

"Impertinent girl. Did I tell you to kiss anything? Five paddles for you. Now finish the job."

"Yes, Mistress." I carefully pulled off her shoes and placed them by her clothes. She was not wearing any panties.

"Good. Now go and stand at the counter with your ass pointed to me."

As I heard her bustling around the kitchen, moisture began to pool between my legs. My Mistress was most inventive.

"Now, you will hold still and count to five."

I braced myself on the counter and as the first slap came, I winced.

Crack!

"One."

"That was for your willfulness."

Crack! Crack!

"These are for your daydreaming. Pay attention or you'll find yourself unhappy for the rest of the evening."

"Two and three. Thank you, Mistress." I hiccuped a sob as the heat crackled in waves across my bottom.

"This one is for my pleasure."

Crack!

"Four," I sobbed, tears running down my face as she hit me particularly hard.

Crack!

"This one is for yours." She rubbed her heavy breasts against my back and brushed her thatch of hair against my flaming ass.

"Five." Thank you, Mistress, for correcting me." Liquid boiled between my thighs as the scent of my arousal flooded the air.

"Good. Now up on the counter and lie flat. I have a special treat for both of us tonight."

"Yes, Ma'am." I climbed up as she'd ordered and lay down.

"Now, what is my favorite drink, my lovely slave?" She was gathering things from around the kitchen and placing them above my head, where I could not see.

"I would think, Ma'am, that your absolute favorite is the salted caramel mocha, if I am not mistaken."

"Good girl. Since I have not seen my favorite slave for a week and I also long to taste my favorite drink, what do you think we should do?"

"Whatever my Mistress pleases."

"I quite agree."

Mistress tethered me down to the counter with soft nylon rope attached to built-in rings. My pulse pounded as she took out the first two squeeze bottles and drizzled something cold across my breasts, belly and just above my mons. The smell of chocolate and caramel tickled my nose and I moaned, delighting in the sensation as her mouth began to move across my flesh.

"Hmmm. Very sweet. Caramel suits you, my dear." She squeezed out some more over my breasts and reached for the salt, shaking it over me. Starting at my breasts, she roamed her way just upward of the apex of my thighs and licked at the sticky caramel and chocolate she had poured across my needful flesh. "Now, I wonder. Are you ready for more?"

I moaned, hungry for her lips to devour me in my most tender of places. She had touched me every place but where I wanted it the most.

"Lovely." She moved between my legs and began to nibble along the side of my moist folds.

I writhed under her ministrations and shrieked as she sucked my erect clit into her mouth, my hips bucking against her face.

"Oh my god. Oh my goooodddd!" I screamed as she gave a long and languorous ice-cream lick down my folds and entered me with three of her fingers, stretching me wide open.

She hammered my pussy with her fingers and sucked my clit into her mouth, sending sparks of electricity through my body. I came, shuddering, against her hand as she mouthed her way back up to my breasts, pleasure meeting pain as she nipped at my erect nubs with her teeth.

Mistress stood and wiped her face with a moist towel, then kissed me long and hard. I could taste myself on her tongue. I moaned against her mouth as she reached above my head for another temptation. Holding up a small cup of ice and a butterfly vibrator, she plucked a piece of ice from the cup and inserted it into my heaving cunt.

"Ohhhh!" I breathed as she secured the vibrator around my hips and positioned it for its fullest potential against my clit. The ice made me writhe against my bonds. She smacked me on the thigh. I began to pant and struggle to get myself under control. The ice burned as my pussy clenched around it greedily.

"Stop." Mistress gave me a stern look and flicked on the vibrator.

Pleasure and pain ricocheted through me as the pulse of the vibrator took over. I could barely breathe.

Mistress smiled wolfishly and turned the dial higher.

"I think it's time we tried a blended iced latte. What do you think?"

I couldn't have agreed more.

BRAZEN

Kathleen Delaney-Adams

I want you to hurt me.

I am kneeling in the parking lot of the bar, already in agony after mere minutes on the asphalt. Although we have been loving and fucking for years, I still dress to impress you (read: make you hard) and tonight I went all out, femme guns blazing, before you swung me up on the back of your bike and drove me to the dyke bar for a poetry reading. Now my slinky dress is hiked up high somewhere around my thighs, surely my pussy is showing and my new heels are no doubt scratched to bits. I hear the chatter and curious mutterings of passersby on their way to the reading. I feel anxious, for I am supposed to be performing at the open mic, and you grabbed my upper arm in your hand and dragged me out here before the andro-mistress-of-ceremonies called my name.

I feel anxious, for I have no idea what you want.

Every time you touch me, my need expands beyond me, outside of restraint. Incapable of controlling it, I dissolve into liquid desire that cannot be quenched unless you hurt me, use your hands on me with a violence I recognize as your love. I am left waiting for your fist to soothe me and break me and bring me back down to this earth. Gravity. Your fist is my gravity.

Your face looks more than slightly dangerous with need, and relief washes over me when I see the smile lurking behind your eyes. That mix of dark and sweet in you had me, claws in deep, from the moment we met. Bad boy with brutal hands or irresistibly charming butch—no matter, I was a goner. Still am. You cup my head tenderly in one hand and unzip your jeans slowly with the other, savoring the sudden gleam in my eye. How I love the sound of your zipper. I tremble as much from anticipation of what is coming next as from the sharp pain in my knees and legs.

The first time you marked my face we had been fucking for days, your cock claiming me as if you had waited a lifetime for my cunt. I pushed you, pleading— it was so big it hurt me, and fear and desire warred inside me. You called me your whore and made me take it, and in that moment, I would have done anything for you.

The first time you marked my face you were slapping it in the front seat of my car, your other hand gripping my hair, calling me *filthy* while I sobbed. The next morning your handprint was visible on my cheek, purple and blue. I felt terrified and elated.

"Do you like to make me feel good, baby?" you croon, and I melt. I nod eagerly, bite my lower lip, want to scream, "Yes!" and throw myself at you. But you don't want that; you have asked me to kneel in front of you and wait for your instructions like a good girl. So I wait, wetter by the minute, my pussy creaming and slick, just the way you like it to be when you touch me.

"Show me how good."

You are stroking your cock languidly. I cannot tear my eyes from you, your hand, your girth. Your cock drives me crazy—watching you handle it even more so—and I gasp, "Yes, yes," as you move it closer to my mouth.

When you say, "Let me come down your throat," I swallow you whole.

I have craved. For an eternity, I have craved. I thought tenderness happened at the moment I broke and began to cry and the person who was beating me stopped to hold me. Yes, tenderness. Now I realize that I was wrong. Tenderness is the moment I break and you push me beyond—beyond fear, beyond limits. Tenderness is the way you carry me into my craving and stay with me while I struggle. A moment snaps inside me and I am flying toward you and you knew all along I could take it.

I have never been so safe in all of my life.

I forget everything but this feeling. I forget the

parking lot, the queers around us entering and leaving the bar, the noise, the nervous rush I feel when you fuck me in public. I forget all of it, and work my mouth on you like it's all I live for. I take you inside me, every inch, gagging and choking, and use my spit to lube you up some more so I can take you in even farther down my throat. I breathe through my nose, and when you are in so deep I can no longer do that, I let the tears and snot run down my face.

"You look so beautiful, baby, so beautiful." Your voice is ragged and so damn sexy I feel weak and grip your legs for support.

You call me "beloved whore" when I please you, and I live for those words, to see the look on your face when I have been a good girl for you, when I take your cock, when I make you come down my throat, when I spread my legs for you without being told. Other times, you call me a filthy whore because I beg for your cock. I cry because I want you to tell me I am good. I cry because a core part of myself needs to be filthy, debased, hurt. And I cry because I worship you and do not know how to make you see what you are to me.

You are moaning now, leaning back against the brick wall, your hands cradling my face, your eyes closed. I am clutching your legs to hold myself up and crying openly, watching you as you begin to shake, violently, a muffled cry, before you come in my mouth and down my throat. Your possession washes over me and inside me. I am yours, and I know in that moment, you are mine.

Your eyes are not leaving my face, my filthy, tear-streaked, makeup stained, puffy and bruised face, and I know, from your eyes I know, I am beautiful. And you are whispering. "My princess," you whisper. And I am precious.

"Mmmmmm. Nice, girl." You open your eyes and wink at me. You pull the ever-present handkerchief from your pocket and hand it to me to clean myself up while you re-tuck your cock into your jeans and zip yourself up. You lift me to my feet, holding me to your chest for a moment until my trembling abates and I stand on my own. Your arm around me, we walk toward the door of the bar. The muffled applause and guffaws from a handful of onlookers grow louder when you pull me into your arms again to kiss me.

"I love you, darling," you whisper in my ear. "Such a good girl."

I am still grinning when we reenter the din and noise. I only hope I have a moment to collect myself before it's my turn at the mic.

STORY TIME

Inara Serene

No. That is just not happening."

"Oh? Are you telling me what to do, cupcake?"

He could have picked a thousand other names that, to anyone else, would have been more degrading. Slut, bitch, whore—even cunt, though I detest the word—any of those would have been preferable. But he had hit on a nickname that genuinely made me squirm. I hated the sickeningly saccharine sound of it, and all that its frosted syllables implied.

The first time he had used it, he sprinkled it casually into our conversation. I don't think he had guessed just how much I would hate that term of supposed endearment, but my vehement response told him everything he needed to know. And once he had hit on something he could use to tease me, to make me uncomfortable and indignant, he sank his teeth into it and refused to let go.

"No. Fuck. I wouldn't say that...I just...please? Please don't make me."

He lifted the corner of his mouth in a sardonic smile.

"You know the more you tell me how much you hate the idea, the more I want to make you do it."

My gaze dropped to my folded hands, and I examined the ring on my left index finger with undue attention. Even the barest hint of suggestion of the threat rendered me pliant and demure. His words traced over the outline of the tattoo he had imprinted on my psyche, making me visibly shake with the knowledge that I was his, and he could do as he wished with me.

"I know, Sir. How about I'll just be good, and then you will have no reason to punish me?" I asked, my eyes lighting up hopefully.

"Oh, Lizbeth. You have so much to learn, my dear. I don't need a reason. And in any case, you *want* to please me, don't you?"

I nodded vigorously, eager to demonstrate my determination to behave.

"Then you'll do exactly as I say, with none of the usual sass."

I nodded again, this time with a tad less enthusiasm.

"So we'll get started then, shall we?"

I looked into his toffee eyes, and reached for the book beside me. I had borrowed the novel from a colleague a few months back. It seemed like an intriguing story: a kinky romance between a blushing virgin and a billionaire. In theory, it sounds hot, right? Yeah, not so much. Two paragraphs in, and it became quite clear that the writing was less than stellar, and after flicking through the pages and sampling some scenes, I wasn't terribly impressed with the actual BDSM dynamic, either. What kind of idiotic dom tells a newbie sub lovers don't need safewords, anyway?

Needless to say, this book was not my favorite, but I suppose that's why Liam chose it.

This was a punishment, after all…

I opened the page and began reading, my voice quavering with nerves. And he just sat there, smiling at me as I knelt beside him and narrated possibly one of the worst erotic novels ever written.

Halfway into the second page, he grabbed my collar—well, *his* collar, really—and forced me to look at him.

"And what are you forgetting, my little slut?"

My eyes flashed at the degradation, and I opened my mouth to protest, but one glance at his face closed it promptly. And anyway, truth be told, I *was* his little slut. I would be anything he wanted me to be.

And I knew just what he wanted.

I traced a hand down my chest, past the ridiculously padded purple push-up bra, and pushed aside my matching purple panties. Taking care to start out slowly, I lightly brushed my already-hardened clit with fingers cold from crisp autumn air. I knew how much Liam liked to tease, and I wanted to show him how good I could be. Even when I gave myself pleasure, I did it to please him, only him.

I painted tight, invisible circles onto my nub, and soon I couldn't stop myself from slipping a finger into my pussy. God, I was soaked.

"Ahem."

My eyes jerked open, and I nervously looked up at him. He did not look particularly pleased.

"Did someone tell you to stop reading, or are you just so dumb that you forgot?"

Well, fuck.

"No, Sir. I mean, I didn't...I'm sorry."

"I suppose I can help you, if you really can't handle the multitasking. And they say women are better at that...but I digress. Would you like that, cupcake? My fingers in your soaked little pussy, and my thumb rubbing your clit?"

"Oh god yes," I practically whimper. I love it when he talks like that, shaping words into vivid stories of what he's about to do to me. "Please, please. Please help me while I read for you."

"Mmm." He was visibly pleased. I think reducing me to begging is one of his favorite activities. "Since you've been relatively good..."

He reached out a perfect, slender hand, so pale in contrast to my darker hues, and easily slipped his fingers inside of me. I could have screamed with relief.

"You're a loud little slut, aren't you?" he taunted.

So maybe I actually *did* scream, just a little.

I began to read again, though it was a Herculean effort. I formed those terribly constructed sentences with parched lips and, between desperate gasps for breath, I read aloud to Liam. Every time I closed my eyes, or forgot to focus on my reading, he abruptly stopped curling his fingers in my wet cunt, and I hastily resumed my performance.

Yes, performance was the right word. Liam played me every bit as beautifully as he played his grand piano, eliciting sounds and sighs and sensations utterly beyond description.

I didn't want to come. I couldn't—*wouldn't*—climax while reading such a crappy excuse for literature. But that wasn't my choice to make, as it turned out. The sheer knowledge that I was actually doing this ridiculous task simply because Liam had asked me to, coupled with his skilled hands, was enough to drive me to the edge of madness.

Every muscle was positively singing with tension, and it was all I could do to pant, "Please, can I come, Sir?"

"Oh, I don't know...*can* you?"

That bastard.

"Please, *may* I come, Sir?"

"I suppose so. Come for me, my love."

That final word of sweetness sent me careening over the edge, crashing hard into an infinite sky of exploding stars.

But when I opened my eyes, I was still in my bed, my solid, soft bed with the man taken straight from both my dreams and my nightmares.

"I'm so proud of you, Lizbeth," he murmured as he held me in his freckled arms.

And as I snuggled into his chest, the stupid book still beside us, I felt proud to be his.

PRINCESS

Amelia June

Today is my princess's birthday.

He's thirty-four today and still rocking the youthful looks. Five o'clock shadow gives him a sexy ruggedness that women like. He's tall and broad and carries himself with the swagger that comes from knowing he's mine. I'm already wet as I watch him sit in the pedicurist's chair.

As I'd hoped, the ladies at the spa fuss over him. They don't see many men, they say. They tell him, "Happy birthday," in that strange falsetto of women who are uncomfortable and more than a little jealous of me and mine. When they paint his nails, I see the shine reflected in his gaze. I can't focus on anything but him. He belongs to me, but his devotion makes me weak in the knees. I'd do anything for him.

The drive home is quick and maddening. He basks in the glow of the pampered, and I send him straight to the bedroom. I have birthday plans.

"It's just that you can be scary," he tells me, even as he strips his clothes off and waits for me. Mostly, my depth of love for him scares *me*. In my dark times I worry he'll leave me and tell the world how awful I am. I fear my own twisted desires will chase him away. I refuse to let this be a dark time.

Plucking a wooden spoon out of a kitchen drawer, I go back to the bedroom. I give an extra swing to my hips so my high heels click on the tile.

When I get into the room, he's eager. His breath comes quickly, his body shaking with the stress of being on his knees. I hold the spoon in both hands, tapping the bowl of it against my palm. For a moment I'm the evil queen to his princess. "Knees hurt?" I ask, arching one eyebrow.

Okay, look, I can't arch one eyebrow. I've tried. But if I could, I'd be doing it now. He knows this, and he gives me a little grin before settling back on his haunches. "Yes, Lady."

"Want to get off them?"

"Please, Lady."

I nod toward the bed.

I'd never tell him that I'm as hungry for him as he is for me, but I promised him a birthday spanking first. I'm nothing if not an evil queen of my word.

The bed creaks under his weight as he settles into

the familiar position. He starts on his hands and knees but by the time I'm done with him he'll be flat on his stomach, clutching a pillow to his face to contain the shouting.

"How old are you again?" I try to make my voice husky but it really isn't. Even when I'm my most wicked, I'm still me—a short, chubby girl with a few self-doubts.

"Thirty-four," he tells me, his voice a whisper. He's nervous, and I can't help but grin. He's cute when he's nervous.

"Thirty-four," I repeat.

I don't know if he knows I need the encouragement or if he simply wants this as much as I do. Whichever it is, he says, "What about one to grow on?"

"Thirty-five. I can do that." I set the spoon aside. Now that he's seen it, he's anticipating it, so I start with my open hand. I kick off my heels and let my toes sink into the carpet. I take a deep breath, then swing. Three loud *thwacks* without much heat in them. Just enough to get the ball rolling.

He gasps, tilts his pelvis up for more. I oblige, settling into a rhythm of spanks and pauses to give my hand a break. I dip my hands between his thighs to fondle him. I blow cool air over the handprints. A blush blooms on his naked ass the more I hit. He's already disappearing into that space where letting go lets him *be*. He's even prettier now as he lets me ravage him and pull every ounce of devotion I can from him. I'm astonished, as always, that he lets me. I think it astonishes him that I will.

"Lady," he says, just when I think he's left planet Earth for dreamier realms.

My arm is already in midswing but I clench my fist and let it fall. "Yes?"

"That's thirty."

Thirty? Already? "Right. Five more then."

"Yes please." A pause; his voice is shaky and he's breathing heavy. "Lady?"

"Yes?"

"Are you going to use that spoon, or what?" The bed squeaks as he repositions, climbs back up onto his aging knees. He has the temerity to swing his ass from side to side, daring me.

I don't need further encouraging. I pluck the spoon from the bed and give him a hard smack. He yelps and dives forward, his face buried in pillows as he lets out a moan. A spoon-shaped welt appears nearly at once on his already-sore ass, standing out in sharp and glorious relief. I was enjoying the spanking, but this makes me shudder with need. His need for pain and my need to give it work together; I'm so turned on my hand shakes as I deliver another and another blow. He's shouting into the pillow, muffled gasps and moans. I don't have to count these because each impact leaves a perfect spoon-welt.

When all thirty-five spanks have been delivered, I seal them with a brush of my lips over each red bump. I trace my fingernails over the spoon-heads that decorate him. He turns over because I nudge him in the shoulder. His cock stands rigid against his belly, straining despite the sharp pain of the last five blows. I hike my long skirt up and dive onto his cock.

He grips my hips but lets me ride him the way I like. I take him as hard as I hit him and in my mind's eye I can see his welts rubbing on the sheets. When he winces, a jolt of sexual need rushes through me. His thumb finds its way to my clit and rubs the way he knows I like. I drive my hips down over and over, taking my pleasure. My orgasm doesn't build, it comes hard and fast, slamming through me and leaving me weak. I clench around him, and though I'm certain his ass must be throbbing he comes not five seconds after I do.

"Happy birthday." My voice is legitimately husky now, from effort and arousal. He puts his arms around me and pulls me into a sweet kiss. I tuck my head into the hollow of his neck. My arm hurts, which only makes me worry. If my arm hurts, I must have hurt him. I slip out of my postorgasmic joy and into the dark place.

Time passes. I worry. "Lady?"

I lift my head to look him in the eye. "Yes?"

A faint redness creeps into his cheeks, and he flutters his eyelashes at me with all the charm he can muster. "Can we do this again on your birthday?"

"We'll see." He knows how to take care of me. He's my princess.

CONTACT

Shenoa Carroll-Bradd

C lare strode into the hotel bar without glancing to either side, as instructed.

No eye contact, he'd said.

She ordered a sidecar, tugging down the hem of the skirt he'd picked out. It wasn't her favorite, but of the six potential outfits she'd sent, this was the one he wanted. While she waited for her drink, Clare slid a compact mirror from her purse and used it to scope out the other patrons. She wasn't sure what to look for; he hadn't sent a picture of his face, just his hands, crossed over one knee.

The drink arrived. She paid, and took a preliminary sip. She'd been disappointed by that photo at first, but the longer she studied it, the more Clare appreciated that glimpse of him.

The slacks beneath his palms were charcoal gray, high quality, and his nails were clean and clipped, not workman's nails. The length of those elegant fingers stole her attention: pale and strong, long enough to wrap her neck like an African collar. Beautiful. Clare prayed the rest of him measured up.

She took a sip as the mirror oscillated, pausing when it caught a tall man in profile, the dim bar light sketching the contours of his jaw and cheekbone in shadow. She closed the compact before their eyes could meet, but not before catching a glimpse of his long, pale fingers. Her hand trembled around the sidecar.

Footsteps approached, then an elegant hand closed over her wrist. "Finish your drink," he said in a rich whiskey baritone, "and we'll go."

Clare emptied it in two swallows.

He guided her from the bar, one hand on the small of her back, and stopped her at the elevators. "Press UP."

"Are we doing names?"

He tucked a lock of hair behind her ear, stroking his knuckles down her neck. "If you like."

The elevator opened and she saw him, just for a moment, in the mirrored back wall. Clare dropped her gaze and stepped inside, letting him select the floor. Her stomach fluttered as the doors closed.

His hands circled her waist.

She leaned back against his chest, reaching up to sink her fingers into his dark curls.

One arm wrapped her stomach, holding her tight

against him, while the other slid up over her breasts to cradle the curve of her throat.

She responded, arching her back and grinding her hips against his groin.

The elevator opened and they separated, his hand guiding her once more. "Remember," he said when they arrived at his room, "eyes down."

"I remember." Clare slipped into the dark room, where moonlight painted the bed silver. The door closed behind her, and she waited for the lights to flick on, but they didn't.

Strong fingers twined into her hair, pulling her head to the side. Her scalp tingled as he kissed her neck, nuzzling her ear and flushing her skin with the heat of his breath.

Clare moaned and reached back for him, tangling her fingers in his hair as his kisses sharpened into bites that left her shuddering and wet, aching at their fierceness.

"Strip," he commanded, releasing his grip on her hair.

Clare obediently peeled away her top and bra, while behind her, she heard the answering whisper of falling fabric. She peeked just enough to catch a glimpse of him bending to remove his shoes, his unbuttoned shirt falling away from a smooth, pale chest.

He glanced up and she turned around too late. He lifted her skirt and spanked her, just once, hard enough to sting. "What did I say?"

"Sorry."

"Off with the rest of it."

She complied.

He turned her around, laying a hand over her eyes as he lifted her face to a fiery kiss.

When he pushed her backward onto the bed, Clare gasped in momentary panic but kept her eyes closed, feeling like she'd slipped into a falling dream.

"Good," he whispered, before capturing her lips again. One hand artfully teased a nipple while the other worked between her legs.

Clare ground against the rhythm of his fingers.

"Ready?"

"Yes." When he slipped into her, she cried out at the sudden joy of acceptance.

"Tell me when you're close," he ordered.

She nodded, pressing her palms against his chest, feeling each thrust ripple through him.

His hands came down and circled her wrists, holding them above her head to either side of the pillow. He lowered his mouth to her neck again, sucking, biting, drawing shuddering moans from her until, at last, she gasped, "I'm close."

"Open your eyes."

They fluttered open, and Clare stared, transfixed, at the stranger above her.

"Don't look away," he whispered. "Not until you come. Don't you dare look away."

She never wanted to look away again. He looked like a Roman sculpture come to life, and his eyes, his beautiful eyes… As the cresting wave of her orgasm rose, Clare's spine arched and her head started to tilt back.

"No!" He released her left wrist and grabbed her chin, holding her face in line with his. "Look at me."

Clare stared into the depths of his blue-green eyes, eyes like portals to an undiscovered nebula on the edge of space, until her vision blurred from tears. The intensity of the orgasm wracked her body, but he held her in place, their eyes fixed together.

He came moments later, then collapsed beside her, drawing her close against his heaving chest.

Clare pressed a hand over his hammering heart, feeling an addictive blend of protection and possession in the wrap of his arms. She never wanted to be out of their reach again.

After a while his breathing slowed, and Clare had to face facts. She couldn't stay. She had an early meeting tomorrow, and, much as she yearned to fall asleep beside him, could not show up to work in the outfit he'd chosen. Plus, she would need a considerable amount of time and concealer to hide all the lovely work he'd done on her neck.

Reluctantly, Clare extricated herself, then crept over to her clothes and began redressing.

"Leaving?" he asked, voice like warm, distant thunder.

"Yes. Sorry. I have to." She heard him shifting on the bed, but didn't risk a glance. She had everything but her shoes on when he said, "How sorry are you?"

She glanced sideways to see him sitting on the edge of the bed. Clare went to her knees before him, smelling the mingled musk of their sex. She caught his beautiful hands, and reverently brought them to her lips. "Very sorry."

He pulled away, stretching out across the bed.

Clare retrieved her shoes and purse.

"I'll be in touch," he said drowsily.

"Good," Clare replied. "I'd love to see you again…"

He chuckled softly. "Nicholas."

She felt a flutter in her stomach. "Clare."

"Yes. It was nice seeing you, Clare."

The sound of her name on his tongue made her shiver. Clare ducked out of the room quickly, before she lost her nerve, alight at the memory of how those breathtaking eyes had laid her bare.

FOR HER ART

Elise Hepner

The houselights flashed against the backs of my eyelids and a zing of belly-tightening fear clenched way down deep. No amount of breath in my lungs would provide an anchor to reality. This was my glitch in time—a way to prove myself while taking pride in my body. Soon the doors would open and my installation would be open to the public. I would be on the best kind of pedestal—one in the works for three long months.

My sharp, jagged inhales made my muscles quake, which twitched the metal harnesses attached to my suspension cuffs—until the tinkle of noise shuddered down my taut muscles, curling my toes. While I focused on my legs spread in a wide V, icy air from the grate far below my feet pressed against my flushed inner thighs. The rush and low babble of people being let into the art gallery sharply snapped awareness into every inch of my burning flesh.

I forced my eyes open with a quick scan of the pool of strangers streaming through the double doors, filling the industrial gallery space amongst the twinkling sconces. Against the tight cinch of my full-body cuffs my pulse tripped and my reality scattered, making my mouth dry. The first set of wide eyes alighted on my naked-ness—a woman with full lips and gorgeous brunette hair cascading down her insanely low-cut dress, barely a scrap of leather covering her cooch. Her cheeks lit up with the sweetest pale-pink flush. Her gaze ate me up. Every second turned into an hour as her lingering atten-tion forced my nipples tight. Awareness tweaked along my naked flesh as if an invisible hand were skimming all over the supersensitive bits.

Our eyes locked. Her tongue slicked across her lips, making me wet. Her irises were wide with need, and I imagined mine mirrored her lust. The scatter of voices and peals of laughter died away. And as some expensive perfume prickled up inside my nostrils, her small mani-cured hand flitted through the air, as if she intended to touch me. But only the tight caress of air licked against my belly. My intent, voyeuristic friend took three short steps to the right—and pressed the button to the side of me with the heel of her palm.

With a slow blink the rest of the room came rushing back when the chatter reached a staccato pitch.

There was no escaping the woman's choice—no

pushing away the next several seconds in my vortex of helplessness. While what felt like the whole world watched, I remained suspended, at the mercy of my audience when the hidden trapdoor in the floor pulled back. The cranks shifted, gears crying out. Meanwhile the mammoth mounted dildo pressed up closer toward my exposed pussy. Still a few inches below my slick labia, another press of the button and the sex toy would flirt with my cunt.

"Interesting," Glamour Girl remarked with a subtle purr. When she eyed the button again my gaze searched outside our circle to the waiting crowd. Would she do it again? Spoil all the fun?

I was in a room full of strangers intent on having my body, on hive behavior and doing whatever they pleased with me. Was there someone to hold her back and give me a chance to regroup? My brain buzzed on a frazzled, needy frequency.

But that was the test—wasn't it? Would they give me what they wanted and give in to their base desires? Or would they look and not touch?

The up close and personal master of my fate moved back in front of me with a coy smile that tipped my helplessness into an emotion ragged with desire. Goose bumps trickled all along my skin, even beneath the suspension cuffs. I couldn't catch a full breath even if my life depended on it. My pussy muscles clenched down, fingers molded into fists. While my body radiated defiance, I wanted to crack because of the hum of machinery below me. One little push, and I was at their mercy, on the cusp of falling into submission while pinwheeling through a gauntlet starting with pride and shifting toward desperation.

The crowd gaped at me. Others milled around, enjoying my paintings that adorned the other three walls. But I was the artist on display, raw sexuality my burden. More people pulled in close and their stares devoured me from my painted purple toes to the rainbow dreads pulled up in a topknot on my head. No need to obscure their perfect view.

They needed to ogle the goods to make a complete decision, before pressing the button that shifted me that much closer to release, and them that much closer to depravity. Would anyone else step up and make me their bitch? Toy with my body for their own pleasure—or even admit they wanted to see me penetrated in front of so many random onlookers?

While my social experiment played out beneath me, the weight of other people's choices pressed on my body like a million mouths, tongues and teeth, teasing me to the point of breaking. Their gazes burned through me. Body language hinted at their indecision while I lay trussed up for their pleasure, to use or not use as they wished. I could still sense the mere inches that separated the toy from being pressed inside me. It was a blessed relief, and yet I was left with no release. Every inch of me on the knife's edge, while my juices were slick and sticky on my inner thighs.

The brunette vixen who held my undoing in her hands skimmed the lines of my body again, as if I were property. Her head tilted, mouth pursed in indecision. But when she winked and blew me a kiss, I knew my night was far from over.

Button, button, who's got the button?

WORKING IT OUT

Roger Markson

Most people say going to the gym is torturous, but they don't know the half of it—unless, like me, they take lessons from Lucille. See, Lucille isn't just a "fitness instructor," she's also a professional dominatrix, and has found a way to combine her two loves. The idea of a session with a domme had never appealed to me. I'd had too many girlfriends who wanted to tell me what to do; why would I pay a woman for that, when I wasn't even going to get laid?

Well, one day last year, when I stumbled into the wrong room at the gym thinking I was going to take a yoga class that would make me sweat and stretch, I got my answer. Under Lucille's tutelage, I sweated, that's for sure, but there was nothing yoga-like about it. Instead, she was dressed in what I think of as catsuit-lite—a tight pair of black latex shorts that shone under the gym's lights, along with a matching workout bra. She sported a ponytail, bright-red lipstick and a whistle around her neck.

I'd just stepped into the back of the room, but Lucille marched right over to me. "Oh no, sir," she said, her tone mocking. "You'll come right to the front of the class. I need to watch you closely to see if you can perform up to my standards. Everyone here is put through his paces. Isn't that right, class?"

The five other men and two women echoed their agreement. Why was my cock getting hard? I soon learned that Lucille offered a bit extra in this class, above and beyond your typical workout routines. I was supposed to sign a consent form, but since I'd stumbled into the class, I hadn't realized. The moment I fell behind in my lunges, Lucille was upon me.

"What's your name?"

"Kyle," I panted.

"Well, Kyle, I have some unusual teaching methods in this class, to keep everyone in line. Are you ready to follow my rules?"

I didn't completely know what she was talking about, but I was curious, and besides, I'd joined this gym because I'd heard they guaranteed results. "Yes," I said. "I'm ready."

"Then drop and give me fifty push-ups. You have two minutes. If you fail, you will be punished far worse than the push-ups. Oh, and count out loud." I didn't even think about it, just dropped to the floor and began. I figured she'd move on and listen from across the room while she surveyed the other students, but Lucille called out instructions to them while remaining very close to me. Unlike every other fitness instructor I'd ever seen, she was wearing shiny black boots. They were so beautiful it was impossible not to look at them. I found myself wondering what it would be like to lick them...

No sooner had my mind drifted than her boot was right under my nose. "Clearly, your mind is elsewhere. Helen, please go fetch the whip." For a second, I was scared, but when I saw the smile on pretty Helen's face, I let myself go with the moment. "I'm turning you over to Helen for the moment—I can't waste the whole class on you, Kyle." Hearing my name from Lucille's mouth, uttered as both a warning and a promise, it seemed, made me even more aroused. I was pulsing with energy. Was this the famed endorphin rush I'd been searching for? I wasn't sure, but I followed Helen to a far corner.

"Now you're going to do jumping jacks, and I'm going to help you. When I want you to go faster, I'm going to use this whip." She let her eyes travel down to my bulging crotch; loose workout pants couldn't contain my erection. "Is that acceptable?" She knew I was going to agree.

My ass and muscles were sore after the class, but the orgasm I had in the locker room afterward, locked in a stall (I simply couldn't wait) was one of the best ever.

That's how I found myself getting inducted into kinky exercise.

The next day, I signed up for private lessons with Lucille. We meet once a week at her home gym, where I get very special tutoring, which she reserves for her favorite students. She's had custom equipment made. To work out my thighs, she'll have me use a leg press, while she straddles my face. If I pause at either pushing the heavy weights or eating her out, I get punished.

Sometimes she'll make me do hammer curls while she runs her riding crop up and down my inner thighs—if I'm lucky, it caresses my balls and travels over the head of my cock. I rarely get to come in her presence—that's reserved for special occasions, like when I beat a personal record. I don't mind, though, because my sessions with her are the highlight of my week—who can say that about their personal training?

Today she invited another student, Maya, to join us (I, of course, don't get a say). Maya was hot, so I wouldn't have objected even if I did get to voice my opinion. She took off her T-shirt and stood before us in just a black sports bra and tight shorts. Lucille wore another of her latex getups, this time in red. "Maya here is doing some special weight training. Why don't you show Kyle?" And just like that, with no warning, Maya pulled down those clinging pants, got on the ground and did a backbend. At first, I didn't see anything unusual, but then I noticed a string dangling from between her pussy lips.

Lucille reached between her legs and drew out a set of silver balls. "We're working up to bigger and bigger ones, training her inner muscles to be as firm as the rest of her. That's a worthy goal, wouldn't you agree, Kyle?" My dick throbbed as I nodded. "I'll let you help Maya get these back inside." Whenever Lucille says she'll "let you" do something, it really means if you don't do it she'll punish you—although, since I love her beatings, *punishment* may not be the right word.

"She's had me wearing them all day," Maya said when Lucille left the room. "I have to squeeze tightly all the time. It feels like everyone can tell."

"Is it making a difference?"

"Definitely. Lucille can now get her second-biggest dildo inside me." For a second, I was jealous, even as I eased the balls inside Maya. She must have sensed this. "You have to be able to squat with two times your body weight before she fucks you." She moaned as I eased my fingers out of her. I smiled. Now I had something to work toward.

"Are you slacking off in here?" Lucille demanded when she returned.

"I told him about what he has to do to get fucked by you," Maya said.

"Well?" Lucille demanded of me. "Get ready to squat. While wearing a butt plug." Lucille is full of surprises—and I wouldn't have it any other way.

CONTROL

Cate Ellink

Visitors at eight, pet." His soft words, laced with command, make my body thrum.

Dashiell Traversham is forty, well-to-do and not unattractive, but the attributes I adore are his domination, quiet demands and disciplines. He makes my cunt weep and my eyes run. He fills my holes with his seed and I love him more with each drop expelled. When he enters a room, it shrinks, filled with his scents of sandalwood and the sea. I don't need to see to know him. I know every lithe muscle. Every dark hair. Every stretch of tanned flesh. How he tastes. How he likes to be touched.

Dashiell's words may sound like he's letting me know his plans, but this is what I hear. "By seven-thirty tonight you need to be completely denuded of hair, except for your head—that hair will be washed and scented, brushed until it's burnished gold. Refreshments need to be prepared and left ready to be served. You're to present yourself to the study at seven-thirty, and without a word to or from me, bend over the padded metal frame until your cunt is exposed like artwork, to be admired by my visitors. You may or may not be touched; you have no say in that. You are to remain silent and immobile until I ask you, by name, to act in another manner."

I spend the day preparing. Tiny petit fours, delicate sandwiches, decadent peppermint molded chocolates set out. My skin exfoliated until it shines. The bar fully stocked. Every hair removed. Coffee ground and percolated. Flexibility exercises complete. Study dusted and tidied until spotless. Hair brushed with three hundred strokes.

By seven-thirty my cunt is swollen, my clit tender with anticipation. I knock once on the heavy wood of the closed study door. At his command, I enter and walk to the padded bar. It will bend me exactly in half, taking my weight when my feet no longer can. The thick padded leather cushions ensure there's no discomfort.

Stiletto-clad feet spread apart, I drape myself across the bar and bend forward. I feel Dashiell watching. My flexibility has increased since the last visitors. I bend in half fluidly.

The leather against my hips and stomach is cool. The burn in the back of my legs increases as I lower my head. A cascade of hair smothers the wooden boards. Heavy breasts strain as I swing forward, dropping toward my lowered head, stretching the flesh across my ribs. My nipples squeeze. Blood rushes to my brain in a pounding rush. When I first tried this, I orgasmed from the rush of blood, but I've learned control. I wonder if Dashiell remembers.

His cane was so quick back then. I earned it often. An orgasm followed by the cane equaled a double coming. Punishment and reward.

My cunt weeps as Dashiell glances at me. He's a man well pleased, which makes my juices seep.

The next thirty minutes are the hardest. I want his touch, yet he's working. I'm desperate for his soothing words, curious as to who's coming, and curiosity always makes me gush.

Finally, the doorbell sounds and Dashiell rises. He walks past me without a touch, and inside I whimper. I'd hoped for a brush of his fingers across my cunt, or a slip of his nail along my open lips, or perhaps the lap of his tongue against my clit.

Nothing.

Voices. They enter. A woman I don't know and Dashiell. The woman strides across the room, heels rapping on the boards, and stares at me as if I am an objet d'art. Only the faintest caress of breath lets me know she's inspecting my cunt. My hole opens as if to stare back at her. Moisture trickles. I worry I'm not pleasing her, not pleasing Dashiell. I want to weep. What if she finds fault?

She has covered shoes with towering, thin heels.

The patent leather shines. I try not to breathe and fog them. Her shapely legs are encased in dark smoke hose; a black dress skims beneath her knees. I'd only glimpsed her walking in; pale flesh, black hair, black dress, red lipstick.

"Of course." Dashiell answers a question I have not heard. Muscles inside me tense, waiting. What has been asked? What must I do?

A crisp floral perfume weaves itself around me but before I can luxuriate in her scent, she strokes the inside of my thigh with her fingernail. Her gasp sucks air across my lips, so I know she's leaning, examining closely. My cunt clenches as I try not to squirm. The thick warmth of her breath brushes over my anus. She's staring intently at my hole. It pulls tight in protest. But a breeze blown hard on my clit has my body jerking, both holes relaxing and a wetness seeping through me. I shudder despite myself, losing the fight to remain still, to keep my reactions internal.

Footsteps patter across the room but they're background noise. I'm focused on my task. A *whoosh* and my attention is brought abruptly back. My cunt clenches just as the bamboo cane strikes across it, hard. I cry out. Pain, shock and a tiny fission of pleasure rip through me. My clit throbs. Nipples tighten. I bite back any other sound or reaction. *Oh dear lord.* Dashiell hasn't caned my open lips in so long. The sting pounds through my body, setting it on fire. My hole opens and closes, like my mouth wants to, weeping the tears I cannot.

A strong smell of candle wax comes to my attention just as a plop hits my anus. At first there's nothing; it lasts but a millisecond. Then the scalding burn forces the breath from me. A scream echoes in my head. A scream not just of pain but of pleasure, too. My clit throbs until I think it may burst. The pain vanishes as quickly as the wax dries. Only tension, in every tightly wound muscle of my body, remains.

"How exquisite." The woman's voice is breathy and husky. The flick of her nail along my cunt lips almost has me twitching, but I stop myself. The nail—I imagine it long and gleaming red—picks the wax droplet from my anus. Spasms hit. Another mini-orgasm. I almost melt into the padded bench.

"She holds herself well, Dashiell." The woman's voice softens as she walks away from me. I hear snatches of her conversation. "A credit to you…I'd like to show her…" I can't put the words together. My head is spinning with rapture, trying to fight not only the physical sensations she's elicited from me, but the mental ones, too. The sheer joy of knowing I've succeeded, knowing I'll be rewarded, knowing I've pleased, is more powerful than the cane, wax and tongue put together. I'm almost unconscious trying to fight the sweeping orgasm threatening me.

But I must wait.

Eyes scrunched in concentration, I count each breath until my body is under control. Under Dashiell's control.

UNANCHORED

Corrine Arundo

I really want you, your sexy deviant mind slamming into mine and making me into more than and less than I am now.

Your last email, about what you think I am—Submissive Vixen you called me. Too headstrong to just submit like a good girl. Too wild at heart to simply control myself. You know me. You know that I need a strong hand. A strong man. I keep running through thoughts of you: your hands on me and your gravelly voice in my ear.

Tonight, I absentmindedly get myself ready for bed. Wearing faded old Bob Dylan T-shirt and Rainbow Brite panties, imagining your hands tracing the curve of my ass. Washing my face brings awareness of the cool rush of water across my skin, making me remember the feel of ice melting on my cane-welted ass that last night before you left. Climbing into bed, I recall a thousand atrocities you visited on me there, at my insistence.

For the twenty-seventh night in a row now, I will get my vibrator out, buzz against my clit, building the tingling and the hurricane of sensation. Building up to the edge—then stopping because you aren't here and it doesn't feel as good without you. I miss you. And I'm mad at you. The tears come, not surprisingly, like they have for twenty-seven nights now. I am empty, wanting you to make me full again. I am aching and waiting. I am unanchored without you to pull me back to earth, back to where I belong, back under you. Missing you and missing my pleasure is too much. I can't do it. Not anymore.

I send you a short text message, knowing you won't respond: *It feels like cheating, but I can't wait anymore. I need to come. Sorry.*

Somewhere, you'll get this message and probably laugh, knowing that I am melting without you. But tears won't stop me now. I shimmy my silly panties off and slip my fingers over my skin, into my wet and too-long-empty pussy. I'm slick with missing you, easily coating my fingers. Spreading my legs wide for the imagined you in my mind, I slide my fingers up to my clit and pinch and push and pulse.

I can feel you over me, dark eyes glowering down at my behavior.

"Such a bad girl." Your voice echoes in my mind as

tears spill from the corners of my eyes, dripping cold into my ear.

"I can't help myself. I miss you so much." I hesitate a moment.

"Well, if you're going to do this, do it right, bitch." A chill runs through my skin at the thought of your harsh words, holding my brain back from thinking too hard.

"Show me how you like to fuck yourself. Show me how you delight your little cunt." I love the words, like sharp pokes into my cerebral cortex, tricking me into forgetting everything else but this moment.

I spread my legs wider, opening myself for my phantom you. The moisture builds more for me, until my snatch feels like a bowl of warm pudding, all gooey goodness, almost liquid, warm and sweet.

"Not good enough. You need a little pain, don't you?" You know me so well. Of course, I need pain. I'd always come so much harder for you when you hurt me, too. I remember being tied tight, legs and arms stretched and you making me come over and over and over for hours, until I felt raw, in my pussy, in my throat, my brain, through my entire self.

"Nipple clamps, clothespins, ball gag, at a minimum. What else do you want?" I know that's what you'd say. I can't think of anything else, just the pain and pleasure and what you would want me to do for you.

I clip my clover clamps onto myself and hold the chain in my mouth, pushing it back when I work the ball gag between my teeth. Another rush of sweetness as the chain pulls tight on my nipples, stretching them up toward my face. The clothespins were always your favorite. Three on each side of my pussy. That last time, you fucked me from behind while I had them on and when I'd get close to coming, you'd pause and squeeze down on one, or pull it off altogether. Your mind is so good for me.

Now, they press down on me, relentless and burning. My fingers trace down in between the clothespins, finding my wetness and my hardness surrounded by my softness, and stroke. Liquid flows down my asscheeks, so sticky and wonderful. I'm remembering your cock filling my throat, cutting off my air until my vision would haze. Your perfect piece in my ass, stroking and stretching, never enough lube that it was completely pain free. But that pain, that special sensation of almost being torn, would shoot right through to my clit, paralyzing me.

I close my eyes, and see your face in all those moments. All the times you bent me over your knee and punished my ass. The first time. I remember the first time, and my pleasure starts to stir more. We had been together for almost three years when we figured out that we'd stop fighting about sex so much if you just threw me down and made me take it. And the glimmer in your eye that first time, when I knew that I was either pushing you so far that it would end us, or you'd find the way to meet me there in the depths of my defiance and make me surrender. Remembering how you grabbed my throat and pulled me to you.

"Just one time, you are going to give me what I want and stop being such a fucking cunt about all this." My shock hadn't even processed before you flipped me around and pushed me facedown onto the kitchen table, flipping up my Easter Sunday dress and tearing my panties off, just the slightest touch of your fingers on my pussy as your laugh echoed through the old apartment.

"You are completely soaked." You laughed and speared your cock into me, no preamble. And that fuck—that fuck, when you planted your elbows in my back and pulled my hair, simultaneously pinning me down and arching me, pulling me backward.

Remembering that now, I feel my orgasm building, so close, so close. Twenty-seven days of frustration and misery lift off of me and I arch my head back again, pulling the clamps tight as I come. Screaming against the gag. Sobbing in the bed, missing you. Missing you. Missing you. And knowing that you're never coming back. Everyone has left now. The funeral is done. You are cremated. I'll spread your ashes when the snow melts. Your parents are back in Jersey. Mine are back in Ohio. Our friends don't know what to say to me now. I am utterly alone and I miss you, in every way.

FUCKTOY

Lady Lucretia

N ow stay in that position and don't you move," she instructed him in a firm voice. He nodded while looking up at her and gave some kind of garbled response. She wasn't sure what he said because of the ball gag in his mouth. No matter. There was a chance that even without the ball gag he wouldn't be forming coherent sentences. She'd just given him a punishment like he'd never had before—but he *did* have it coming. Rules were made for a reason, and if they weren't enforced, what was the point of having them?

She went through the bag and found the plug she was looking for, lubing it up before going back to where he waited on all fours. She noticed a puddle of drool on the hardwood floor. "Look at you drooling all over the floor," she commented, knowing that her mentioning it would make him feel even more humiliated than he already did. She made a mental note to make sure he cleaned the puddle up when she was finished with him.

"There you go," she purred as she gently inserted the weighted silver plug into his ass. It took a little time to work it in since it was bigger than the one he was used to. He moaned and she had no doubt he was sore as he adjusted to the fully inserted plug. The shiny silver loop stuck out of his puckered hole. Both sides of his asscheeks were bright red from the wooden hairbrush she'd used on him as punishment earlier. Beautiful. She smiled and removed the ball gag, letting it fall to the floor into his spittle.

"I want you to keep that plug in your ass. If you feel like it's coming out, you let me know." He nodded, still unable to speak. It didn't surprise her since she knew that while his body was present for the punishment he'd endured, his mind had gone to some other place. Climbing onto the bed, she motioned for him to come near her. "Get over here and eat my pussy." Lying down, she watched him climb onto the bed at her feet. She opened her legs wide and he practically dove into her pussy, licking, sucking and eating her in the same submissive way he always used when he went down on her.

She pushed his head into her pussy and he drank her juices eagerly, making noises as he concentrated on his task. He moved his hand and inserted a finger into her. Grabbing a fistful of his hair, she pulled his face away from her. "Did I tell you I wanted you to finger-fuck me, bitch?" she demanded. "Did I?"

"No, no, Ma'am," he stammered back. "I just thought you might like it."

"I don't need you thinking for me. I tell you what I want you to do and you do it. I said eat my pussy. How hard is that? Follow my fucking directions."

"Yes, Ma'am. I apologize," he said before she shoved his head back in between her legs. He was so good at eating pussy. He would suck her clit and run his tongue along her pussy. She knew if she let him keep going she would come right in his mouth. But that wasn't what she wanted. Not this time.

"Stop and go get a condom out of the bag on the table. I want to use your cock to fuck," she instructed him. He got up quickly and found a condom, putting it on fast so she wouldn't have to wait for him. He knew from past experience never to make Mistress wait. "Bring me the hood, too." She noticed his slight hesitation before he went into the bag and pulled out the black hood. He was familiar with it, having worn it during other playtime sessions with her. The hood was made of shiny Lycra, with only a mouth hole. She knew wearing it cut off his sense of sight and caused him to lose his sense of self, making him feel like a thing.

He walked back to the bed holding the hood. "Once your cock is in me I'm going to put the hood on you and then I'm going to use you to get off."

"Yes, Ma'am," he answered as he got back on the

bed and positioned himself over her. "May I enter you now, Mistress?"

"Yes, you may." She couldn't help but moan a little when she felt his cock penetrate her. If she loved his eating her pussy, she loved his cock inside her even more. God had given him the gift of being fantastic at fucking. "I want this on you now," she explained as she pulled the hood over his head. She adjusted it so the mouth hole was in the correct place, allowing him to breathe freely. "Right now, you're not you. You're not even a person anymore. All you are is my fucktoy. All I want is your cock to get me to come. Do you understand me, bitch?"

"Yes, Ma'am. All I am is your fucktoy," he answered.

She adjusted the hood over his face and head, then pulled him close to her mouth so there was no mistaking he could hear her through the hood. She spoke directly into his covered ear. "Fuck me, bitch, but no making your own mess."

As he started fucking her, she knew he'd heard her. She reached around and grabbed his ass with both hands. A loud groan erupted from him, but he never stopped his momentum as he fucked his Mistress. His ass had to be sore from the punishment she'd administered earlier—and the plug. While he was thrusting, she reached up and started pinching and twisting his nipples. It was a very sensitive area for him and any sort of stimulation of his chest always caused his dick to become rock hard, a turn-on of his she'd discovered early in their relationship—and taken full advantage of every chance she could.

As soon as she came around him, she'd order him to stop fucking without letting him make his mess. She'd announce to him she was done with him and remove the hood and the plug from his ass. Then she would let him choose which strap-on cock she would fuck him with that night. She still wasn't sure if she'd let him make his mess at all, even though he'd be begging for some kind of release. But whatever she decided, it was her choice and not his. He never had a choice. He never had a say in any part of their relationship. That wasn't how their relationship worked. He was her submissive, her slave, her most beloved and owned boy. And on nights like these he was her personal fucktoy. She smiled and felt the first wave of her orgasm start to wash over her. It was good to be the domme.

CARAMEL

Kathleen Tudor

He's wanted me since the first day he saw me, but I held him off. That's the power of a submissive—she decides when and where and how to give herself over. The dom is in control, but only after she says he is. And even though I wanted him right back, I waited...

It was the dungeon's kinky Christmas party, and even though there was no drinking on the premises, it was pretty clear that some people had spiked the eggnog before they'd shown up. Julia was on her hands and knees in the lounge and her Master was behind her, fucking her slowly with a candy cane and pausing every so often to give it a good lick. She was just asking for a yeast infection, if you ask me.

One of the party hosts was circulating with a challenge: name the reindeer in alphabetical order and win a prize. And *he* was taking on the challenge. Thomas. A big man, muscled all over, with arms like a superhero, and those tight leather pants showed something else at heroic proportions as well.

"Blitzen, Comet, Cupid..."

I set down my paper cup full of punch and moved behind him as he went through the list, breathing deeply enough to make my breasts swell over the top of my corset, even though the effect was wasted for the moment.

"...Prancer..."

I leaned forward until my breasts just brushed his back, and breathed, "Vixen." The room seemed to stop, and even silly Julia choked back her exaggerated sounds of pleasure to see what we would do. I'd ruined the game and finished for him; would he win? Would he be angry? What would our esteemed host, Blaggard, do?

Thomas turned to glance over his shoulder at me, and his smile was sharp. "So you are," he said. Then he turned back to Blaggard, and whatever was in his expression made our host grin.

"Well, since you two shared an answer, I guess you can share the prize. An hour's reservation in the blue room. You can have it now if you want it."

"We'll take it. Come on, then, Vixen, if you're brave enough..."

He held out his hand in invitation, waiting for me to give him the power. Mine still, until the moment my palm touched his. Then his hand closed over mine, his feral smile overwhelmed me and the room burst back into the sounds of several conversations, Julia's breathy sighs and a few knowing chuckles as Thomas led me away.

The blue room. It was closed to regular dungeon guests, open by reservation only. There were real sheets on a real bed with a nice, heavy frame for bondage and a selection of toys and implements for borrowing. And there was the bag, which Thomas had stopped to grab from his locker, teasing me with its mystery. I didn't have to wonder for long.

The bag was full of rope in a rainbow of colors and a variety of lengths. My skin flushed and my breath grew shallow as he guided me to the bed and positioned me how he wanted me. My skirt and panties were taken away. My corset and heels were left. Soft, intractable knots were formed, sealing me in place with ribbons of pink and green and white. I shivered as each one breathed over my skin, immobilizing me by degrees.

"I've wanted to tie you up like this for months," he said, finishing the final knot and stepping back to admire me, trussed up on the bed, helpless before his desires.

"I know."

"What will you say if you want me to stop?" he asked, moving around the bed. The formerly heroic bulge in his pants was absolutely titanic now. I shuddered and felt tingles growing between my legs; the man hadn't even touched me yet, except to impersonally position me for the ropes.

My regular safeword was *red,* but it seemed so ordinary. Thomas deserved something special, something as sweet and heady as he was. "*Caramel.*" It reminded me of the color of his skin.

He smiled. "Caramel." He drew the word out like he was tasting it, and my mouth watered. "All right, Vixen. You've been teasing me long enough. Tonight, as payment, I'm going to take your virginity."

I laughed. "I'm not—" But my breath caught as he pressed one slender finger to the exposed pucker of my ass. Oh.

"Or you could say it..." *Caramel.* I wouldn't. I'd offered him this power. I wasn't ready to take it back.

He smiled at my silence and fetched an XL condom and lube from the bag of rope. I whimpered. What a first date!

But my mouth was watering again by the time he had peeled the leather away and slid the rubber on over that intimidating pole.

He didn't kiss me, or tease me, or run a finger through the pool of liquid heat that was already dripping down my crack. He just smoothed some lube onto his cock, and used what was left to ease the entry of one thick finger. I moaned as he penetrated my virgin hole, and strained against my bonds, wanting to play back.

He didn't finger-fuck me for long, though. I gasped when he shifted, bringing his cock in line with my tight bud. "Already?" I asked, my voice trembling.

"You could always make me stop."

I moaned. He thrust. I screamed. It was like a lightning strike, sparking and painful and exciting, electrifying my entire body, tearing me in two. I gasped for air, and he laughed.

"That was only the tip. You ready to give up, Vixen?"

"Never!"

"That's what I like to hear." He rocked against me and I cried out with each thrust, feeling him sink into me, so huge, so deep, it was as if part of me must have been displaced. It was a desperate feeling—ecstatic and agonizing and even a little empowering. After all, I could make it stop whenever I wanted. I held the power.

Finally, he was rooted in me, so deep I could feel the tickle of his hairs against my ass. He thrust slowly at first, picking up speed as he began to reach for my pleasure, teasing his fingers across my clit as he took me.

I soared toward climax, but Thomas watched me closely, moving his fingers away every time I came too close. I was nearly weeping with frustration as he brought me to the edge again. "Say it. Say it and you can come."

He plunged into my ass, and I clenched around him, taking my power back as I forced him over the edge with me, crying out as I did so, "Caramel!"

THE BULLDOG
BREED

Lisette Ashton

D ani whistled in soft horror. The door was left open. Someone would pay.

She stepped warily into the office. Ted Powers, owner of Powers Investments, was aggressively proactive on the subject of security. Dani had heard the bald-headed, broad-necked man berate many of his young secretaries for accidentally leaving the office door ajar.

He had a daunting presence that left Dani weak from the prospect of earning his wrath. Even though she worked for Simmons Stationery on the floor below, she still felt more fearful of Ted Powers than of her own boss. Some days, when her office was quiet, she could hear Powers shouting at his underlings with a bellowing roar. If she'd had to put up with a boss like that, she knew it would be akin to living with the constant threat of retribution.

Closing the door behind her, she thought about how livid Ted would be if he discovered that one of his staff had failed to adhere to his security protocols.

Dani considered calling to announce her arrival.

She'd opened her mouth to ask if anyone was about when she heard someone moan.

It was an exclamation of obvious pain.

But there was something else in the sound: something needy, obvious and sexual. It was a sound Dani knew well, a sound that often reverberated from the walls of her own bedroom.

She stiffened.

She glanced back toward the door, planning to make an escape before she was discovered. She turned and caught her hip against a corner of the reception desk. The collision caused a small thud.

"Is someone out there?"

It was a man's voice.

It was the voice of Ted Powers.

A stack of papers had sat on the desk. She saw them teetering and reached out a hand. Because she was still holding the package, a small brown parcel of stationery addressed to Ted Powers at Powers Investments, she ended up pushing at the pile rather than steadying it.

Pages and books fell to the floor.

A stapler that had been perched on top of the pile clattered noisily against the reception desk. To Dani's mind, the noise could not have been louder if it had sounded from a klaxon horn.

She groaned.

"Who the fuh…?"

Ted Powers appeared from the doorway behind the main reception area. His cheeks were flushed. His eyes were hidden behind dark glasses. In one hand he held a wicked-looking length of cane. His shirt was undone. The front panel of his pants was distended by a fat and obvious bulge.

Dani snatched her gaze away.

"Dani?" He sounded surprised and pleased.

She nodded, too frightened to speak.

"Was the door unlocked?"

She considered her options and knew she couldn't lie to Ted Powers. "Yes."

He sighed with obvious frustration.

Although she couldn't see his eyes she knew he was glowering disapprovingly back into the room behind the reception desk. He nodded at the package in her hands. "Are those the goods I ordered this morning?"

She glanced down at her trembling fingers and saw she was still holding the parcel. "It's your bulldog clips," she told him.

"Close the door," he told her. "Then come back here."

Dani didn't like being given commands but she didn't dare disobey. She hurried to shut the door properly, drop the deadbolt and then hurry to where he stood at the door behind the reception desk.

A whimper came from inside the room.

It was a woman's voice. The tone was one Dani recognized. The woman's appetite was being sated by pain.

"Please, Mr. Powers." She spoke in a low, breathless whisper. "Not this."

Ted gestured for Dani to join him.

Still holding the box, she followed. Her heart raced.

Inside the room was a naked woman kneeling on a desk. She was on all fours, her backside held high in the air. Her lowered face was hidden by the cowl of brunette hair hanging down. Her breasts hung pertly beneath her. Her bleached anus and smoothly shaved labia were directly at eye level with Dani as she entered the room.

Dani swallowed. There were stripes across the woman's rear. The bright red marks sliced with agonizing beauty across the pale mounds of both asscheeks. A dewy sheen of arousal colored the lips of the woman's sex.

"Alison," Ted began, addressing the naked woman. "This is Dani. She works for the stationery company downstairs. Say hello to Dani, Alison."

Alison muttered a mortified greeting.

"Dani," Ted continued, "Alison is being punished for her lack of attentiveness to the job she is supposed to do for me. I've already striped her backside, as you can see. Do those marks look painful to you?"

Dani studied the marks.

They were more dark pink than red. They cut across both cheeks of Alison's ass in lines that curved with the swell of her buttocks. Dani imagined they had been an agony to receive. She couldn't resist the urge to reach out and stroke her fingers against one of the lines.

Ted Powers smiled with obvious approval.

Alison winced beneath her. Dani could sense the woman's electric excitement beyond her surface discomfort and embarrassment. She didn't know if it was the musk of arousal that spiced the air, or if there was something else in the atmosphere, but as she traced her finger over the raised weal of reddened skin, Dani knew this was something darkly exciting that she needed to experience. It didn't matter whether she was wielding the cane or suffering the brutal sting of its kiss: she yearned for this torment just the same.

"The marks look delightfully painful," she whispered.

Powers nodded as though he approved of her word choice.

"Could you open your package?"

She hesitated. Was that a euphemism for undressing? She remembered she was holding the stationery supplies and cursed herself for the arrogance that had made her think Ted Powers might have any interest in someone like her when he already had a willing sex slave on his desk.

Dani opened the pack. Her hands shook so badly that she scattered the contents from the box of bulldog clips across the desk.

Alison groaned when she saw what had been brought.

Dani had no idea why the woman might dread the small clips—springs of black steel fitted with nickel-plated handles—but she could hear the moan of dread in Alison's voice.

"Apply one," Ted told Dani.

She took a moment to work out what he was suggesting. When she understood, a wave of raw desire rushed through her body. The surge was almost enough to make her swoon.

"Where?"

Confidently, he reached between Alison's legs and teased her pussy lips together. Pulling lightly, drawing the labia closed, he held the lips between his finger and thumb.

"Put one of the clips on here," he said. "Do you have any other questions?"

She plucked one of the clips from the table and squeezed the handles so that it opened. Turning to face him, and studying her own reflection in the dark lenses of his shades, she said, "Yes. I do have one other question. Do you have any vacancies in this office?"

MISTRESS RAVEN

Olivia Archer

I am hers. But she is not mine.

For the past year I have been allowed to serve Mistress Raven on the evenings that she entertains in her beautiful mansion. I am one of her manservants. The parties continue long into the night. I steal glances at her as I move around the room, passing appetizers and filling glasses, wearing only a collar. I wait for approval, for acknowledgment. From her.

She is always magnificent in her black thigh-high boots, sporting one of her array of leather dresses. Her simple makeup is set off by deep-red lipstick; her dark hair is secured in a single band. No further embellishments are needed. At times she carries a whip, but often her words are her only tools. They cut as sharply as any implement.

Finally she singles me out, and I advance beyond the role of a waiter, for just a moment. "That one, the boy with the long brown curls," she commands, pointing at me.

For the entertainment of her guests, I am brought to stand before her on a low pedestal. Maybe she sees my freshly scarred back, but she says nothing. People surround me, talking, touching. As I bow my head, someone runs a nail along the edge of my wound. The pain excites me.

Mistress Raven clears the crowd back and makes a show of circling me slowly, electrifying my body with teasing touches from the braided leather cord of her whip. Then I feel the true sting of it across my ass. Once, twice, three times. The room falls silent.

When she stands before me again, she runs the handle along the underside of my rock-hard cock and, with an exaggerated frown, says, "Oh, no, we can't have this."

The partygoers laugh and move in closer as I concentrate, trying to control my seemingly uncontrollable cock. But over the past few years, my mind has grown stronger as my desire to become a submissive has taken over. Proudly, I become flaccid.

My limp dick elicits a round of applause, then the attention turns away from me because another manservant is called forward and I am replaced. As I walk to get a new plate of canapés, her words stop me. "Pretty Boy, go home."

Disappointed, I spend the next few hours riding my

bike through the dark streets, analyzing this surprising turn of events. Suddenly my phone vibrates against my body. It is a text from her. *Return now. Buzz at the gate.*

I pedal there quickly and am led in by a man who just points through the foyer's dark silence to the staircase. In the absence of lights, in the absence of others, the house is hushed and welcomes me into its shadows. Climbing the sleek marble stairs, I become one of its secrets.

My Mistress is in the first room. When I enter, the sight of her bare skin halts my breath. Never is she seen naked. The heat and scent of her recent bath have followed her into the bedroom. Though the flickering light of the room hides as much as it illuminates, it cannot keep me from absorbing the luscious curves of her full breasts, the way her body narrows at the waist, and the graceful bow of her hips.

"Boy, come here," she instructs as she sets down her empty glass on the table beside her bed.

"Yes, Ma'am." I approach several steps, my eyes downcast as they should be in her presence, willing myself to take in no more of her beauty.

"I've been watching you. Your long lashes can't hide those hungry eyes. So I've decided that I want something different from you. Strip," she instructs.

"Yes, Ma'am." Her words stir me as I shed my usual attire: jeans, T-shirt, hoodie. Though my pulse races, I control my breathing, my actions, my erection.

"Why do you work for me?" she asks while watching

my every move. Her voice is a smooth blend of power and seduction.

"Because you allow it." Is she dismissing me? Here and now? As I stand naked before her, wishing only to drink her in?

"One more time, Boy. I want to hear *why* you do this for me. I do not pay you. I do not pleasure you. Yet you continue, unflagging. Should I be concerned that you are *too* devoted?"

My automatic responses will not serve me here. I hesitate because she *does* give me pleasure. The moments draw out as I stand in her large bedchamber. I am comfortable in the role of silent submission and do not expect her questions.

"Answer," she demands, "Or leave."

I try to give voice to my inner desires, to explain to this woman—my very opposite—what it is like to be me. But I do not think of this often. Or ever. It just *is*. The only answer I can summon is, "I need it, Ma'am."

I feel her eyes probing me as I continue to look downward. "Kneel," she commands. Then her bare feet pad across the hardwood floor until she is inches from me. I can feel her heat and become light-headed with ecstasy. My cock jumps up; I cannot control it anymore.

"Is this what you want, Boy?" she asks pressing her cunt within an inch of my face.

I whisper, "Yes. Yes."

Mistress Raven leans down, her heavy breasts

brushing my skin, and breathes these words in my ear, "Show me."

Unsure, I look up at her for approval and she nods. Gingerly I touch her thighs—so smooth—then I begin to explore her sweet pussy glistening before me. Its musky smell now overpowers the flowers from her bathwater. My senses awaken to this nirvana.

With my thumbs, I gently part the wings of her beautiful butterfly, then I reach forward to taste its nectar. My cock bobs in the open air, wanting to rub against something, anything.

She sighs and grabs the locks of my hair, pulling me into her. Her pelvis tilts forward and I service her deftly with my tongue. My hands knead the womanly curves of her ass, urging her deeply into my mouth with each thrust. Faster and harder, until I feel her body tense. And then it releases into the waves of orgasm.

Mistress Raven leans against me, panting and stroking my long curls. My cock brushes the side of her leg and that brief bit of contact is enough to make me erupt onto the floor.

"Beautiful," she says in a hushed voice, and steps back to look at me.

I wonder what she means, but I don't dare ask.

"Boy, you may go now," she declares, back in control.

"Ma'am?" I inquire, my overstimulated mind needing her to repeat the directive.

"You may go," she repeats. "For now."

I turn, picking up my clothes, and walk away, not knowing what to expect next. My destiny is hers to control. Just as I desired.

I am hers. But she is not mine.

FOLLOWING ORDERS

Jade Melisande

C ara stood on the threshold of the door that led into the hearth room, surveying the other partygoers within. They stood around sipping drinks, checking each other out and talking idly, just like guests at any other cocktail party.

Except that at this party there was a woman dressed in a latex catsuit, stroking the head of a naked man at her feet; two men stood by the fireplace discussing the merits of jute rope versus hemp while one of them tied a woman's wrists; and elsewhere a man traced a knife slowly down the arm of the woman standing next to him without breaking her skin.

Yep, just another kinky party at the Pleasure Dome, as their hosts liked to refer to the house where they held weekly play parties for the local BDSM crowd.

Van gave the leash attached to a collar at Cara's neck a tug, and Cara followed him obediently into the room. Frank followed after, a hand in the small of her back, before heading over to the bar to get them all drinks while she and Van settled themselves on the couch. He returned shortly, a whisky for Van in one hand and white wine for Cara in the other, then retrieved his own drink before perching on the arm of the couch next to Cara. She smiled and wriggled back into the couch pillows a bit: just where she liked to be, snug between her two men.

They took a moment to relax, drinking in the sights and sounds around them, Frank casually stroking Cara's arm, Van with a hand on her thigh.

Finally Frank broke the companionable silence. "Have you masturbated yet today, Cara?" he asked.

Van had recently decreed a new rule: she should masturbate once a day. Prior to doing so she was to text him for any special instructions, such as whether or not she was allowed to orgasm, but mostly it was so that he would know that she had obeyed. "No," she admitted, feeling her cheeks heat up a bit—and not from the crackling fire in the fireplace. She hated to be caught out.

Frank's eyebrows raised and he looked pointedly at his watch. "It's eleven-thirty," he said. "When were you planning to do it?"

Cara frowned up at Frank. Their relationship was an interesting thing, a fluid mixture of teasing and fun, in which he topped her at times without ever domming her, and frequently played the role of "troublemaker"—

deliberately getting her into hot water with Van, with whom she shared a more traditional Dom/sub dynamic. It was all in good fun, but even "funishments" could be painful or embarrassing.

"I…"

She didn't have a good answer. In all the excitement over the party, she'd plain forgotten. "I forgot," she finally admitted, chagrined at herself, and at Frank for calling her out.

"That's too bad," Van said.

"I'll do it when we get home," Cara said quickly. "I'll even put on a show for you two," she continued, trying to sound seductive. She'd rather not get Van's cane cold tonight, or perhaps have him decide on some other punishment later.

She felt Van meet Frank's eyes over her head.

"Yes," Van said. "You will."

Cara breathed a relieved sigh, and couldn't stop herself from shooting Frank a tiny, triumphant smile. *Ha! Try to get me in trouble, will you?*

But instead of looking downcast, Frank just grinned back at her. Then, softly, he said, "Spread your legs, Cara."

Cara shot a startled look at Van. Frank was seldom the "bossy" one, preferring to let Van instigate things. But she saw a gleam in both men's eyes that made her stomach clench and her breath come short. That the command also made her pussy throb was a point she couldn't deny either.

"Did you think I wouldn't notice that you hadn't texted me today?" Van asked, his voice low in her ear. "Or that I wouldn't care?"

She gulped. She hadn't thought about it at all. She shook her head mutely.

"Now do as Frank says," Van ordered.

Cara's eyes swept the room. There were occasional glances their way, but no one paid overt attention to them. Still, she felt her cheeks burning as she spread her legs in her short skirt, revealing her naked pussy. Van seldom dictated her clothing, but tonight he'd told her not to wear underwear. It was becoming apparent why.

She'd been set up.

"Do it now," Frank said.

Cara looked pleadingly over at Van. "Now?" she whispered. "Here?"

He nodded sharply, the glint in his eye brighter, an almost-smile tugging at the corner of his lips. She looked over at Frank to see him grinning smugly. They were both enjoying her discomfort far too much.

Offering to masturbate in front of the two of them had been edgy for her, and they both knew it. Masturbating made her embarrassed, even when she was alone, and having to text Van every time was an agony, especially if he gave her special orders, like taking pictures, or once, even recording herself.

"Please—" she started, but bit her lip at the frown that came over Van's face. Yes, it was fun and games, but the reality was that she hated disappointing him.

A further reality was that obeying him, even in something as embarrassing as this, turned her on. She could smell her own excitement wafting up to her already, could feel the slickness between her thighs, and a glance over at both men's trousers revealed that neither of them was unaffected either.

She slid her hand down her blouse and slipped it under the waistband of her skirt, which, she acknowledged, was a little ridiculous, since her legs were spread and anyone looking their way could see exactly what she was doing. But it gave her the illusion of invisibility.

Her pussy was indeed wet, her copious juices smearing her thighs. Her lips were swollen, and when she stroked her fingers across her clit she couldn't stop the gasp of pleasure.

Around them, the party continued; people drank and talked and pretended not to see her, but she caught their covert glances.

"Do it," Van growled in her ear as she hesitated. "Make yourself come."

Cara moaned, laid her head back and began to stroke herself in earnest.

Her fingers pumped, circled and rubbed the sensitive nub at her center as the orgasm began to build. She panted and closed her eyes, knowing that they were watching her—Frank and Van and the others. Embarrassment flooded her but she couldn't deny the tension, the tightness, the building, blinding ache between her legs. Her belly and cunt clenched as she fucked her fingers into herself faster and faster, until the orgasm finally crashed over her and she turned her head in to Van's chest to stifle the scream that tore from her.

Moments later she lifted her eyes to see every head in the room turned her way.

She turned to look up at Frank, who smiled widely at her. "I could get to like giving orders," Frank said. And she could definitely get used to following them.

WRITER'S BLOCK

Kitten Boheme

C laire stared at her laptop, fingers drumming on the keyboard. As usual, she was the last patron left. The shop was closing soon and she was still no further in her writing than she'd been when she'd sat down.

"I need an idea," she sighed, beating her forehead against the keyboard. She suffered a chronic case of writer's block. "Any idea…" Her computer typed gibberish each time she smashed her head into the keys. It wasn't productive, but it was more writing than she had done all day.

"How's it going?"

Claire whimpered.

"That good, huh?"

She looked up. It was Alex, the barista. She smiled sheepishly, always startled by how attractive he was.

"Anything I can help with?" Alex asked.

"Are you a creative genius who only moonlights as a barista?"

"Sorry."

"Then just more coffee," Claire sighed, holding out her empty mug.

"You need a distraction," Alex suggested, returning with a full mug. "When you stub your toe you forget all about the pain in your hand."

She looked at him quizzically, not really sure that stubbing her toe could help.

"Watch." He took Claire's hand, laying it palm down on the table and holding the cup above it. Intrigued, Claire gasped as it poured over the back of her hand. She couldn't move from the table, instead riveted as she watched coffee pool around her fingertips. It wasn't hot enough to burn, only warm enough to make her skin blush. She was surprised at how much she enjoyed the momentary pain.

"You've forgotten your writer's block, haven't you?"

"I suppose." She looked at her hand. "More?" Claire surprised herself with her eagerness.

"I'm closing up shop. Stay as long as you want, so long as you listen and do what I say. If you don't want this say, 'Starbucks is better,' and walk out the door." Alex grabbed her by the face, his thumb and forefinger straddling her chin, pulling her gaze up to his. "Understand?"

Claire nervously agreed.

Alex released her. "Good girl." He slid a hand up the nape of her neck, grabbing a fistful of long hair as he pulled her out of her chair and up on her feet. "Let's go lock the door."

Claire didn't move, unsure what he wanted from her.

"I don't repeat myself," Alex growled. Taking his free hand and running it down her thigh, he delivered a sharp slap to the back of her knee. She lurched forward, her skin tingling, her knees weak. She walked, almost automatically.

"I'll show you how the door works." Alex locked the door, giving it a push; it opened a crack. "It's locked from the outside. No one gets in, but you are free to go."

Smiling, Claire flipped the sign on the door to CLOSED. The shop may have been closed, but she was open for something new.

"Good." His breath was hot against her goose-pimpled flesh.

"Follow," Alex ordered. She followed, surrendering to him. When they reached her table, she sat. "No!" Pulling her up by her hair, he swept the chair away deftly with his foot. "Bend over, and put *these* on the table," he said, slapping her forearms.

Claire obeyed. She turned to watch Alex remove his apron. He put a hand on either side of her face, directing her gaze straight ahead; he positioned the makeshift blindfold over her eyes, tying it tight. Taking her hands, he guided her fingers to the home row of the keyboard.

"Write," Alex said, grabbing the hem of Claire's skirt and flipping it up over her back. From under the blindfold, Claire tried to envision everything he was doing. She felt him take hold of her panty hose, pulling until they ripped from waistband to crotch.

"Type!" Alex gave her a sharp spank.

She began, writing furiously, revealing every thought and sensation—the stinging pain from his hard slaps; the way she could feel his eyes on her body, admiring her like a trophy. The more she typed, the wetter she got; she could feel her pussy dripping. She wanted to plead for his cock. She turned to look back at him. Her fingers slipped off the keyboard.

"Put your hands back." The punishing slap was hard. Claire whimpered, scrambling to replace her fingers on the keys.

He was silent as he pulled away. She realized just how cold and vulnerable she was without his firm hands against her near-naked skin.

"Panties off."

She hesitated. His hand was on the back of her head, closing around another fistful of hair, pulling her ear to his mouth. "You will do what I say or you will get out."

Quickly removing the ruined panty hose, Clare shimmied out of her panties and presented them, craving his approval.

Alex took the wet panties from her hand. "Mouth open."

She parted her lips, and he slipped her panties in, gagging her. Soon Alex's hand was on her back, forcing her back down over the keyboard, forearms on the table, fingers on the keys. She cleared her mind, ready to type.

His zipper rasped. Anticipating a hard cock bumping up against her, Claire moaned, the sound muffled by her gag. Alex thrust himself into her. She bit down hard on the panties, thrilled by the pain of his sudden entrance. She concentrated on his every motion, transcribing it moment by moment.

All too soon, Alex pulled the panties from her mouth. "Read."

"*He entered me from behind, his hard cock filling me up. Each thrust methodical, his hands on my backside, spreading my cheeks apart for a better view as he slipped his cock all the way in and all the way out, enjoying complete control of my pussy. Another hard, stinging slap against my thigh, and my knees buckled. I righted myself, ready for him again. He gripped my hips and started to thrust harder and wilder. He stopped, commanding me to turn my head. I obediently turned. I could soon feel him standing next to me. He seized my face and pried my mouth open, slipping his cock in; I gagged as he pushed it deep into my throat, forcing me to swallow it. I struggled to keep my fingers on the keys, to keep typing. Grabbing my hair, he forced my head up and down, barely allowing me a breath between strokes. There was a hard crack against my face as he slapped me; I was terrified and wanted more. He slapped again, his cock still working deep inside my throat. He held my face against him, his come hitting the back of my throat. Finished, he pushed me away. I swallowed, wishing I could see him."*

Claire stopped reading and waited.

Alex removed the blindfold. She could tell her makeup was smeared and runny, her hair tangled and knotted. Claire beamed at him, grateful she'd given him what he wanted.

"I've cured your writer's block," he said.

Another wave of wetness hit as she looked at her screen. She watched as Alex disappeared into the back room. She selected the whole document and hit DELETE. The page went blank. She smiled, knowing she would be back tomorrow. With writer's block, of course.

HELP! MY WIFE'S A FORMER DOMINATRIX!

Angela R. Sargenti

Never marry a former dominatrix.

Unless you like to be beaten, of course, and then it's pretty fun.

Painful, but fun.

Usually.

This time, it wasn't so fun.

It was just a normal Sunday evening, where we cap off the weekend with my weekly punishment. My wife takes my discipline very seriously, and as usual, she made me take a shower and put on my pajamas.

After that, I had to meet her in the living room, where she let me watch TV until she was ready to spank me.

There she sat on the couch, quietly doing her needlepoint. Something seemed to be bothering her, since she was quieter than usual, and she made me sit there on the floor with my teddy bear for a very long time.

Finally, she set her needlework aside and said the words I was dying to hear.

"Shut the TV off and come here, Dave."

"But, Ma'am…"

"Now, young man. Or do you want to go to bed directly after your spanking?"

I shook my head and turned off the TV, and then I dragged myself over to stand beside her.

"Pants off, Dave. And I mean all the way off."

"Even my undies?"

"Yes. Those, too."

Well, this was something new. She normally starts my spankings over the top of them, and once I'm warmed up, she pulls them down for the real thing.

The most she's ever done before is make me take them down at the same time as my pants.

My heart pounded fiercely as I watched her spread a clean towel across her lap. When she glanced up at me again, her eyes bored into me.

I tried to hide behind my teddy bear, but she yanked it out of my hand and flung it to the floor.

"Go get me that hand lotion over there," she ordered.

"What for, Ma'am?"

"Just never you mind. Go get it and get your ass down here before I really get mad."

I obeyed her immediately, and once she had me over her lap, she let me have my bear back. I clutched it to my chest and positioned myself with one hand on the floor, up on my tiptoes.

It's amazing how my wife's hands can be so hard and yet so soft at the same time. She sensually worked the lotion into my ass. It felt pretty nice having my butt massaged like that, but all of a sudden, she smacked me hard.

"Well, Dave. What've you been doing with your week? Anything special? Like ditching work and going to the ballgame with Bob?"

How the hell she found out about that, I'll never know, but I swallowed hard, wondering why my mouth was so dry.

"That's right, Dave. I know all about it. I know how you lied to me and let me think you were going to work, when all you did was call in sick and jeopardize your career. Didn't you?"

"Yes, Ma'am. I'm sorry, Ma'am."

"Yeah, I know, Dave. You're always sorry. But this time, sorry doesn't cut it. You *lied* to me, Dave. Do you know how much that hurts?"

And she *did* sound hurt, which almost made me want to cry myself.

"A lot?"

"That's right, Dave. It hurt a lot. And that's why I've decided *you* should hurt, too. A lot. Now shut up and hand me the bath brush."

"Oh, Ma'am, not the bath brush. Please?"

"Let's go, Dave," she told me. "I have things to do."

So I obeyed and reached down for the bath brush, which lay on the floor in front of me. It's heavy and solid and one of the worst implements we own.

"Hmm," she said.

I pictured her sitting there admiring it, turning it over and examining it from all angles. My calves were starting to ache, and I wished she'd get on with it.

"Very nice, Dave. I'm pleased with your obedience."

"Thanks, Ma'am."

For a moment, my wife remained silent, and then she placed the nice, cool wood upon my skin, rubbing it against my soon-to-be roasting ass.

"So tell me, Dave. How many runs did your team score?"

"Eleven, Ma'am."

"Eleven? My goodness me. That just so happens to be the number of swats you're getting, too."

"Oh no, Ma'am. Please?"

"You know I hate it when you beg. Just for that, we'll make it an even dozen, and I want you to count each one and say, 'One, I'll never lie to you again, two, I'll never lie to you again.' You got that, Dave?"

"Yes, Ma'am."

"Good. Now let's get started."

And with that, she struck the first blow. Fire spread immediately through my left buttcheek, searing me so badly I almost forgot my instructions.

"Count, Dave. Now."

"One, I'll never lie to you again."

"Good boy. Keep 'em coming."

The next blow brought my feet off the ground, and I twined them together to bear the pain.

"I swear to god I'll never lie to you again, Ma'am."

"Hmm. I bet you won't."

Blows three, four, five and six were quick but devastating. I choked back tears as I counted them off, and my wife waited until she heard each one clearly.

Seven almost broke me.

"Ow! Please, Ma'am. I won't lie to you again. Ever."

But she showed me no mercy. I thought I'd lose my mind, they hurt so bad, but still she made me count, the evil bitch.

"Please, Ma'am. No more."

"Nonsense. We're celebrating your team's big win."

"But they lost."

"Really? What a coincidence. So did you."

And though I couldn't see her face, I knew her expression was grim and forbidding. She hauled back and let the next one fly.

"Oh god," I wept shamelessly. "I can't take any more."

"You can and you will, Dave. And after I'm finished here, back in the corner you go. I'll set the timer for ten minutes, and then I want you ready for the prison strap."

What?

You don't know what a prison strap is?

Then let me enlighten you.

A prison strap's a thick and heavy piece of leather shaped like a fraternity paddle. It has a handle that's perfect for small hands like hers, and it gets its point across very quickly.

Thank god.

Since it's so heavy and cumbersome, her arm got tired fast, so all I had to endure were a few swats.

A few swats were enough, though.

Trust me on that.

I stood there in the corner waiting for the timer to ring. Ten minutes might not seem like a long time to you, but when your nose is planted against the wall and you're standing in an awkward position, it's an eternity.

Such an eternity I was almost *glad* when that timer rang.

But having to face that prison strap?

No one could be glad about that.

No one.

THAT
MOMENT
WHEN

Martha Davis

There was that moment when I first saw his ass. Tight enough to bounce a quarter off, highlighted in tailored gray suit pants. Above it, under a white shirt, broad shoulders and a well-muscled back, not overdone like baby-oil-soaked bodybuilders, just strong. He returned my appreciative gaze with eyes so rich they'd make Hershey's beg for the recipe.

"Hi. I'm Alicia. This is my second year teaching first-year Algebra."

"Wes." He shook my hand, held it a moment longer than necessary in a grip that made me simultaneously soak my panties and have to lock my trembling knees to maintain balance. "First year English Lit."

Wes asked me out and over the next couple of months he proved himself witty, intelligent and beyond charming. I spent many a daydream moment—there was just something about this guy.

But the newness of me and Wes began fading, revealing all his secrets from his life before there was a me and Wes.

"You aren't his normal type," said one of his old college buddies the first time we were introduced, "but you're adorable. I can't help but like you."

Later, I asked, "What did he mean?"

Under much prodding, he confessed a past in which he tied up his lovers and did totally indecent things to them. My charming, sweet-tempered, easygoing Wes—who would have thought? How intriguing!

"Why don't you do those things to me?"

"I don't do them to anyone any more."

"Why not?"

"Sometimes subs don't realize they can push a Dom's limits, too."

"So you retired? How sad."

His eyebrows arched.

I surfed the Internet for days, studied the pictures I found, fantasized. Wes's mouth dropped in amazement when I tossed a picture in his lap and said, "I want you to do that to me."

"We'll see."

Wes's version of "No comment."

A full week passed, making me half crazy wondering what else I could do or say. I researched even more. He acted like nothing happened. Then last night, after dinner and a movie, we returned home and I found a dusty cardboard box sitting on the living room coffee table. He must have put it there before we left when he came back in for his forgotten wallet.

"Take all your clothes off. Turn slowly while you do so I can see every curve." He spoke soft and deep. "Then get on your knees with your hands clasped behind your back. Open your mouth wide enough to hold a dick."

I couldn't stop grinning as I did what he instructed, complete with lots of hip wiggling and butt bouncing. My show earned me a hard smack on my bare butt. I squealed and petted the spot where he struck me, relishing the new feeling. My ass burned from the single contact, then melted into a warm heat across my whole bottom. I'd been officially spanked and, well, I liked it.

As soon as I got into position on my knees, Wes took a finger and stuffed it deep in my mouth.

"Suck it like a cock. Flick your tongue on the creases between the digits. Yeah, that's a good girl."

He braided a hand in my hair to hold my head still while he forced me to take two fingers, then three. I could see his growing erection through his jeans. When my hands left my back to reach for his zipper, he momentarily let go of my hair and smacked them back down to my sides.

"You don't have permission. I see I'm going to have to train you from the beginning."

He went over to the box and pulled out leather handcuffs and tethers, pushed me facedown on the floor and held me there while he cuffed and tied me, face and upper body against the floor, ass stuck in the air. He stroked his cock through his jeans, dry humping my right asscheek until my pussy grew so wet it smeared my thighs. I wanted him to fuck me so bad.

He rose, walked over to the computer desk in the corner and signed on, completely ignoring me.

"Wes?"

"Don't make me gag you. I don't do that on a first date, but if you keep talking, you'll leave me no choice."

That was my WTF moment. Yes, I wanted exotic and hot sex of the extreme sport variety, but tossed on the floor and forgotten? I struggled in my bonds and my tummy fluttered with the thrill of my complete helplessness. My pussy grew even wetter. The passing time only let me meditate and mentally masturbate on my predicament.

"You really need to delete your browser history. The things you've been studying? Good for me to know, but makes me wonder about the educators of our impressionable teenagers."

He reached in the box and pulled out a black leather paddle. "How does it feel to be tied up like that little computer glossy you gave me? You like it?"

"Yes, Wes. Fuck me please."

"You are not in any position to give me a list of demands. Fuck you while you're trussed up like a wild animal on my floor?" He ran a finger down the length of my spine. "Really?"

He smacked my butt with the paddle. First one cheek, then the other. Tears formed in my eyes and ran down my cheeks. When I grew to expect it on one side, he changed his pattern and landed another blow in the matching spot on the opposite cheek.

"Are you actually getting wetter as I spank you? Now that kind of naughty behavior *will* get a girl fucked."

He positioned himself behind my burning ass and stuffed his entire length into me, withdrew almost to the tip of his cock and plowed into me again. He gripped my tender buttcheeks and made me wail as he rode me. I came like that, faster and harder than I ever had before. Instead of petting me and coaxing me down from my orgasmic high like he usually does, Wes upped his game and made me come again, sooner than I ever thought possible, then pulled out in the seconds before his own hips shuddered and smeared my ass with his come like they do in the porn I'd been watching.

"This is a good beginning. I would like to go deeper with you, but I need you to understand something. I enjoy giving you a little pain with my pleasure, but I won't permanently harm you. Cut you. Scar you. I love you, Alicia, but if you feel like you need those things, I can't give them to you."

Finally, there was that moment—the one when my reddened bottom, sticky with his come, wearing sensations I'd feel for days, every time I tried to sit down, spoke to me. That moment when I knew beyond all doubts that I'd fallen in love. There would be no other for me.

"I'm not your ex, Wes. I only want what you're willing to give."

I sobbed into the shag carpet, loving his hands petting my hair and his gentle kiss soothing the small of my back.

THE DINNER

Erzabet Bishop

C omfortable?" Sir's cool gray eyes stared into mine over our glasses of house wine. I had to struggle not to fidget.

"No." I flinched, gasping, as he powered up the vibrating egg he'd placed inside me before we left the car. My pussy began to clench around it and I had to grit my teeth not to cry out as his hand reached underneath the table to stroke my leg. I was so close to coming, it wouldn't take much to push me over the edge.

"No, what?" His words curled around me like smoke as his hand slid up my inner thigh. I hitched my breath as it eased closer and closer to my bare pussy. Tonight he'd insisted I go completely bare underneath the dress.

"No, Sir." I looked down at my barely eaten salad and groaned as his fingertips brushed against my mound.

Thankfully, the lighting in the restaurant was dim. It was one of Sir's favorite destinations when he was feeling adventurous. Glancing up at the table closest to me, I was relieved to see the couple talking amicably. The din of the other guests and clatter of silverware on plates combined with the soft classical music playing helped to disguise my moans. He flipped the switch again and eased his finger just inside my slick opening. I ground my pussy against his hand. As my clit brushed his thumb, my release thundered through me, uncontrollable in the force of my body's need. Waves of fluid doused my inner thighs and I bit my lip, knowing he would be very displeased.

"You were not to come without permission. You are being a very naughty girl tonight, Arin." Sir watched me behind hooded lids, no doubt assessing the delicious torment he had in store. Pussy throbbing, I was ready for more.

Trying to control my breathing, I reached for the glass of wine in an effort to calm myself. His touch was making me into a puddle of want. Picking up my fork, I stabbed some lettuce absently, preparing for what was to come next.

I paused with the fork in midair; it quivered in my hand as I met his eyes. "Yes, Sir." His finger edged inside of me once again, one finger becoming two, and I gave up all pretense of trying to eat. When he turned up the control on the egg, my fork clattered to the plate. Sucking in my breath, I looked up in alarm as a warning cloud settled on his features.

"I think I was away on business too long." He took a sip of wine, his eyes trailing over my breasts as they pushed out against the snug fabric of the dress.

"Yes, Sir." He withdrew his fingers and wiped them on the tablecloth.

"I want you to get up, Arin, and go into the men's room, remove the egg and wait for me there."

Panic caused me to suck in my breath. *The men's room*? I hesitated in getting up and his stony expression darkened further. *Uh-oh*. I scrambled out of the seat and pulled my dress down as I stood on shaking legs. Not looking at him, I felt the thrill of whatever he was planning shiver down my spine. His two weeks out of the country had left me pining for his touch.

I walked past the seated guests and made my way down the dark hallway to the restrooms. The bustle of the waiters and the laughter of the guests made the scene even more surreal.

Opening the door to the luxurious bathroom, I was relieved to find no one inside. Making my way through the lush carpet and comfortable couches in the lounge area, I came to a stop in the main area of the bathroom. The marble counters and granite floors were breathtaking, but it was the mirrors that really made the pulse race in my veins. Reaching between my legs, I eased the small egg-shaped device out, wrapped it in a towel and placed it into my small clutch purse.

The expansive wooden door opened behind me and in came Sir. He latched the door behind him. I swallowed.

His full mouth had spread to a thin-lipped smile and his massive shoulders filled out the suit he was wearing for the evening. He removed his dark-gray jacket, hanging it on a coat hanger. His shock of black hair had mussed slightly; I had an urge to run my fingers through it, but I knew better until we were at home.

"I shouldn't have to discipline you here, my pet, but it seems you are woefully trying my patience this evening." He rolled up the light blue sleeves of his dress shirt as he approached, moving like a caged tiger. "Lift your dress above your ass and bend over the counter."

A shiver of alarm sent electric pulses of desire through my lower body. My nipples tightened. I eased the dress over my hips and leaned forward, ass out. Sir undid the belt from his pants.

"All right, kitten. Four lashes for coming before you were instructed. You will count with me."

I nodded, afraid to speak.

He lifted his arm and brought the belt down over my ass.

Whack!

"One." My voice wobbled as I blinked back the prickle of tears caused by the stinging heat.

He raised his arm again, aiming for the other cheek. *Whack!*

"Two. Thank you, Sir." My eyes met his, before I noted the tenting in his trousers.

"Good. Now again."

Whack! Whack! The belt singed my already tender

flesh with fire. I yelped as the last two cracked against my asscheeks in rapid succession.

"Three!" I panted. "Four!"

"Good." Sir placed the belt on the counter. I could hear the sound of a zipper as he moved in close behind me. As I watched him in the mirror, his eyes crackled with heat when they bored into mine. His cock sprang free and rested in the crack of my ass.

"Arin," he breathed as he found my entrance and mercilessly shoved himself inside of me. Thrusting deep, he stopped, our eyes never breaking contact in the mirror as he held me in place.

"Harder," I whispered, moaning as he teased me with his length. "Please, Sir. Fuck me."

"Yes," he hissed. His hands dug into my hips, the fabric of his suit pants rubbing against my sore ass. His hips bucked, our bodies meeting in a frenzy of need.

My breasts swung with each movement; his fingers grazed over them as he embedded his cock deep inside me and thrust with short, almost violent bursts. Moaning his need into my hair, he fucked me hard. His finger brushed my clit. "Come now." My pussy spasmed around his cock as he filled me with his essence.

"Lovely," Sir whispered as he withdrew, sliding my dress down over my hips. He put himself back together and smoothed his hair, a devilish smile on his face. "Well, how about some chocolate mousse cake to go?"

I grinned. "Yes, Sir. I couldn't think of anything better."

ROOM WITH A VIEW

Rose de Fer

I bought the binoculars for bird-watching. Honest. But the wildlife is scarce on this row of terraced houses, and I always forgot to pack them when I went walking. I thought they'd just sit in their box forever. Then the new neighbors moved in.

The previous tenants took the curtains with them when they went, leaving the inside of the upstairs flat opposite mine quite exposed. At first I simply enjoyed watching through the window as the couple moved in. They arranged furniture, put books on shelves, sorted clothes into dressers. Seeing the details of these little domestic chores was surprisingly intimate. Most of all I liked watching them assemble the fancy iron bedstead with its scrolled rails at the head and foot. The rest of their furniture was rather plain but the bed was a showpiece. It was what finally made me grab the binoculars.

It sat in the center of the room, dominating the space like a stage. They made it up with satin sheets and a silk duvet all in red and black, topping it with a scattering of pillows. And when they were done they did what all loving couples do on their first night in their new home: they fucked.

At first I felt guilty, and I put the binoculars down. But even without them my eye was drawn back to the naked window and the nakedness I could see through it. The man was slightly older. Older than her and older than me. Handsome and athletic. I couldn't have appreciated that piercing gaze without the binoculars. It was little wonder his lovely wife had fallen under his spell.

So I sat in the dark by my window, my left arm propped on the sill, the binoculars pressed to my eyes and my right hand pressed to my sex. Afterward, of course, I put the binoculars away and promised myself I wouldn't spy on them again.

Promises, promises.

A week later they had unpacked completely but the window was still bare of curtains. I wondered if they had any idea just how much I could see. I should have done the neighborly thing and told them. Gone over with some tea and biscuits and a casual, "Oh, by the way, you do know I can see absolutely everything from across the road, don't you?" But of course I didn't.

One evening they looked dressed for the opera—he in an elegant dinner suit and she in a lovely, clingy red satin gown. They never left the flat. They had a long, intense conversation in the bedroom and even without the binoculars I could tell there was a strange dynamic. Their body language intrigued me. She hung her head, clasping her hands nervously behind her back while he frowned down at her. Then she knelt on the floor before him. Heat surged through my body as she lifted her arms, offering him her wrists. He tied them with a little silk scarf and suddenly I understood the scrolled iron bed frame.

My sex pulsed as he led her, not to the bed, but to the door. He pushed her back against it and looped her bound wrists up over the coat hook. Her face was flushed as she arched her back and rolled her hips invitingly. Then he tore open her dress at the front, exposing her breasts. I gasped at the sudden violence, as if the exposure were my own. With firm hands he traced the swell of her bare breasts, each dusky pink nipple stiffening beneath his touch. I pressed my legs together as he held up the riding crop.

I could actually hear the muffled slap of each stinging stroke as he brought the little leather flap down, first on one breast, then the other. She yelped and tossed her head, her face flushed, her expression full of lust. I lost count at twenty.

When he was done he piled the pillows high on the

bed and fucked her ass. Nothing could have torn my eyes away.

After that I watched them every night.

Tonight it's a new game.

She stands before him in a pleated tartan mini-skirt, a generous expanse of thigh on show between her black stockings and the hem of the skirt. Her tight white blouse is knotted together beneath her breasts, flaunting even more skin. He crosses his arms with frowning disapproval and shakes his head. I can guess what's coming next.

He seats himself on the side of the bed, facing the window. The authority in his expression makes me squirm. It makes her squirm too as she moves to his side and places herself across his lap. He strokes her back, running his hand down the curve of her spine, making her shudder. Then he lifts her skirt. Her girlish white knickers are a contrast with the rest of her sexy outfit, but he doesn't let her keep them. He peels them down over her cheeks, baring the peach of her bottom. She's trembling. So am I.

When he starts to spank her I slip my hand down inside my own knickers, not at all surprised by the wetness I find there. It's all I can do to hold the binoculars steady.

She kicks her long legs and struggles as his hand comes down again and again on her bare bottom. Even in profile I can see her pale skin blushing to a rosy pink, then shading into red. The slaps ring out in the room but I'm not sure if I'm really hearing them or just imagining it. The binoculars make me feel as though I'm right there with them, nervously waiting my turn. I can almost feel a sympathetic sting in my own bottom.

When he is satisfied that she's been punished enough he lets her up and sits her on his lap. She wraps her arms around his neck, wriggling her bottom against his legs. No doubt she can feel the bulge growing in his trousers. After a moment she leans her head in and whispers something in his ear. She is smiling. He nods. Then he looks up, toward the window. Straight at me.

I jump and almost drop the binoculars. I'm completely in shadow, hidden from view. How is it possible...?

Quickly, I raise the binoculars again, convinced I'm imagining things. But no. A slow, wicked grin spreads across his face as he meets my eyes through the magnified lenses. He points directly at me, emphasizing what I already know. They've always known I was watching. I blush to the roots of my hair, embarrassed, terrified, exhilarated. He crooks his finger, summoning me. I don't dare disobey.

FITTING ASSIGNMENT

Marie Rebelle

C laire walked into the huge branch of a well-known
lingerie store. She felt as if everyone in the shop was
keeping an eye on her and knew the real reason for her
visit to this store. An assignment. To calm her nerves
and try to blend in, she wandered between the racks
filled with lingerie, women's wear and other sexy things.
She pretended to be interested in several items. When
she walked to the back of the shop toward the fitting
rooms, she had two dresses, two nightdresses and two
sweaters to try on.

A friendly young woman took the items from her
as she got to the counter at the entrance to the fitting
rooms.

"You can take four items into the cubicle with you,
miss," the friendly woman said. Claire nodded.

"I'll bring the other two items once you're done trying these on," the woman added. This remark increased Claire's nervousness. She did not want to be disturbed. She needed to be left alone. Claire did not care to try on those last two items—information she could not share with the fitting-room assistant.

She smiled at the woman just before the cubicle's curtain fell into place. The two black dresses and the sweaters hung on hooks inside the cubicle. Claire had no intention of seeing how they looked on her. Against the back wall was a narrow bench. She unzipped her bag and took out her smartphone. Claire rummaged through her bag to find the special cradle that she'd bought earlier. She put the cradle in the corner of the narrow bench, switched the phone on, entered her PIN and activated the camera function. The phone had two camera lenses, one each in the front and back. Claire activated the lens in the front. When she put the phone in the cradle, she saw herself—no, she saw her skirt.

With a nervous glance at the curtain, she double-checked that no one could see her from the other side. Claire pulled her skirt up as she looked back at the screen of the phone. Image by image, she appeared on the telephone screen: her stockings, the garter belt, her naked pussy. Claire had one more thing to check before she could continue with her task. She took a small step closer to the phone and put her left foot on the bench. Yes! The image on the screen was what she had in mind. The lighting in the cubicle was perfect. Light from the ceiling reflected in the mirror and back at her. The image was without shadows. Every detail of the folds of her pussy was visible on the screen.

Claire took the phone from the cradle and changed it to RECORD VIDEO. When the phone was back in the cradle, she put her foot back up on the bench and started to stroke her pussy. His voice was inside her head: *Do it slow. The images must be clear. If the image is blurred, there will be consequences.* She pinched her outer labia, rolling them between her thumb and forefinger. The inside pink of her pussy appeared on the screen in the cradle as she pulled her labia. *Pinch those cunt lips. Pull them. Hard.* With her fingers spread, she pushed her pussy lips aside and watched as more of her wet pinkness appeared. *Spread your lips. Show me your lust.* The sexy images on the screen caused her nipples to harden in reaction.

It took every inch of her self-control to move her fingers over her clitoris at a slow pace. The intimate images made her horny. The adrenaline coursing through her body made her itch to move quicker. She spread her fingers once more, opening her lips, looking at the glistening of her soft flesh. Claire pushed her fingers into her wetness and smeared her fluids to her clitoris. *Push your fingers in deep.* Her clitoris ached under her fingers. Her body begged for more. She breathed harder. The assignment was clear: *You will masturbate in the fitting room and film your climax. I want proof that you have executed my orders.* As nervous as she was, she'd thought it would take long to reach her climax. She'd been wrong. The familiar tingling of an orgasm building and her increased breathing told her different. Just a few seconds more…

"Are you succeeding in there, miss?" she heard the voice of the fitting-room assistant call out to her as she approached.

Damn! For the love of…! Why now? Why hadn't the woman waited just two more minutes?

"Um…" she faltered, "um, yes, everything is fine." Her voice was husky with lust.

Her skirt had just dropped into place when the curtain opened. She took the clothes from the hook and gave them to the woman. The woman had questions in her eyes. Claire was sure that her body obscured the view on the telephone. The assistant looked surprised when Claire almost grabbed the two nightdresses from her hands.

"I will try these on now," she managed to say in a voice quivering with desire. The curtain fell back in place.

Claire dropped the nightdresses to the floor and turned back to the screen. In one smooth movement, she pulled her skirt up again and rested her foot on the bench. Claire sighed as the image of her intimate folds appeared on the telephone screen again. No shadow. Just the glistening of her pinkness. Her fingers pushed in deeper and spread her wetness toward her button. She pulled at her cunt lips, pinching them. Claire kept her eyes fixed on the tiny screen. *I want to see every move-ment, my horny little slut.* Her fingers rekindled the fire in her clitoris.

With agonizingly slow circling movements, she touched her clitoris. She pressed harder. Pulled her clitoris and circled it again. Her nipples ached. She wanted them touched. Pulled. Pinched. Her fingers danced over her throbbing nub. Her knees went weak when she climaxed. A low moan escaped her mouth. With her foot still on the bench, her legs spread wide, Claire supported herself against the side of the cubicle. Her hand covered her throbbing pussy. Inhaling deeply to catch her breath, she tried to calm herself before leaving the cubicle.

Claire sensed movement and turned her head side-ways. There, on the other side of the curtain, was the fitting-room assistant, watching her through the crack between the curtain and the cubicle wall. The rawness of unvarnished lust in the woman's eyes had Claire hoping she'd be granted permission to return and pursue that look.

SPIDER

Valerie Alexander

Siobhan twisted and writhed on the bondage table, her long, pale legs flexing as her red hair fell toward the floor. I could see her toes flex as the dom fucked her with a candle, moving it in and out of her swollen, wet cunt just an inch or so until she wailed in frustration. She was lost to the sensation, oblivious to the men gathered round to gawk at her. Their cocks were hard. I wondered if she was going to get fucked by all of them.

My boyfriend nudged me. "Don't you know her?"

"Kind of." The aloof makeup artist who worked at the mall was barely recognizable here, naked and moaning and desperate to be degraded. Hopefully it wouldn't be awkward the next time I saw her at the store. I really didn't know what the protocol was. Play parties weren't my usual cup of tea.

"Kate, Devon, you made it." The bearded host appeared with a smile. "Come out back and I'll show you the kind of cross I can make you."

I kept a cool face as we passed a caged girl, a shirtless man with red welts crisscrossing his back, and another girl bridled like a pony. We were here because the host made bondage furniture, and Devon and I were commissioning him to build us a St. Andrew's cross—if we could afford it, that was. Bondage furniture tended to be expensive.

I ignored the doms eyeing me and smirking. Though I'd been sexually submitting to Devon in private for eight months now, I'd never had the desire—or the guts—to take part in the scene, as people called it. Somehow I didn't think I could get turned on by a spanking or whipping here the way I did in private.

Two voices rose in argument and the host excused himself. Devon looked at me and shrugged. Much as he liked mastering me at home, play parties weren't his thing either. Nor was he an especially dominant presence in the real world; tall, slight and bespectacled, Devon always struck people as the young professor type, not a man who liked to truss up his girlfriend in rope and nipple clamps.

We passed into the backyard. Electric candles were glowing in lanterns hung from the trees but they didn't illuminate the shadowy figures moving around with cups of beer in their hands. I smoothed my dress over my ass and spied a hammock tied between two trees.

Perfect. "Let's hang out here," I suggested, and climbed in. To my surprise, the hammock sagged beneath me. I immediately rolled onto my side. I tried to push myself up but found it embarrassingly hard.

The host stepped forward from the darkness. "That's not a hammock," he said.

His smile was kind but I still felt like a neophyte, tangled in this odd rope swing that seemed rigged to trap me. "How do I get out of this?"

"You don't," he said, stepping up and rolling me over in a circle. "That's the point."

I was completely entangled in the rope swing now, facedown and facing away from the party. Which was partly good, because at least people couldn't see my face burning with embarrassment. But it was also partly bad, because my ass and legs were facing the guests and I knew my dress wasn't quite long enough to cover my panties in this position. What a rookie move to make—mistaking some kind of bondage swing for a hammock and getting tangled in it.

The surrounding men had noticed, and I could hear them drawing up behind me and assessing my ass.

"Take her underwear off," one said.

"The dress too," said another one.

"Devon," I snapped.

He was laughing. "What? You're the one who climbed in there."

The bearded host looked at him. "You want me to get her out?"

"Hmm, I don't know," Devon said. "She does looks appetizing all bound up like that."

"I'll make a deal with you—she provides some entertainment and I'll give you a hell of a deal on that cross."

Devon grinned. Goddammit. Of course I wanted the St. Andrew's cross as much as he did, and getting a break on the price would be great. But what did "entertainment" mean?

"You don't have to fuck anyone," the host said, reading my mind. "But putting on a show would be good."

An electric bolt went through me. The one thing playing with Devon couldn't provide was indulging my exhibitionistic streak. I nodded hesitantly.

The host rolled me over once more. I was firmly trapped in the ropes now. My arms were bound at my sides, with only my head free at one end, and my ass and legs emerging from the other. Devon moved behind me and pushed my dress up to my waist, tucking it into the ropes. Then his fingers hooked into my panties and pulled them all the way off.

I gulped. My face felt hot and my whole body trembled. I'd never been so helpless in public before, especially in front of strangers.

I swallowed hard and spread my legs.

Devon's fingers brushed my clit. I moaned and the men laughed. Then two stepped up and apparently posed on either side of my pussy; I couldn't see them but

I could hear the camera phones clicking. "Can I touch her?" asked someone else.

Devon ran his fingertips up my thigh and stopped. "Kate...?"

I nodded. "I want to be fucked," I whispered, so only he could hear. "But safely."

It was the most shameful confession of my life. I was spreading my legs at a party for a bunch of strange men, making myself available to be used by any interested taker. Getting gangbanged: that was something only the biggest sluts did. My face and body were burning as Devon said something to the men about what I wanted, and a collective dirty howl rose up.

"Oh god," I muttered as the first man stepped between my legs. A faceless, anonymous stranger was going to fuck me, and one after that, and one after that... My nipples ached with the pain of desire repressed as his condom-wrapped cock pushed inside me. My blood pounded through me like a hot flood. I was breathing hard and totally bound, and as he began driving in and out of my pussy, I succumbed to my own powerlessness. I was just an object, helpless to resist the men lining up behind me; that degradation set every nerve ending in my body on fire. I moaned and twisted feverishly in the ropes. The first man groaned and shook; a second man replaced him, but he came too quickly and then a third began fucking me, slapping my ass with every thrust.

"You're so lucky," one of the men said to Devon.

And as I began to come in euphoric throbs, my pussy squeezing the anonymous cock inside me, I smiled because I knew he was right.

THE CHROME-PLATED CONNECTION

Ginger F.

D on't you think that's enough computer time for tonight," says his deep voice from behind me.

"In a minute," I reply, while working on the paragraph I've been laboriously constructing for the past five minutes.

"No," he says. That word makes me flush. I stop typing. He beckons me to follow him out of my office, and I do. "What had you so focused?" he asks.

I'm in the bedroom when I look at the clock. Heat crawls up my neck and turns me red. It's almost an hour after our agreed upon playtime. I've screwed up.

"I'm sorry," I say, "There's no excuse, but—" With both of us working from home we've had a hard time maintaining balance, and our connection has suffered as a result. In an effort to remedy the situation we've set working and playing hours with each other. This evening I had clients who required a late meeting. After the meeting I found myself on a certain kinky social networking site, and lost track of time.

"You see, Sir, someone was wrong…"

"Oh, on the Internet?" he asks, smirking. We laugh, but his face quickly returns to stern.

"It's not—"

"A good excuse? No."

He takes me by the nape of the neck, pulling me closer to him. The kiss is languorous, his mouth working at mine, his thumb caressing my neck. "You can make it up to me in service," he says, whispering in my ear.

I press my cheek to his, and breathe him in. "Yes, Sir."

As my clothes begin to disappear, so do his. I leave my panties and bra on, knowing his preference for this aesthetic. "It looks like you weren't entirely unprepared for our date," he says, placing his hands on the band of my black lace panties and toying with the upper part of my ass.

I suck in a large helping of air. "Thank you, Sir."

His hand is at the base of my skull and his fingers dive into my hair, not so much pulling as guiding me in the direction he wants me to go. He places me on top of the bedspread and reaches into our bedside drawer. Items clatter as he gropes for his desired object. When he acquires it, he leaves it pooled on the pillow, glittering in the light of the lamp.

It is time for me to serve. I smile.

Everyone needs his release and my Master finds his in controlled pain—his control over the person giving him the pain: me. My fingers caress the cold metal object left on the pillow. Picking up the nipple clamps, I let them dangle in a line of chrome delight, swaying gently.

He smiles.

He's lying down, and I straddle him. His hands clasp my hips, still toying with the line of my panties, and make me squirm. I let my nail drag over his nipple, and with a deep breath and a smile, I begin to play.

I start by pressing the clover clamp to his nipple. I can hear him suck in a breath. I use my other hand to start toying with the other nipple as I tease my Master with the lightest pressure from the clamp, opening and closing it at intervals. His eyes are shut and he's pressing his head back, but his hands remain firm and unyielding on my hips. When his fingers dig in I know it's time, and I let the first clamp establish itself on his flush flesh.

Now I press my lips to his other nipple, licking and biting at it, but he takes me by the face and taps me on the cheek with his open hand—an almost slap. "No biting," he says, but he's smiling. I place the next clamp, and begin to tug and play with them. I can feel him relaxing beneath me, his cock hard against my lace-clad ass. Extending my arm, I play with it, teasing it. I move to the side of his body and take hold of the chain that connects the clamps with my lips. "Good girl," he moans, his eyes opening to watch me.

He reaches out a hand and tugs my panties down, then spreads my legs. His fingers dexterously work my clit til I'm moaning and forgetful of my duties. My hand becomes still on his cock, and the chain begins to slip from between my lips. He removes his hand from my slit and shoves his fingers into my mouth. I am awake again. I lick my wetness from them, the metal from the chain nudging my teeth.

"Thank you, Sir," I attempt to articulate from between his digits.

He closes my lips around the chain. "Quiet."

My cunt is dripping, and I want to come, but I know better than to speak. I spread my legs wider and try to keep my head in the same position, with my lips connected to the chain. I sit back a bit farther, hoping he will see how swollen I am. I can't help whimpering, and I reach out to stroke his cock, so he will be pleased.

"Should I let you come tonight?" he asks. "You can't have wanted it too much, if you forgot about it."

"Please, Sir."

He cups my chin and puckers my lips so that I release the chain. He removes one of the clamps from his chest and removes one of my breasts from the bra, to attach the clamp to its nipple. I press my chest forward, aching for the feel of more of him on more of me. We're linked.

I lean into the sensation, straining the chain between us. "Good girl," he praises again. Then, pressing his hand to my shoulder, he pushes me down, and follows me. His hand reaches between my legs, and it's all I can do to not call out to him. As my breath begins to quicken, he enters me unceremoniously, but I am wet enough and instantly begin to throb. He keeps his thumb on my clit. The chain goes taut and then lax as his body moves with his thrusting, making both of us writhe. As I watch the glittering light of the chain between us, I feel pressure building inside of me, threatening to spill over.

"Please, Sir. Soon, it's going to happen soon. Please, Sir, please say I can. Please."

"Yes," he says, and I do. My body spasms beneath his. As the throbbing begins to subside I can feel him pulsing inside of me. He collapses, and we gently reach across our bodies to remove the clamps. They sit between us.

"Was it a hard day for you?" I ask, yawning.

"It was," he says, stroking my hair. "Yours?"

"I managed," I say, scooting forward to be closer to him, and moving the clamps out of my way. His arms wrap around me.

After some silence I whisper, "Thank you, Sir."

"For what?"

"For letting me serve you...and for the orgasm."

Warm arms and his scent surround me. His face is peaceful, and our legs intertwine for sleep.

HOW TO FAIL

Laurel Isaac

First he was spanking me with a paddle. It got very intense very fast, and it hurt. A lot. Like being skinned, like getting kicked repeatedly. I was past being able to cry, just stuck in the pain, knowing I couldn't take it, but not knowing how to talk.

Aside from the thwacking, the bedroom was very quiet. The roommate was out of town. Daddy Owen was focused and moving about swiftly. My gasps into the bedspread had gotten quieter and quieter; it was as if someone had lowered the volume on my thoughts. A loose panic wove through my mind, spiking occasionally, but I almost couldn't hear it, distracted by the intensity of the spanking and muddled about what exactly I was supposed to be doing. Owen was like a machine, completely on task. He had his favorite hard cock strapped beneath his jeans and was whaling on me, his bare-ass boi (to everyone else, a proper butch dyke). I could tell he was enjoying himself. Working up a sweat, on a mission.

All I could think was how I must be doing something wrong. I must have forgotten some technique I usually use, or there must be something wrong with my body that the feeling good wasn't kicking in. Maybe if I waited a little longer it would start to. Maybe this was how it always was in the beginning? If only he'd slow down I might be able to figure it out, but the paddle abruptly landed squarely in the middle of my right cheek. The throbbing felt like it had shocked me right in half. I let out a sob. And there it was again, and again. If only I had a minute, I might be able to...but the strokes kept landing, bludgeoning, deafening. The Tegan and Sara poster went fuzzy before my eyes. I began to feel like I was being swung around the room, seasick and powerless.

Ashamed, I asked, "Could you lighten up a bit?"

I didn't know if it was my tone or what, but Owen pulled his solid body back fast and then was staring right at me, interrogating me.

"Has it been too much for a while?"

Or at least it seemed like an interrogation. I felt stuck, afraid to say anything in case that meant he wouldn't come back. We were silent, both of our queer hair mussed, the bed askew.

"Kinda," was obviously not the answer Owen was

looking for. He sighed dramatically and seemed pissed.

Owen sat down on the bed. I stood around feeling awkward, naked. He took another deep breath.

"Boi, come here." He opened his tattooed arms so I could climb into his lap. I wrapped my legs around his torso, bare against his clothed frame.

"I'm so sorry," he said.

He ran his warm hands over my back and kissed the top of my head.

Owen hugged me to his chest, smooshing my cunt against his belly. I worried about leaving a wet spot, but he didn't seem to care.

"I never want to hurt you," he said. "I'm really sorry."

I didn't understand. I felt like a failure—not like anything bad had happened on his end. But slowly it started to sink in. It had been scary. Heavy strokes coming out of nowhere so fast I couldn't assimilate them. Having to act tough when I was in so much pain. I sniffled and collapsed onto his shoulder, tearing up. Owen reached for a soft blanket and wrapped it around my back. I'd been really scared. I hadn't known what was going on or when it was going to stop. Tears moistened his neck as he stroked my short hair. I'd felt so alone. It was only in being so close to him now that I noticed my vulnerability, which had been there all along. I curled into him.

"Safewords," Daddy Owen began in a gentle voice, "are not just for catastrophes." Daddy spoke softly about communicating in scene and how we were still getting to know each other. I closed my eyes and rested. He smelled really good, like wood fire. I felt like I could breathe him directly into my core. If I breathed enough of him in, maybe I'd have him inside of me, protecting me like this all the time.

By the time Daddy was finished talking, I was enjoying how warm my butt was and wanted more.

"Please, Sir, would you spank me again? I promise I'll tell you if it gets to be too much."

Then I was back in the saddle, bent over, breathing in his clean bed.

The slaps came slowly. Daddy hit my bottom with his hand and rubbed away the pain. Ever so slowly, he increased the intensity, so I was rocking into his fingertips, wanting to feel every crawl of the sting across my flesh.

I was drifting into a very happy place when the strokes started coming in a long train close together. A tremendous sadness entered my body.

"Sir," I murmured. "I think I need more time between strokes tonight; I think that's the problem."

"Thank you for telling me, boi," Daddy said.

And then, quick as magic, I was flying. Daddy pulled me tight against his hip, clasping my labrys tattoo. A paddle landed over and over in surprising and perfect rhythms and locations, bringing symphonies of sensation—like coming, like eating. I could taste the leather in a hundred different flavors. The pain wiped my palate clean.

I was right at home, drooling on the bed, whimpering.

Daddy interspersed some strokes with rubbing my clit, but not enough so I could come.

"Aw, you want to come? So sad for you," he mocked, and returned to beating me. His hand cupped the heat of my ass.

Then his hand was gone, wrapped around something new and snappy and I was going to scream.

My butt was so hot, my whole body was sweltering. My cunt was dripping down my thigh. I was shaking, some part of me close to maxing out.

"Please, Daddy, not much more," I got out.

Daddy took this into consideration. Four more, he decided. He said I could take four more. And then I did. Four big crashes that felt amazingly good. In one, two, three, four, I was beaten out of myself and then back in. I panted.

Daddy's hand reached for my clit. I needed to come, but was falling over. Daddy moved me onto the bed, then jerked me off. *Daddy stroking boi's cock, dirty dirty. Claiming ownership of boi's whole body.* Massaging the shaft, flicking the tip. Until I came, rapidly, curling into a ball with the force of it. The spasms pricked sharply like needles; I squirmed and groaned. My come leaked everywhere.

Daddy pulled me under the covers and spooned me, palming my tits. Suddenly I was buried under quilts of love. "I'm so proud of you. You're beautiful." Daddy held me tight.

"When you've recovered, I want you to suck me off."

And I couldn't decide what I wanted more—to stay harnessed to his heart or to have my mouth between his legs immediately.

CRUSH

Giselle Renarde

She comes home to find him wearing her panties and snaps, "Get those off."

"Why? I'm not stretching them."

"I don't care. Get your own underwear."

"I *have* my own underwear. I like yours better."

She rolls her eyes and crosses her arms, but she can't help smirking. He looks damn good wearing nothing but sheer red underpants. They cling nice and tight to his otherwise naked body. All she can focus on is the rising swell of his erection.

The panties are mesh and see-through from the right angle, like cling wrap cradling his big dick and his balls. He's hard already. God, is he hard! The bulbous head of his cock pulses like a heartbeat. She can actually see that through the fabric.

One step forward and she's wet. The gusset of her panties—the ones *she's* wearing—is already slick with juice. She walks closer to him in her vicious spike heels. They *click-clack* across the parquet, backing him into the bedroom. She doesn't usually wear shoes in the apartment. The people downstairs complain a lot. But just for this, just for him, she keeps them on.

"Get down." She strips off her jacket, unbuttons her blouse. "Down, on the floor. Go."

He sits on his ass, with his back against the bed.

"Spread your legs," she says, dropping her skirt. "Wider. Attaboy."

Red panties cradle his balls like ripe fruit. They looked good enough to eat.

She licks her lips. "I know what you want."

"Do you?"

Pushing his head against the side of the mattress, she straddles his face. "You want to taste my pussy."

"No," he says, innocently.

"Brat."

"I will if I have to," he tells her. "But it's not what I *want*."

"Do you want to torture yourself?" she asks, taunting him. "Is that what you want?"

"No."

He doesn't hesitate long before biting her cunt, right through the tight layer of black lace. She hisses. It's better than good. His nibbles send shock waves down her legs and up to the nipples hardening inside her black bra. She likes to coordinate.

"I wish I could fuck you with my clit."

He glances up at her. "Fuck me where?"

"Your throat," she says. "Your ass. If my clit grew big and hard, I'd slap it across your bratty little face. I'd smack your cheeks. I'd spank your ass."

A whining noise emerges from his throat.

"You want a nice little taste?"

When he nods, she pushes down her panties and steps out of them. His nose disappears beyond her thick black bush. When his tongue finds her clit, it's so hot she gasps. Hot, thick, and soft as velvet. She breathes deeply, trying to hold herself together. His tongue is too much. Much too much. She'll come if he keeps at it.

She takes a step back, and he looks at her, pleadingly. "More?"

"Later."

He grins, opening his legs wide. She stands between them, watching his cock throb. All she wants is to fall on the floor and let his dick impale her face, but she knows what he wants, and his wants are her most vital concern.

Setting her foot in position, she lifts the toe of her shoe. The stiletto heel slides closer to her panties—the ones *he's* wearing—until he hisses in anticipation. He drives his palms firmly into the floor, like he can feel the pressure already.

It's going to be good. She'll be firm with him. Unforgiving. She knows what he likes.

"Crush," he says, drawing out the *shhh* sound.

She's doing his bidding. Might not look that way to an outsider, but she is. This is what he wants. He needs to feel the base of her shoe against his hot cock. She nudges his swollen tip with her patent-leather toe, and he hisses, knocking his head against the side of the mattress. She sets her weight on him, little by little, building pressure.

The expression on his face would look like pain to anybody else. But she knows what he likes. She strokes him with her shoe, up toward his cockhead. Pressing her toe against his tip, she lifts her heel off the ground.

"Does it hurt?" she asks. She's crushing his swollen head. Of course it hurts.

He says, "No."

"Well, then." She sets her stiletto in the center of his ball sac, lowering the heel slowly, torturing him. "I guess I'll have to do better."

A sound emerges from his throat, somewhere between a screech and a howl. He's a prey animal, caught in her clutches. She sinks her heel into his balls. Her weight remains mostly on the other foot, the one on the parquet, but she's digging into him good and hard. Every time she shifts, even slightly, he whimpers, pressing his palms harder against the floor.

"You're never going to come," she tells him.

"No?"

She shakes her head. "No."

Not for a while. Not for a good long while. She sinks her heel a little deeper into the fleshy mass of his balls, and he squirms, whines. The pain is so blatant she can taste it on her tongue.

Tongue…

She'd almost forgotten…

"I'd like to come now, I think." Dislodging her heel from his crotch, she straddles his body, pressing her pussy against his mouth. "You're going to make me come."

He looks up at her in reverence. When he nods, his lips brush her clit. He opens his mouth and she rides his face. His tongue strokes her—liquid warmth—and she melts all over his cheeks, spreading juice down his chin.

She thinks about his hard cock, about his huge, swollen balls. Why is it so fulfilling to press a cruel heel into the most sensitive part of his body? Is it the rush she feels when she's certain her stiletto is about to puncture him? Or the thrill of knowing he would never ask anyone else to provide this sort of pain? He would never *trust* anyone else to do what she does.

Cupping his head with both hands, she thrusts her clit against his tongue. She's so close. He's going to make her come.

HOUSEBROKEN

Laila Blake

Her kitten was lying in a patch of sun on the hardwood floors. Her eyes were closed against the bright light but she had her arms stretched out into the air above her, moving slightly this way and that. It looked just as if those beautiful, nimble fingers were trying to spin a dreamlike, golden fabric out of the millions of little dust and glimmer particles in the air. Or maybe like her arms and hands were bathing sensuously in the sunlight trying to wash away the stale, grimy winter pallor in the early spring sun.

The tiny bell on her kitten-collar chimed whenever she moved her head a little this way or that, sparkling like her pink lips with their ubiquitous honey-scented gloss. All of her seemed to glow as she lay there ivory-pink, her knees pulled up in a shallow angle, leaning against each other, her toes wriggling a little. She never did lie completely still—for that she needed ropes and cuffs, commands and punishments. For the moment, though, Imani allowed it, smiling at her kitten's antics and the way, in her apartment, her kitten could let go completely, with no care in the world but Imani's pleasure and her own, attaining the purest sense of freedom humans could find.

Sitting in the old-fashioned rocking chair she had picked up at Camden Market from a grisly antiques dealer for ten quid her first week in the country, Imani swayed gently. It was a comfortable Saturday morning, the kind that passed almost without her noticing the perfection of its simple pleasures. Imani's breasts were full and warm outlines under the flowing white kaftan robe she had pulled on to make breakfast a few hours earlier. Her long, proud legs were open, one thigh resting on the side of the chair, a cup of coffee balanced on her knee. The bright color of the translucent fabric contrasted starkly with the deep, dark color of her skin.

Softly, like the kiss of a butterfly she ran the tip of a peacock's feather over her kitten's stomach, smiling at the little movements that showed her pleasure, the tingling of the bell and the tiny whimpers. She found the arch of her rib cage and traced along its path. Her kitten flexed her stomach and released again. Imani ticked her belly button, trying to drill the feather into the small, tight hole to make her do it again. She was rewarded with a tiny squeal and little kicks into the air.

Her kitten's nipples hardened at the soft contact as she arched up her chest for more. The silence in the room was only broken by her shallow breaths and the soft chimes of the bell on her collar. Her hands were on the side of her body now, palms pressed flat on the floor to support her billowing chest.

"Touch yourself," Imani said in her characteristic quiet voice, her accent dripping like honey and cream. "Slowly. Not your clit yet. Touch inside, push as deep as you can."

Her kitten smiled up at her; her little English rose. She was chubby and short where Imani was thin and tall. Where her kitten's face was round, with pink cheeks and bright blue eyes, Imani had the strong, noble features of ancient tribes, only accentuated by her proudly shaved head. Her kitten's hair was long and silky and always in tangles; she found it everywhere when she vacuumed or shook out her pillows. The way she was sitting with her legs apart gave her kitten just a peek at the dark, creamy wetness between her legs. Wiry curly hair grew on her mound but she kept her kitten's shaved, preferring an unmarred expanse of pink.

Curling in a little, the kitten reached down, obediently circumventing the top of her slit, and pushed two fingers deep into her cunt. She whimpered at the slippery warm wetness she found there, then pulled back and pushed down harder. Her body curled in on itself even more as she gasped.

"Stop," Imani all but whispered; she didn't need to

raise her voice to establish her dominance. "Taste it, suckle your fingers."

There was no hesitation, just an immediate movement of her arm and a moment later her fingers were in her mouth and she was sucking at them noisily, just the way Imani liked. She smiled to herself.

"Good kitten," she cooed approvingly. She loved her yielding sweetness, her smiles and her eagerness, the way she sought touch and praise with every fiber of her being. Stretching out her long leg, she ran her toes over her kitten's stomach and nonchalantly, taking a sip of her coffee, she slipped them between her labia. The kitten moaned hard around her fingers and Imani rubbed her toe hard over her clit until her kitten couldn't keep still anymore, billowing and wriggling under the onslaught of pleasure.

Imani tutted; her foot stilled and she pulled it away. With the elegance of a dancer, she moved her leg again, gently brushed her toe over her kitten's pink nose and left a trace of her juices.

"Clean," she commanded her; the arousal had slowly trickled into her voice as well, making it hoarse and more accented. There was a soft popping sound when her kitten pulled her fingers from her mouth and started to lap at her toes instead. Imani closed her eyes and exhaled a shallow breath, fingers gripping at the side of the chair.

"Fuck yourself again," she exhaled as she pushed her toes harder into her kitten's mouth. Her swirling tongue was hot and wet and felt deliciously dirty around her toes. The sensations doubled when her moans added a layer of vibration to the connection.

"No, not your clit. No coming yet."

She wanted to ride that beautiful mouth raw but she had all day—all weekend—to enjoy her pet. She could make herself wait. Fucking her mouth with her toes gave her that tingling dirty feeling that her kitten knew so well how to arouse. She only pulled them out when her leg started to ache. Immediately, the noise level rose. There was no sight quite like this one: her kitten, rolling on the floor and fucking herself at her behest.

"Do you want to rub your clit, kitten?" she asked, a little breathless herself. Unsurprisingly, the kitten nodded hard, yowling softly in as much elaboration as she could manage in that state.

"I want you to recite that poem," Imani whispered, "the one I like. And you make yourself come for me."

Her kitten whimpered and scrunched up her forehead for a moment, lining up the beautiful words all in the right order before she let her fingers pull back the hood of her clit.

Imani leaned back again and smiled. She had always thought that the sound of abandon and orgasm fit the melody of Keats like nothing else.

STRONGER THAN STEEL

Alva Rose

Even when he's on the edge, even when he finally breaks and his hands grip me a little tighter, he's quiet, strong, restrained. Always the picture of control.

Tonight, when he comes home from his week on a remote construction site, I'm going to take that away.

He is always rewarded by the sound of his name coming breathless and distorted from my mouth, by the hard upward curve of my spine and the bucking of my hips, the slickness that spreads pale, wet butterfly wings on my thighs, and tonight I will get mine. I will see his strong, tanned brow wrinkle, his jaw with a week's hair growth falling open, pulsing veins stretching up his aching forearms. I will leave him no choice.

I've been studying his body, putting together the teeny-tiny pieces: the very point on his cock that, when pressed with the tip of my tongue with exactly the right amount of pressure, causes the shaft to go a little more rigid; which sounds that bubble out of my mouth at the moment of climax cause his eyes to flutter closed; what happens the second before he stops letting me have my way and wrestles me onto my back or my knees; what might otherwise make him lose control.

I started a mental log of the times he would come up behind me and grab my ass while I got dressed in the morning. It reliably happened when I wore a particular pair of lace boy shorts, the lime-green ones with a single bubble-gum-pink bow that stopped just above the crease that forms between my thighs and my ass. If I happened to stand on my tiptoes and lean over my vanity to grab a bottle of perfume or an eyeliner pencil, he'd spring out of bed, lock his arms around me and growl into my ear, baring his teeth and pushing his hips against my lower back. He'd wet his finger with his tongue, slip it between the lace and my skin and with quick accuracy pinpoint my clit and circle it over and over. I'd feel the smooth head of his cock separated from my cunt by millimeters of bunched-up fabric, pushing back and forth between my thighs until he hooked his fingers around the crotch of my underwear, tugged them aside, and parted my lips with his swollen manhood. And when moisture began spreading over its surface, that's when he'd push into me, so slowly, making me feel every ridge and vein as it stretched my soaking hole.

And I would writhe and gasp and pound the vanity

with my fist, yelping his name and pushing back to take him deeper, trying to gain some tiny scrap of control, trying to find a hair-thin crack in his composure as he worked me into unhinged ecstasy. I never found either.

I know exactly how the night goes whenever he returns from a week away on a job. He's always aching to touch me, to smell the faint floral notes of my moisturizer and run his toughened hands over the smooth flat of my back. When he first gets his hands on me, he's as close to abandon as I have ever seen him, as vulnerable, as sensitive to my voice and my touch as he can be. But he regains himself quickly, because more than anything, he wants to make me come, and for that, he must focus.

He has tried a few times to let go and hand me the reins, but he just can't. He says he wants to, with great sympathy in his voice, but he's used to control. His will, his instincts and his arms are too strong to let that happen.

But he is not stronger than steel.

A pair of shiny double-lock handcuffs are dangling from the center of our curly forged-iron bed frame. As soon as he left on Monday, I went out and bought them, and every evening, I held them and clicked them shut and unlocked them over and over again, acquainting my hands with the curves of the smooth, cold steel. I'm quick with them now—hopefully quick enough.

When he gets inside, he'll wrap me up in his arms, kiss me, breathe against my neck, then run into the bathroom and whip off his filthy, sweaty shirt. He'll scrub his hands with pumice, and return to the bedroom smelling of oranges. He'll lie down next to me and take a few minutes to bask in the comforts of home: clean, well-worn sheets, privacy, leisure, love, and a bed he shares with his adoring wife. Once he's done that, he'll pull me on top of him (and even in doing this, direct me just where he wants me at that moment) and rest his hands on my hips, give me those few moments to do to him what I please, but he won't be ready for what I do tonight; he'll never see it coming. And that's how I'll get the upper hand.

The lights are dim. The waistband of my lime-green boy shorts just barely peeks out under my black yoga pants, and the dryer is buzzing downstairs. As I begin making the bed, I hear the deep rumble of his car coming up the driveway, its headlights shooting beams of light across the pale bedroom wall. I feel myself tensing up, blood beginning to redirect itself between my legs as I put the pillows in their cases and tuck the fitted sheet around the corners of the bed.

I've planned everything so carefully. I'm so sure of what I'm going to do once he's immobilized beneath me. Tonight, I'll say his name once and only once. Tonight, I get mine.

Just as I arrange the pillows high at the head of the bed—the cuffs safely hidden behind a deep layer of soft, inviting fluff—I hear the front steps creaking. I hear his keys jangling as he selects one from the ring, the lock turning and clicking into its open position, the whoosh of the door separating from its airtight seal, and him sighing as he finally returns home from a long, hard week.

I sit down on the edge of the bed, calming my nerves with one last, deep breath as he crosses the house. He steps into the bedroom, and I rise to my feet.

He wraps those big, powerful arms around me, kisses me again and again, then breaks away to wash his hands. When he rejoins me on the bed, he stretches out next to me, lying with his head inches from the nightstand. On it are two new silver keys on a small ring.

But in the dim light, he hasn't noticed them.

He has no idea.

STUDENT
BECOMES
MASTER

Rob Rosen

He'd looked almost the same—older, of course, but the face of the teenager I'd coached years earlier still rose to the surface.

"Let me out!" I hollered. The gym's closet door was shut tight, leaving me in utter darkness.

He banged on the wood from the other side. "Mister Jones," he replied, voice muffled. "What do we say?"

I gritted my teeth and yanked at my tethered wrists. "*Please.*"

I waited, beads of sweat dripping from my brow before stinging my eyes. My bare knees ached as I maintained my crouched and bound position. He'd surprised me, showing up after school had finished for the day, the last student long gone. He'd surprised me even further with his wrestling skills, considering how weak they'd been the last time I'd seen them.

The door creaked open, a shaft of light momentarily blinding me. "Good boy," he cooed. I squinted up at him, sucking in my breath as yet another surprise greeted me. He was naked now, hard as granite, billy club of a cock swinging as he strode into the closet, a hand quickly rising before slamming into my exposed rump. I stifled a moan as best I could, but my rigid prick gave me away. "Good boy," he repeated.

"John," I managed. "Please."

He grunted and smacked me again. "Not John." *Smack*. "*Mister* Matthews."

My cock throbbed. He smacked that next. Ass to cock, cock to ass. "Mister Matthews," I reiterated. "Please untie me." Even to my own ears my plea came off sounding rather weak.

He crouched down, our faces barely an inch apart. "Funny, your voice says one thing, but your prick says something else." He got on his knees and rubbed his dickhead against my lips before smacking my cheek with it. Again I moaned, body quaking in rapt anticipation. "You were a fucking sadist in my youth, Mister Jones. What's happened to you?"

He rammed his stellar cock down my throat. I gagged as the aroma of crotch sweat filled my sinus cavity. A tear then streaked down my cheek as he extricated his meat. "Is that what this is about?" I rasped. "Revenge for teaching you how to be a man?"

Again he grunted, his dick thwacking my cheek, left

side, then right. "Sure, we'll go with that," he replied. "And now it's my turn. Student becomes Master, Mister Jones. Think you can pass the test?"

A rush of warmth spread through me. He was right, of course; I had been a bit of a sadist, but a good coach teaches by discipline. Guess I taught him too well, by the looks of things. Like he said, student had become Master, in more ways than one. Funny thing was, I'd never known how much of a masochist I could be as well. Go figure.

"Not much of a fair fight," I said, locking eyes with him.

His face moved into mine again, his hot breath hitting my mouth. "I was just going to leave you here. To be found in the morning." He bit my lip, teasingly at first, but then with enough force to make me yelp. "Until I saw how much you were enjoying yourself. Little head always gives the big head away, you see, Mister Jones."

I smirked. "*Both* your heads look awfully big these days, Mister Matthews."

He pulled my lip with his teeth, then replied, "Guess I grew up a bit since you last saw me. And out." He stood, cock hovering above my head. "As to that fair fight, here's your lesson for the day: life ain't fair; get over it."

He scooted behind me, yanking my bindings even tighter as he went. Each pull and tug sent an eddy of adrenaline coursing through me, pain and pleasure combining as one. "You always were a bad sport, *John*."

Fine, I was egging him on. But the slap I got across my ass was well worth it.

"And you were always a prick." He grabbed my prick as he said the word, yanking it between my legs, causing my back to arch and a fresh bead of sweat to trickle. He smacked the head, my body tensing each time flesh met flesh, until my brain swam in glorious pain.

"And is revenge as sweet as they say it is, *John*?" I asked, as he spat at my exposed hole. I winced in expectation, again as double digits thrust deep inside of me. He rooted around in there. "Are you planning on finding your answers up my ass?"

He didn't reply at first. When he did, it was with a sigh. His fingers then retracted. Suddenly, he was face-to-face with me again. This time the kiss was soft, his eyes open all the while, searching. When our lips parted, the sigh repeated itself. "I already got my answer, Mister Jones."

I stared at him, confused, cock so hard it felt like it would burst on its own accord. "And what is that?"

He smiled and stood. "That I'm better than this." He moved to the door. "Than you."

Out he walked, the door closed behind him, darkness again complete. "John!" I hollered. "Mister Matthews!" I rolled over on my side. "*Please.*" It came out a whimper.

A minute went by, two. Thankfully, the door creaked opened again. His cock was in his stroking hand. "But maybe not that much better." He strode over and stood above me. His body spasmed a moment later, a soft moan escaping from between his lips as he shot his hefty, aromatic load onto my face. I licked it off my lips, my own cock suddenly erupting as his spunk hit the back of my throat.

I gazed up at him and winked. "When's my next lesson, *Master*?"

He smiled down at me, then turned and left, leaving me to my sticky humiliation.

WHERE THE SUN DON'T SHINE

Corvidae

It was one of those rare luxuries for San Francisco: a warm, sunny day, and Elise had the afternoon off to enjoy it. By the time she got home, the sun was hitting their small outdoor deck just right. She wasted no time before stripping off her clothes, strapping on a bikini, anointing herself in lotion and spreading out on a striped picnic blanket on top of the warm wood.

Elise sighed deeply. She had been looking forward to this all morning. The heat of the sun dissipated the tension rooted in her back and shoulders while a light breeze wicked away the clean sweat beading on her skin. It felt like her skin was purging the suffocation of the stuffy suit she had been confined to all morning. Her mind retreated as she stretched luxuriously across the blanket, her thoughts awash in a warm glow like the pink light leaking through her closed eyelids. She was just starting to drift away when her phone buzzed.

She sighed again, this time in resignation, and groped for it, praying it wasn't work trying to contact her. But she relaxed when she saw her boyfriend Jordan's name in the heading of the text message. *Hey babe! How's your afternoon off?*

She wanted to tell him in detail how perfect everything felt right then, but a picture was worth a thousand words, and a lot easier than squinting at the phone's keyboard. She grinned as she took a shot of her current view: her body stretched across the deck under blue sky, the golden swell of her hip, long muscular legs sprawled across the bright blanket and the tiniest triangle of fabric perched on her mound at the center of it all. Satisfied, she sent it, amused at how it would tease him to see something like that while stuck in the office.

The phone buzzed again a few minutes later. *I don't like the look of that suit. You're going to get tan lines. You know I don't like anyone but me marking your skin, Pet.*

A thrill shot through her. He wouldn't have called her "Pet" unless he had some sort of game in mind. She hesitated, then replied. *What would you have me do...Sir?*

There was a longer delay this time, but when his reply came it was short. *Take it off. Now.*

Her breath caught in her throat. She sat up and looked around. Their house was on a hillside, with a commanding view over the city, but they were surrounded by other houses and buildings that had a clear line-of-sight view of the deck. She couldn't see anyone at the moment, but it wasn't impossible that someone else might be home early in the middle of the day. Someone could even be watching her right now from the shadows behind their windows. Her stomach clenched uncomfortably at the thought.

Her phone buzzed again. *You better do as I say, Pet, or your spanked ass will be worse than a sunburn after I get home.*

She shivered, suddenly feeling terribly vulnerable. But no matter how anxious she felt, pushing herself would please him, and pleasing him excited her.

Slowly, she lay facedown on the blanket. The thin bars of the deck railing didn't obscure much, but she could at least keep a low profile. After a deep breath, she untied the strings of her suit and wriggled the two halves of the bikini off.

She grinned to herself, pleased at following his instructions. Then another text came through. *Send me a picture, Pet. Faceup. I want to see the sun on those glorious tits.*

She stiffened and took another nervous look around. A light breeze tickled her butt, teasing her as she worked up her nerve. Finally, she rolled over onto her back, sprawling as flat onto the blanket as she could.

She lay there, heart pounding. The sun was indeed shining on her breasts, and the warmth helped her relax again. Another puff of breeze licked her nipples, reminding her that she was now exposing skin that hadn't seen direct sunlight in who knew how long. Her vulnerability started to shift from terrible to delicious.

She held her phone up at arm's length for a picture, cupping her breasts with the other arm and smiling shyly into the camera. She sent it to Jordan and waited for his reply.

Minutes passed. She waited nervously, gradually enjoying the sensation of sunlight warming her secret places. She gasped lightly when a colder breeze rustled her fluffed pubic hair.

Finally, the phone buzzed. *That is very lovely. Now I want you to worship yourself properly, Pet.*

Her breath quickened again. He could only mean one thing by that. She had never exposed such an intimate act to broad daylight, but submitting herself both to Jordan's will and the open sky excited her. She ached for warmth to fill her inside as well as out. She cast one more furtive look around, then slowly spread her legs, opening herself to the light and the sun.

The warmth hit her inner thighs and lips and sank deep into her, as insistent as the touch of a lover. She reached down and explored herself, slick with sweat and excitement. She slid her fingers inside, first one, then two, engulfing them in her velvety heat. She spread her legs wider, all concerns of her neighbors disappearing as she thrust while stroking herself with her thumb. Her dampness spread across her thighs and leaked down between her cheeks, creating cool patches on her skin as it evaporated. Her free hand stroked and teased her sun-ripened nipples. She braced her feet on the blanket and tilted her hips, working her wrist harder. She could almost feel Jordan's approving gaze as she writhed under the sun. The thought pushed her closer to the edge.

Just as she was about to release her ecstasy to the heavens, her phone buzzed again. She groped for it with her free hand. *Very good job, Pet. Come inside now.*

She stared at her phone for a moment in confusion, then turned to look into the house. There, leaning nonchalantly on the back of the couch, just on the other side of the sliding patio door, was Jordan. He was still dressed in his work clothes, one hand holding his phone and the other idly stroking himself through his pants. His dark skin helped him blend into the dim light inside the house, but she could see his Cheshire-cat grin even through the glass's glare.

Her thoughts flashed from surprise to amusement. All of her nervous glances around and not once had she looked at the windows right behind her. She smiled and locked eyes with him as she slowly drew her hand out from her pussy and licked her fingers clean before texting a reply. *Why don't you come join me outside, Sir?*

OBJECT

Regina Kammer

W ell, it was embarrassing, really.

Intriguing, beyond a doubt. But mostly, at this stage of the affair, Nigel was a bit abashed and a tad uncomfortable. Especially his prick.

He was supposed to be having dinner at *the* most exclusive restaurant in San Francisco. "Ten-thirty, Tuesday," his girlfriend had said.

"Seems a bit late for a Tuesday."

"Look, that's all I could get. It just opened. Everyone wants reservations."

"All right, I suppose that will have to—" He had stopped. She hated when he quibbled.

But Mandy had smiled. "God, I love your accent. I could listen to you talk all night." Had patted his cheek. "I'm paying, by the way. Remember, Nige, ten-thirty.

I'll meet you there. It's down the street from the BART station." Good thing. He was hopeless at finding his way around the city.

And, in typical nouveau-exclusive fashion, there was no sign on the door. He wandered up and down the block a couple of times, checking addresses against his scrap of paper. He knocked tentatively on an ornately carved wooden door with a number scrawled in chalk.

The door cracked open. A stern female face scrutinized him up and down. "Yes?"

"Number seventeen?"

She gave him just enough room to slip inside to the pitch-black entryway. Before he could get his bearings, fingers prodded from behind, forcing him to stumble up the stairs to a dimly lit landing opening onto a narrow hallway. He glanced around futilely for the dining room.

His staircase tormentor appeared at his side, a petite but muscular woman in tight jeans and a tank top, hair shorn like a sheep. She indicated the bathroom, a Victorian water closet with a single lightbulb hanging stiffly from the high ceiling.

"You gotta take a piss?"

It took a second to comprehend the abrupt American invitation to urinate. Perhaps a bizarre culinary trend? "I suppose—"

"Be quick about it."

She stood in the open doorway as he relieved himself.

He'd barely gotten his fly up when she jerked him into a dark, overly warm space thick with the stench of cologne and locker room sweat.

Nothing like a restaurant.

His skin crawled at the eerie sense of other people, unseen, unheard except for labored breathing and the occasional clanking.

"Take off your clothes."

"Sorry?" This was most irregular.

"Take off your clothes," Shorn said pointedly. "Give 'em to me. Jen'll take it from there."

And when he was completely nude, Jen took it from there. She was over six feet, with a weightlifter's body and a smoker's voice. He felt compelled to do whatever Jen said and to keep quiet about it.

"Against the wall." She provided an encouraging shove.

The wooden wainscoting was cold against his bum, a sensation quickly overshadowed by Jen's insistent lifting of his arms above his head.

"Stop fidgeting."

"Yes, Ma'am."

"And stop talking."

A challenging task indeed. Questions swam in his head as Jen wrapped metal bands around his wrists and ankles.

She grabbed his prick. He yelped.

"I guess the ball gag'll go on first."

Ball gag? Definitely *not* a restaurant.

The contraption engendered discomfort and drool. Jen stroked his cheek in a stern, motherly sort of way. "Relax your jaw."

Which suddenly became rather difficult when she once again pulled on his genitalia to place a ring against his groin, tightening it, fussing with it in the dark.

He swallowed, awkwardly, as she slid something smooth, wet and hard over his cock, like a fitted, rigid condom that clicked shut.

Jen slapped the wall above his head. "We're a go!"

The lights rose slowly, their soft, sensual glow discordant with the startling surroundings. Nude men lined the walls of the otherwise respectable parlor, restrained in the same manner as he, arms manacled above, ankles fettered below, mouths gagged, cocks encased in clear plastic sheaths with tiny padlocks.

The men were of every hue and decoration typical of San Francisco, yet each of them honed to perfection, their proudly displayed bodies supremely ripped, waxed, and glistening.

That's when embarrassment for his beer bulge, profusion of hair, and pasty skin nagged at Nigel, competing with the unpleasantness of the blood rushing from his hands and the saliva dripping down his chin.

Feminine titters and giggles filtered from the hallway, followed by shushing and admonishments.

And then women swarmed into the parlor, their eyes wide, their gasps gleeful, their bodies seductively swathed in latex and leather. They took in the sight of each man, their gazes palpable and heavy, raising brows in appreciation, or, in Nigel's case, bewilderment.

Such reactions kept his growing arousal in check.

Jen and an equally formidable counterpart stood as sentries at the entrance. "Keys will be auctioned off in fifteen minutes—"

Keys? Nigel studied the wall across from him. Above each man was a number and a black ribbon holding a set of keys. He glanced down at his imprisoned cock and farther to his shackled ankles.

"—so make your choices now. Until that time, look all you want, but don't touch."

Bollocks. His freedom was in the hands of total strangers, his competition a dozen buffed guys. He couldn't even use his charming English accent.

The room continued to fill with women, their voices, their fragrances, their breasts, their thighs, their tight bums peeking out from under short skirts. His cock throbbed and ached.

They stared and conferred, pointed and whispered. Most left after the appointed gawking period. A minute later, shouts and cheers filtered in from down the hall.

The auction. Nigel closed his eyes in despair. His stomach growled. He had expected dinner.

Shrieks of delight roused him. Two women in red leather catsuits bounced excitedly before a tanned, hairless hottie, running their fingers across his rippled abs, playfully swatting his confined cock with a leather crop. More women entered, eager to torment their prizes.

And then Mandy sauntered in, red lips smiling wickedly, wearing the shortest damned skirt ever, high-heeled boots climbing above her knees, her breasts straining against a leather corset, a scantily clad girl on her arm. She held his eyes as she straddled the naked thigh of her friend, rubbing herself, leaving a trail of wetness. The girl wrapped an arm around Mandy's shoulders, drawing her closer, kissing her full on the mouth, massaging a breast as Mandy moaned and writhed.

Well, fuck me. Nigel's cock hardened, twitching painfully as it struggled to break free.

Mandy pulled back from her friend, surveying his reaction. She went to him, tilting her head with a chiding smirk, then tickled his needy flesh with her black lacquered nails.

"God, you look miserable."

He was trying to convey relief. Mandy had said they should kink up their sex life. Apparently bondage and a threesome were on the menu that night.

His heart and cock thrummed in excitement as Mandy's girl retrieved the keys and worked on his shackles, her touch gentle and reassuring.

Mandy kissed his nose as she removed his gag. He dared to catch her lips with his, tangling his tongue in the warm wetness of her mouth.

She moaned her approval. "Hungry?"

"I'm bloody starving."

"Good. Dinner's just down the hall."

THE CONTROL TOWER

Olivia Summersweet

Fog was everywhere that morning—covering the runways, obscuring the view of the bay and fraying nerves in the control tower. The pilots couldn't maintain visual separation, so we were clearing planes for takeoff one at a time instead of in pairs, as we usually did at San Francisco International.

I was working local control, giving pilots takeoff instructions. Brad, standing to my left, was working as radar coordinator, feeding me flight-progress strips— slips of paper bearing each plane's call sign, destination and squawk code, logged by controllers as the flights made their way through departure or arrival. We were an assembly line, mirroring the movement of airplanes on the runways below.

I was one of the few women in the business. I was

tough, one of the guys, holding my own among the macho men of this profession. But not around Brad. Around Brad, I stuttered. I lost self-confidence. I melted into a puddle. There was something about Brad.

That morning, as he stood next to me, I could smell his cologne. I looked straight ahead at the runways but in my mind's eye, I saw only Brad: his dirty-blond pony-tail, his pecs, his sweet smile. I imagined him stroking my naked body, making me feel warm and soft. He would pay particular attention to my ass. He'd caress my inner thighs, millimeters from my pussy, stroking my asscrack. I would give myself up to him and my labia would swell and moisten; they were, in fact, doing just that as I thought about him. And after I surrendered to him, Brad would violate me in the dirtiest, nastiest, sweetest, hottest ways imaginable. He would spank my naked ass. His finger would stroke my cunt, and touch my asshole, and...

Damn.

"United 830, cleared for takeoff, contact Norcal departure," I told a pilot through my headset, getting him off the runway just seconds before a landing plane set down.

Another close call. These fantasies about Brad had to stop. This month I'd already created a "golden towbar," two planes nose to nose that had to be towed apart because airplanes can't back up. I'd been the laughing-stock of the tower. I'd been mentally sucking Brad's cock at the time. I'd never actually seen Brad's cock, but I imagined it as just a bit longer and thicker than average, with a large, shapely, purple head. Perfect for sucking. My mouth watered again just thinking about it. *Please let me suck it, please.* I closed my eyes.

Shit. A pilot with a French accent was talking frantically at me through the radio. I opened my eyes. The Air France jet was taxiing toward the intersection of two runways, while a Lufthansa plane headed the same way from the opposite corner. They were on a collision course. My stomach tightened.

"Flight 235 heavy on papa, cross two-eight left, hold short of two-eight right," I said quickly.

Air France made it through in the nick of time. I took a deep breath.

I was in the process of exhaling when I felt hands behind me, pressing on both sides of my waist. I turned around; it was Brad. My heart began to pound. He'd barely spoken two words to me before, let alone touched me. What on earth?

With a small smile on his face, he pushed a flight-progress strip toward me on the counter. I glanced downward: it was a flight-progress strip, all right. But instead of flight data, there was a handwritten note: *I am going to punish you for that ;). 8 tonight, my place.* There was an address.

I looked up but he was gone. His shift had ended and Martin, a biker type, had taken his place.

I was stunned. Obviously, he thought he could get away with this. Obviously, he knew how I felt about him. For the rest of my shift I couldn't stop thinking about the note, trying to deconstruct it. What nerve. What did he mean, "punish?" And why, more to the point, did that word turn me on?

I got through the day without further incident and rushed home to my Noe Valley flat. I was famished but too nervous to wolf down more than an apple and a piece of cheese. I showered, threw on fresh underwear, jeans, a black T-shirt, boots and my bomber jacket and drove to the address in the Mission.

I rang, was buzzed in, and walked up a flight of stairs. At the top, in an open doorway, stood Brad, barefoot, wearing jeans and a T-shirt.

"Hi," he said. "C'mon in." He smiled.

I walked in and he closed the door behind us.

"You know I'm going to punish you," he said, and stroked my face. "You nearly crashed three airplanes today."

"What do you mean?" I said. I couldn't—*wouldn't*—let him see that I wanted it. It was too humiliating.

He turned me around and slapped me on the rear, giving me a push toward his living room, where he sat down on the sofa. He pulled me down next to him. He stroked my hair and grazed my nipples, then squeezed both breasts.

"Here," he said, patting his lap.

I just sat there, uncomprehending, not wanting to comprehend, until finally, unbelievably, he pulled me over his knee.

"You've been nearly crashing planes for as long as I've known you," he said. "What's up with that? It's about time you were punished for your mistakes. Don't you think?"

I was silent.

"Say it," he said quietly. "Say, 'I deserve to be punished.'"

I heard my own voice, as if from another world, whisper, "I deserve to be punished."

Brad pulled his hardening cock out of his pants and put my hand around it. He yanked my jeans and panties down below my hips and petted my ass. I moaned. He spanked me once, twice, three times. Once for each nearly crashed plane.

"Count," he said, continuing.

I began to count.

"Say, 'I'm sorry I nearly crashed those planes,' with each count," he said.

I giggled.

"You think this is funny?" he demanded, and spanked me harder.

"No," I whispered.

He spanked me twenty times, and each time, I made myself say, "I'm sorry I nearly crashed those planes." His cock was hard in my hand. I was so wet I nearly came.

He sat me up. "On your knees," he said. I fell onto my knees and he pushed his cock into my mouth. "Suck."

His cock was beautiful, just as I'd pictured it. He

came in my mouth, then kissed me. He stroked and petted me gently all over, just as I'd imagined.

I got home thinking the whole thing had been a dream.

The next morning, the weather was beautiful; planes moved majestically on the runways and taxiways, glinting in the sun.

"United 816, cross runway two-eight left, contact ground point eight," I told a pilot.

I looked down; there was a new strip in my pile: *8 p.m. See you then ;)*.

I smiled.

A Japan Airlines jet took off on 28 left, flew over the bay and headed toward the Pacific.

LONG SKIRT

Gigi Frost

I want to be good for you. I want to show you, through my self-control, how much I want you. We've only been together once and I loved your strength, how you didn't tell me where you wanted me, you just put me there.

But I have a different kind of fantasy, an idea of a way to offer myself to you, if you want it.

In my fantasy, I am wearing a long, slim black skirt made of sensible jersey, the kind I used to wear in high school and college, back when I thought that showing my legs would mean being taken less seriously. I dug this particular skirt out of my thrift-store pile after our second date, when you told me I could write a story for you, telling you what I dream about you doing to me. I've been holding on to the skirt, and now it's about to serve a far different purpose than it used to.

* * *

I stand, alone, in the center of the room. There is only an inch of leg showing between the hem of my long skirt and the ankle straps of my shoes. You walk around me, appraising. I duck my head and look up into your eyes, then away again. Then you are behind me.

I grip the sides of the skirt in each hand and lift it, ever so slightly. I am going to give myself to you, expose my flesh for you, one inch at a time. I practiced in the mirror this afternoon, trying to learn by muscle memory what an inch feels like so I could do this accurately, the same way I use a mirror in rehearsal to learn what height to raise my leg, where to place my hands.

I take a deep breath and try to ground myself, connecting with the floor as best I can in my heels. You start with something thin and stinging on my ankles and calves. I'm not used to being hit so low on my legs but I find it relatively easy to stay in control, to keep breathing and lifting my skirt exactly one inch higher after every blow.

Then you reach the backs of my knees, which you strike with a leather strap. It stings and stays with me and suddenly I am much more turned on than I was before. I start to feel greedy. I want you to strike me again and again. I want your hands, your strap, all over my thighs and ass. I want to lift my skirt all the way up to my waist, or better yet, take it off entirely.

Instead, I lift it another inch. It's hard to stand here, trying to keep my balance, trying not to move, with nothing to lean against. Soon I'm going to have to ask permission to bend over and hold my ankles, at the very least.

Inch by inch we travel together. It's awkward, all this material bunched up in my hands, but I can't seem to get my brain and my hands to work together enough to roll it up neatly and get a good grip. I've reached the point where I need to keep reminding myself that I want this, that I want to go slow, that this is an offering I've chosen to make for you, that taking our time is always better than instant gratification.

You reach the tops of my thighs and I stumble. I can't remain standing anymore. My cunt has been speaking up very loudly for a while now. I'm shaking and moaning and breathing heavily. Still, I push myself through one more inch, one more blow, before I find my voice, coming up so quietly from the depths of my submissive state. "Please, Sir, may I change positions now?" I would love to simply bend over and stay on my own two feet, with nothing to brace against. But I'm also hoping that you'll soon be doing things to me that will make it impossible for me to continue unsupported. So when you ask me what I want, I pause in dreadful silence, unable to decide.

I gamble on the old standby: "Whatever pleases you, Sir."

But you're not letting me get away with that easy out. "I want you to tell me, girl."

Another interminable wait while I collect myself.

Finally I come to a conclusion. "Please let me bend over a chair, Sir." You indicate that I should bring one over. I try to hold my skirt level with one hand as I drag the chair with the other.

I bend over, with no support from my arms, which are still holding the skirt at my hips. You run your hands over the backs of my thighs. I shiver and raise the skirt another inch, exposing the tender crease between my ass and thighs. You tell me you want me to stay still and take five blows on that spot, and I acquiesce gratefully.

I love being told to hold still. I love how it takes every bit of my concentration to obey. Being still makes me more vocal. I cry out and thank you again and again for taking me this way, for pushing me to take more, for hurting me.

After five blows I take a deep breath and reveal the next inch. You take my uncovered ass in your hands and tell me to grip the seat of the chair. You lift my skirt to my waist and I am ready for anything and everything that might come next.

BREATHLESS OBEDIENCE

Cèsar Sanchez Zapata

She arrived shortly after three in the morning.

My Mistress, perhaps you might call her. I'd not had occasion to call her much of anything yet. Our relationship (whatever it was) had developed more organically. It was far more visceral, like a chain reaction—stray dominoes falling one upon the other.

She strolled in, as she was wont to do, having picked the lock with the pin she kept tucked in her hair. I was nearly asleep by then, but the click of razor-sharp stiletto heels on the tiled floor woke me. Through parted eyes, I watched her cast off her wool coat and set the taser she carried—not for protection but reserved for extreme punishment—next to my badge on the foyer table.

She donned the black corset—marvelous choice—and thigh-high stockings held by threadlike garter belts sprouting from her crotch. The silk lace skivvies did their best to rein in the sweeping curves of her superbly bulbous backside, as her breasts swelled against the décolletage, overflowing the bodice with warm, supple flesh.

She was sporting the brunette look tonight, which meant she'd made a pretty little bugger of one of her regulars from the Upper East Side. She tossed the wig, and her long, golden tresses cascaded over her shoulders as she approached.

"You're ready for me, precious?"

Without waiting for an answer, she tested the latches securing my hands to the headboard, then the cuffs on my ankles. She tugged on the intricate riggings lobbed through the ceiling rafters, thus towing my legs up until I was spread obscenely for her pleasure.

She read my mind, purring, "Oh, I *am* quite pleased, precious."

Now I was strung up just as I'd found her, months ago, during the raid. Strapped to a bed, wonderfully and completely opened wide, her mouth gagged, chest pulsating with excitement.

Two men had stood over her then, in that room off the west corridor of the club, one wielding a riding crop, the other an enormous black dildo that was grazing her pussy. They froze even before I spoke, jaws dropped, yet the sight of me, the pistol in my hand leveled on their pricks, didn't quite register. She, on the other hand, took it in with mild amusement.

Poor saps—once they sorted it—wet themselves.

I hadn't been able to stop gawking, not for one second, even then—on the job. I'd circled the bed, breathless, soaking her in as her eyes followed my every move, never blinking, never shifting.

At first, I didn't realize Ramirez had stopped in the doorway behind me. "Sir, building is secure, we've seized business records, the manager's in custody…" He trailed off, processing the vision in front of him. "My, my—Lieutenant, what've we here?"

I holstered my weapon. "Take the trash out, Sergeant. Leave her."

Once handcuffed, the johns were led from the room, and I shut the door. Then I moved back to the bed, lowering myself beside her. There wasn't a trace of fear anywhere in her expression. Even as I reached over her naked body to release the gag, she gave only a tiny scoff and chuckle.

"Am I to be the spoils of war?"

I don't remember how long I sat there, wordlessly staring, as she did the same, gazing unwaveringly back at me. She was as exposed as any human being could possibly be, yet she retained the power at all times, sure as anything.

"It'll be your pleasure, Lieutenant."

She caught me off guard, I'll admit, when she broke the silence. "How's that?"

"This type of work—is unsavory. Oh, I don't much mind the illusion, but it's just not my role to play, you understand. Still, a girl's got to make a living." She

trained her eyes on me, all at once mocking and pene-
trating my soul. "It *is* rare in this town to find an honest-
to-god pet worth a damn."

"I couldn't afford you."

"Serve me in other ways." She'd knitted her brows
together, smiling, tongue slithering like a serpent.
"Release me this instant. My precious."

I obeyed. Against all judgment, I'd felt that immediate, consuming urge to collapse on my knees in prayer,
to worship and relinquish control before that blessed
altar betwixt her thighs. I'd unlatched the binds post-
haste, and watched, transfixed, as she dressed her
luscious body in front of me, never bashful. Pure, unbri-
dled confidence.

Then I watched, helpless, as she flounced out of the
room.

To this day, I don't know how she managed to exit
the building undetected.

I met with the local police shrink recommended by
a friend on the force. The hack spent nearly the whole
afternoon going over my service record, family history,
childhood, my brief marriage. All a waste—if he'd had
a kernel of merit he would've seen my "condition" right
away for what it was.

Not two weeks after the raid, she woke me in my flat
for the first time. I'd never given her my address, but I
suspect in her work, it pays to be resourceful.

That night changed everything for me.

The long and short of it: I'd never met a woman who

could dominate me. That desire had never materialized, but the moment I laid eyes on her, a trigger was pulled. Hers was a raw, unmistakable energy. I was paralyzed by the knowledge that she could strip me of everything... and that I *wanted* that.

Before her, my life had been a series of menial snapshots strung together like a cat-o'-nine-tails: wake, drink coffee, drive to work; evidence boxes, scene photographs, fingerprint analysis and blood reports; drive home, eat dinner and sleep. When she had me, really had me, she took that away—yet, inexplicably, gave my life purpose.

After a decade of "protect and serve," I was finally serving. Unconditionally.

I didn't notice the leather collar in her hand until she clasped it around my throat then took a step back, admiring her handiwork with a wicked grin. She pulled a two-tailed tawse—how perfectly old school—from beneath the mattress, and crawled on, drawing her exquisite legs on either side of my waist, nestling my cock between her thighs.

Leaning forward, crushing her breasts against me, she hooked the belt behind my head to lift up my face. I parted my lips for a kiss, but she merely licked and bit, teasing my tongue until I was positively frantic. As if from a far distance, I heard my own pleas. Whimpering! The anticipation always got to me. She knew that, and relished it, I'm certain, more than anything else.

With a mere roll of her hips, she had me, now fully

engorged, flush against her cunt, slavering on our fusing honey. As soon as my cock brushed the slippery nub peeping through the curtains of her sex, she let out a gasp—that particular sort of gasp, stretching out like a dozen whispers, that turns a man's brain to shit.

"Are you ready to serve?" she said, already scaling my body.

Moments before she covered my mouth with her pussy, I managed, fighting for each wisp of air, to promise her what she demanded—full obedience.

MINE

Roxanna Cross

Y ou have been a very naughty slut today. Don't deny it. I saw you after the board meeting. With Jason. Did you like it when he hugged you? Squeezed that sweet little ass of yours? Dragged you over the bulge in his suit trousers? Tell me slut, did your pussy get wet?"

I couldn't respond. I couldn't breathe. With each of his savage accusations his cock pounded inside of me with almost violent force. I moaned deep in my throat.

Colt's fingers tightened around my ponytail, sending shards of wicked pain straight to my skull and dancing along my nape and spine.

"Answer me, slut," he said through clenched teeth.

"Yes, I liked it. Yes, my pussy dripped," I breathed between heavy moans.

He pushed my torso hard against the glass separating

his plush office from the boardroom we had exited moments before. My already hard nipples extended and beaded even more at the cool touch.

"You like being on display like this, don't you? Your perky nipples begging to be sucked. Your swollen clit rubbing against the glass. It thrills you beyond words, doesn't it?"

Colt's words heated a fire deep inside of me. He knew me so well—how I needed to be possessed, how I craved being watched while I come, how I liked to be called a naughty dirty slut, how I loved the feel of his nine-inch cock filling me until I thought he would rip me in two.

He never disappointed me.

Ours may not be the usual Dominant/submissive relationship, but he understands my need to be taken, claimed and branded, and I understand his need to control me with his cock, his touch—at times soft and tender, or, like now, hard and cruel.

He never ceases to amaze me. He responds to my needs thoroughly, seeing to them one hundred percent. Even if I'm the one submitting to his control, I know I hold all the power. He's proven it to me time after time by fulfilling any number of my crazy fantasies, this one being the latest.

I felt the orgasm build in my lower abdomen as he kept up the cruel rhythm of his punishing plunges.

"Speak!" he commanded.

"Yes, I love everything you said. My nipples are so hard they hurt. My clit is pulsing. You can tell better than me how hot and wet and tight my pussy is."

"And if Jason were to walk into the boardroom?"

"I...I..." I closed my mouth, unwilling to express this part of my fantasy to him. What if I pushed too far? Revealed too much? Would he still want to possess me?

"You'd rub that pussy of yours over that glass, beg him to come closer and lick you through the thin barrier. You'd grind your pussy on my cock and come in long trembling gushes."

Of course he knew. He always knew.

"I should be angry with you for wanting another man to give you pleasure." He slapped his open palm across my derrière. "But I'm not." Another slap. "I love that you're such a slut." And another. "My slut." His next slap reverberated all the way to my clit. "Mine," he said savagely.

His words got to me.

His total possession of my body broke the dam. The orgasm I'd been holding at bay rocketed trough me.

My breath came in ragged pulls.

So did his.

His cock moved in and out with primal need, force and speed.

Colt's fingers released my blue-black hair and dipped down my belly. They found my pulsing clit. Rolled it. Pinched it.

"Mine!" he said again with one final, urging thrust.

I cried in ecstasy as another wave of rolling bliss crashed over me.

He grunted through gritted teeth.

Both of us panted and trembled as our juices filled my pussy to the point of overflowing.

"You. Are. My. Slut." He whispered each word distinctly as he pulled out of my hot wet confines and zipped up.

Not given the permission to move and rearrange my clothing, I stayed plastered against the glass.

Nipples hard.

Pussy dripping.

Almost as if on cue, Jason walked in the boardroom. I bit down on my bottom lip and watched in silence as he deliberately scanned the floor-to-ceiling glass wall like someone had told him he would find something there. His eyes bugged out of their sockets when they noticed me—by this reaction I assumed I'd been wrong, and he hadn't been told what to expect. The slick juice still oozing from my pussy perfumed Colt's office; even though I knew it was crazy I swore from the look on his face that Jason could smell it through the glass. When I would have backed away to cover myself, Colt's words froze me in place. "Let him watch you."

I watched Jason walk back to the door. He turned the bolt, locking himself inside. He slowly made his way toward the glass, then lifted his finger and traced my shape.

Never before had I been so aroused.

The man of my latest fantasy was on his knees before me, adoring me. The man who for the past eleven months had had full control over my body, had fulfilled my every carnal need, no matter how slutty, stood behind me, devouring me.

My pussy constricted around a phantom cock. My pulse raced in my chest.

"Colt," I begged.

He chuckled in my ear. "This is what you wanted?" His sultry voice caressed every inch of my skin as his slacks-covered pelvis rocked into me.

"Colt," I begged again. "I need to feel you inside."

I heard his zipper being pulled down. His pants hit the floor with the clunk of his belt buckle. His hands gripped my hips, and he plunged deep inside my sopping wet heat.

Jason's tongue licked my clit through the glass. His fingers reached up to close over my cherry-sized nipples. The illicit movements from the other side of the thin barrier separating our flesh were hauntingly erotic.

"Don't forget. You. Are. Mine." His cock fiercely possessed my pussy. His hands, his mouth, his teeth, his tongue, were everywhere on me: my throat, my earlobes, my shoulders, my breasts, my belly, my waist, my hips, my clit, my thighs, my ass. No part of me was left untouched. Unclaimed.

I forgot about Jason on the other side of the glass.

I was Colt's.

His alone.

To brand and dominate.

SECOND DATE

Alice Gauntley

D
o you own any strap-ons?" Jamie asks, her engineer boots playing footsie with my worn Chuck Taylors.

I shake my head. "I'm more of a bottom. As I'm sure you know." This is only our second date, but our first was at a play party, so I feel like the normal rules of propriety don't really apply.

"A bottom in the kink sense, sure," says Jamie, her leather-clad heel pressing so hard on my toe all of a sudden that I almost let out a whimper in the middle of this hipster-student café. "But I didn't see you complaining when I shoved your fingers into my cunt last weekend. I seem to remember you were very...enthusiastic about it. Or were you just being obedient?"

Jamie takes a sip of her soy chai latte. I love that she likes such fancy coffee—love it the same way I love that last time I unbuttoned her 501s, I found a lacy thong barely covering a thick growth of pubic hair. Jamie has so many layers, and I'm already dreaming of uncovering them all.

"How about you?" I ask, deflecting.

"Of course," she says, "and I'd like to strap one on you and tie you to my bed and ride you as long and hard as I want."

I feel my nipples stiffen under my T-shirt. No one's ever suggested that to me before. My lips part, and I try to hide my growing arousal by taking a big gulp of searingly hot black coffee.

Under the table, she reaches a hand up my skirt to pinch my thigh. "Would you like that, being my fucktoy, my slutty little piece of ass?" she asks, raising her own mug oh-so-casually to her lips. I mutely nod, parting my legs to give her better access.

"God, I've been imagining that all day," confesses Jamie. "You really want to?" For a minute I see through her bravado dominance to the horny girl underneath, nervous that her new date won't be into her fantasies. Then I nod and smile, and she digs her nails into my leg and I lose myself once again in this world we like creating, where I give her power and she spins it into something terrible and glorious for us both.

"Finish your coffee then," she says, withdrawing her hand. Obediently, I drain my mug. She does the same.

"My house is a block away from here," ventures Jamie.

"And you'd like to take me there and fuck me?"
Jamie nods. I smile. "Lead the way."

Ten minutes later, Jamie has me pinned on her bed, her
fingers in my hair, my clothes scattered around us. Her
bed is the kind I've been circling in IKEA catalogs for
the past five years: sturdy metal, it seems to be made
entirely of tie-down points. She's affixed leather cuffs to
the four corners, and I wonder if she leaves them on all
the time or if they're especially for my benefit.

Jamie's hands roam over my breasts, twisting and
pinching. I whimper. "You like that?" she asks. I can tell
she really wants to know, worried, despite the beating
she gave me last weekend, that I'm not actually into
this stuff. At the party she reminded me of my safeword
three times. She's cute, this one. Very gentlemanly.

"Fuck, yes, I like it when you hurt me," I assure her.
"I like seeing that look in your eyes when you—ah!" She
slaps my tits, needing no further encouragement. I can
feel my flesh growing red under her eager palms. I grind
against her leg, and she pulls off her shirt and slams into
me, hands taking temporary ownership of every inch of
my body, mouth tight on my lips, legs clamped together
over my thigh.

I'm wondering if we'll just end up making out, quick
and dirty, when she abruptly pulls herself off me, opens
a drawer in her bedside table and takes out a harness.
She slips it up my legs and tightens the straps, securing
a medium-sized purple dildo into place. I've never worn

a cock before. I try to imagine having a dick, being so visibly aroused. It feels so much more vulnerable than the discreet wetness and fullness of my pussy, a whole different kind of bondage, of submission.

Jamie is working on my wrists and ankles now, strapping me down so I'm spread-eagled on her mattress. She looks at me, her face gleeful. Her hands grab at my tits, and I strain against my bonds. She pinches my nipples so hard I cry out.

"You really like that, eh, slut?" she asks, still gripping the hard buds firmly between her fingers.

"Mmph, yes," I manage to moan.

"Then can I put these on those sweet tits of yours?" she asks, rummaging around in her magic drawer and holding up a pair of clamps connected by a chain.

I nod eagerly, and she affixes them to my already sore nipples. She kisses me again, her tongue invading my mouth, then slips the chain between my lips. I clamp down without having to be told, sending a shock of pain to my breasts and a wave of pleasure to my cunt.

"I'm going to fuck you now," Jamie informs me, and I moan as she pulls off her jeans. This time, her panties are plain and white, but they're still incongruously femme. She pulls those off too, and I see that her pubic hair is matted with wetness.

She slowly rolls a condom down over my cock, then squirts lube into her hand and milks me as though she's giving me a hand job. I move my hips to meet her, but she takes her hand away and straddles me instead.

I gasp at her solid weight. She begins to ride my cock, her movements fast and rough, a hand once more in my hair, the other rubbing her clit. I watch that hand, the way it dances with practiced fingers, and start thrusting back at her, wanting nothing but to help her get off, to let her use me just the way she promised she would.

Her fingers in my hair are clenched so tightly I can feel tears coming to my eyes. She thrusts hard against my tender clit, and then, so soon, she's coming, her face titled back, her mouth open in one long, wordless cry. I think she comes twice, or maybe her orgasm just keeps going and going, but finally she collapses onto me, panting and grinning.

After a moment, she looks into my face. My teeth are still clenching on the chain.

"You haven't come yet, have you?" she asks. I shake my head.

"Good girl," she says approvingly, and I realize I've narrowly avoided punishment.

"I might let you come," she informs me, letting go of my hair to slap my throbbing tits, "after I've gotten myself off a few more times." She starts to ride me again, that diabolical smile back on her face.

This one's a keeper, I think to myself. I wonder how long I should wait before asking about our third date.

TABLE
MANNERS

M. Marie

My knees are aching and my arms are beginning to tremble, but I don't dare move. Her instructions were for me to hold my position, so, despite the discomfort, I do just that.

Rosa's making it difficult for me, though.

When I arrived for today's session, she immediately led me, without a word, into her study. My eyes went straight to the large mahogany desk. I eagerly began to anticipate receiving a complement of pleasure and pain while bent over it, but my partner had other plans.

Silently, she placed a hand on the small of my back and guided me toward the leather couch under the window. The coffee table that normally sat in front of it was absent. In a cool voice, she instructed me to strip nude and kneel on hands and knees in the vacant space, before turning and leaving the room again.

Somewhat apprehensively, I obeyed.

I always wore a loose sheath dress for our sessions, so it took only a moment to pull the light garment over my head. I was nude underneath; Rosa preferred it that way. Stepping out of my heels, I slid the shoes out of the way, then folded my dress and placed it on the corner of the desk. I let my hand linger longingly on the cool wooden surface a moment, before obediently turning back to the couch and lowering myself to the floor as directed.

She didn't make me wait too long.

The door creaked, announcing her return. I was facing away from the doorway, but the click of her heels as she crossed the threshold from the carpeted hallway into the office sent a shiver through me. She crossed the room slowly, letting her footfalls fill the expectant silence. When she finally reached the couch, she didn't immediately acknowledge me. I heard her set a few objects down on the small end table beside the couch, before sitting. The leather cushions squeaked under her.

Soon, I felt a hand on my left shoulder. It slid down the curve of my back. Her touch was cool, but my skin burned under her caress. Reaching my hip, her palm cupped my left asscheek, while her thumb traced the cleft between my buttocks.

Her other hand was touching me as well now. She stroked the front of my thigh, upward, and then caressed the gentle swell of my stomach. My breath shuddered as she found my breast and squeezed it slightly. My nipple stiffened against the palm of her hand. Pulling her hand away, she flicked her painted nails against the stiffened peak until I bit my lip to keep back my groan.

Rosa's other hand was moving again. It slid down my crack to explore the spreading arousal between my legs. My pussy was already wet, and my swollen lips parted open eagerly as her fingertips trailed down my slit.

"You're eager tonight," she purred, pleased.

Her voice only added to my arousal. I was breathing hard and risked a peek under my arm. All I caught was a glimpse of sheer black nylons and gorgeous red pumps before Rosa demanded in a sharp voice, "Eyes down!"

Her order was emphasized by a hard smack against my upper left thigh. I dropped my gaze immediately, but that didn't seem sufficient assurance for her that I wouldn't sneak another peek. Her hands pulled away and there was a rustle of fabric, before a strip of dark satin was slipped over my eyes and tied behind my head.

A whine escaped my throat. I *hated* being blindfolded, and she was well aware of that fact. My complaint fell on deaf ears, though; her hands had already abandoned the tight knot and were sliding back down my spine and over the round curve of my ass. As her fingers found my wet pussy and slipped between the lips, I forgot all grievances.

Moaning, I clenched my muscles around her fingers as they scissored inside me, stroking and stretching my inner passage. Her preparations took only a moment, but I was already breathing hard when Rosa slipped her fingers out of my pussy and slid a thick, pulsing object inside me in their place.

I recognized the feel of the vibrator, but was confused as an additional weight suddenly pressed down on my back. It was flat, rectangular and warm. The question was on my lips, but Rosa spoke before I could voice it.

"Last night you brought your BlackBerry to dinner. Again," she reminded me, coolly. "Before we play today, I've decided that you need to learn a lesson about ignoring people."

She began to tap the surface of the unfamiliar object, and the clicking of keyboard keys filled the small room. My mouth fell open, and despite the blindfold, I turned my head to look over my shoulder in disbelief.

"Is that your *laptop*?"

The typing stopped and her palm slammed down sharply against my backside. "Quiet!" she commanded. "You will hold still and keep quiet until I finish my work. Is that clear?"

She punctuated each word with a smart smack, and it took all my self-control not to try to crawl away from her punishing hand. It was rare for Rosa to bring personal issues into our private play and that fact brought a heavy weight to the lesson she was trying to impart.

I wanted to please her, so I nodded; the spanking stopped and the typing resumed.

* * *

I've been kneeling silently since. *How long has it been?* It takes only a moment for my hands and knees to begin to protest this position. Any fidgeting is answered by a sharp slap, and I know the more I move, the longer this lesson will take. The machine grows hotter on my back with each passing minute, and as the heat sinks through my skin, it enflames an arousal that needs no further encouragement. Already, the steady pulsing of the vibrator has teased me to the point of frustration. My entire body aches for relief from the pressure.

The vibrations suddenly increase. It's a multispeed toy, and Rosa has begun to dial up the frequency. The typing stops.

"Keep still. Keep quiet," she reminds me.

The speed intensifies again, and her open palm seeks out the center of my ass. She spanks hard, targeting the divide between my cheeks, where the base of the vibrator is visible. Each slap drives the shuddering object deeper inside. I tremble violently and a strained keening sound escapes my throat as my control starts to slip. I bite down on my lip and lock my elbows; somehow, I manage to stay quiet and still as my body climaxes.

Rosa lifts the laptop and removes the toy. She leans forward to pull off the blindfold and whispers, "Good girl."

I let myself collapse onto my side, exhausted. Muscles ache loudly throughout my body, and I want nothing more than to lie still until my arms and legs stop trembling, but Rosa's voice commands my attention again.

"Are you ready to play?"

I look up, and she nods toward the desk, smiling. Fatigue instantly forgotten, I pull myself eagerly to my feet.

TEDDY, BARE

Jere Haken

Bottom bare."

Adam places the leather armchair in the center of our otherwise empty living room floor, and I think I might faint. My stomach is tight and hard, tied up in knots. He's going to do it. He's really going to do it. I want to flee, but I know I can't. It isn't only the new collar around my neck and my sense of submissive duty that keep me from it—it's also the sure knowledge that my trembling legs would betray me.

"I'm sorry, Adam," I say meekly. "I'm really sorry."

"I know, Teddy. Do as I say, please."

My fingers shake as they fumble with the snap of my jeans. I can't get them down. I want so much to please him, but my tense body refuses to cooperate. I close my eyes and swallow, biting down hard on my lower lip.

"*Now*, Theodore!"

The formality of my given name rings in my ears and prompts me to obey. Adam has always been gentle, but tonight his first responsibility as my new husband will be to punish me.

My fingers are cold and clumsy as I shove my pants to my knees. As instructed, I didn't bother with briefs when I changed out of the tuxedo. Adam liked me in my fancy clothes, but he loves me in my normal, comfortable wardrobe. Plain T-shirt and plain jeans for a plain boy.

Adam kneels before me, and my breath catches in my throat. His hands caress my bare legs as he slowly peels my jeans all the way down. I step out of them, and his gaze rests on the fresh bandage adorning my right calf.

"The hospital," he mutters. "Other husbands whisk their lovers straight to bed after the wedding. I get to take mine to the hospital."

"It wasn't that bad, Adam," I say. "Really, it wasn't!"

Angry eyes flash up at me.

"It's my right to know," he says, his voice low and dangerous. "Anything that happens to your body is my right to know. You should have called me immediately."

"I didn't want to ruin things. I'm always ruining things. I couldn't be late for my own wedding! Besides, the car barely grazed me, and it was my fault anyway. I'm so stupid. I forgot my cummerbund, and I dashed back through the crosswalk to get it, even though the light had changed, because I thought I had time—"

He slaps me, hard, on the back of my left thigh. I flinch and fall silent.

"The time for excuses is over," he says. "There is no excuse. You hid an injury and deceived me on the very day you took a solemn vow to always honor, obey and respect me."

He stands and slowly unbuckles his belt. I grip the back of the armchair and wait, struggling to breathe as I watch him double the leather in his hands.

"Nose to the cushion," he orders. "Now."

"Yes, Sir," I say, my timid voice cracking on the words.

"Wait!"

I freeze, and he presses a kiss to my temple.

"I love you, Teddy bear," he whispers. His lips are soft against my ear. "I didn't mean to be harsh. It's just...I don't know what I would have done if that accident had taken you from me."

He clears his throat and steps back. His eyes are shining, bright and stern as he studies me.

"I love you, too, Adam," I say, flushing from the intensity of his gaze.

I turn and force myself to bend over. I grip the front of the armchair, pressing my forehead into its cool, soft seat. My naked bottom rests atop the chair's low back. The cut on my calf throbs in time with my pulse, but I don't dare mention it. Adam's belt buckle jingles as he takes up position behind me.

"You must never keep anything from me," he says. "No matter how small."

"Yes, Adam."

He places his hand on my back, and I'm grateful for the comfort.

"You've accepted my ring," he says quietly.

"And with it your discipline," I finish.

The words have barely left me when I hear the hiss of his belt as it cuts through the air. I gasp at the sound of the solid smack against my bottom, and then I sob as the first wave of sharp pain surges through me. Adam has never whipped me before. He could have if he'd wanted to. It was his right as my dom, and there were certainly other times when I'd deserved it. But Adam is a romantic at heart. No sex before marriage, and no correction before collaring.

The second swat lands just below the first, and just as hard. Three strokes are all it takes for his belt to completely stripe my bottom. He begins again from the top. Three more methodically delivered bands of fire burn into my flesh, and I cry out. Three more, and the tears roll down my cheeks and drip onto the chair.

In my fantasies, I'm vocal. I beg, plead and make elaborate promises as Adam takes his belt to me. The reality is different—and far better. I submit completely, surrendering myself to him mind, body and soul. All the anxiety and apprehension melt away. I don't need to fear Adam. I am his sub, and he is my dom. I am his husband and he mine. He will punish me, but he will never hurt me.

"Teddy," he says, and only then do I realize the whipping has ended. "You are forgiven. Stand up."

I obey him in a dreamy haze, reveling in the sweet pain that has cleansed me of my guilt. Adam places one finger on my chin and turns my face toward his. His eyes are dark with arousal as he leans down and brushes his lips against mine. His thumb sweeps a lingering tear from my cheek.

"I want to see you," he says. "I want to see my beautiful husband."

He slowly strips the shirt from my body, leaving me nude save my collar and wedding ring—and the bandage on my leg. He's once again on his knees before me.

"Does it hurt?" he asks, examining my leg.

"A little," I admit.

"Allow me to kiss it better."

Adam places a gentle kiss on my calf, just above the bandage, and then rests his cheek against my soft inner thigh. I shiver at the tenderness of his touch, and my cock stirs from the warmth of his skin against mine. I want him inside me so badly I'm shaking, and if I have to wait another minute I think I might burst.

"I know we don't have a bed yet," he murmurs, "but if you're willing..."

"Yes," I say. "Yes, Adam. Please. Right here. Now. I can't wait any longer."

Adam allows me to undress him, and we lose

ourselves in a tangle of desire in each other's arms. For the first time in my life, I am not only loved, I am owned. I am Adam's Teddy bear.

His Teddy, bare.

THE PROBLEM IS, I'M A BITCH

Corrine Arundo

Y ou will do what you are told. Without hesitation, without question." My potential Mistress walked a slow circle around me. Shorter than me and very thin, with small breasts, wild blonde hair and an eastern European cast to her features. She wore a leather corset, cinching her waist to almost nothing. Amplifying her breasts. Her thigh-high dominatrix boots clicked as she walked around me.

Mistress Anya had taken me under consideration, and this was our first session together. I'm a little taller than her, with short, shaggy, dark-blonde hair. B-cup titties, a swimmer's physique. My butterfly had paid my college tuition.

If I wanted to I could probably take her in a fight, I thought.

It was sometime in college when I realized I liked a certain kind of pain. I'd get a rush from a paper cut or a good pinch. And when my coaches would smack my wet ass after a swim, I'd always wish they'd done it harder, with more bite. That was when I first tried out BDSM. But it does tend to raise some eyebrows, coming to swim practice all bruised up. And that shit is year round.

The problem is, I'm a bitch. I have friends who play the brat game; I'm so much more than that. I want to make my dominant really hurt me. I have a smart/stupid mouth that gets me into trouble. Anya knows this even as we go through the ritual of her expectations and my promises to meet them. Both of us know that I won't, and she'll get/have to punish me. I don't want to waste time. I want to get destroyed. Regularly.

"Right, Anya. I know." My tone was flippant, verbally rolling my eyes at her bullshit domme posturing.

She stopped directly behind me. She grabbed my hair and pulled me so I bent over backward, then she kept pulling, until my knees hit the concrete slab in the play space. She left her fingers twined in my hair, pulling hard enough that I felt a few hairs pop out, stinging.

She huffed a big breath. "So, you need a lot of work. Let's get started."

Okay, there's a brief note of steel in her spine, but I bet she hits like a girl. My thoughts were the precursor to the words that were about to get me in trouble.

She pulled my back farther, so I was leaning against her legs, head resting against her abdomen. It felt curiously cozy and then, *smack*. A red handprint blossomed on the side of my little titty.

"Is that enough for you, little Nikki? Or do you need more to believe that I can and will break you?"

I didn't answer her. I was still reveling in the sting. And, well, I wanted to piss her off more. After a ten-second pause, she reached across my chest, pulled my nipple out away from my body and then smacked my breast again, knocking the nipple from her clamping fingertips. I took a deep breath, peace settling over me. *This might be good.*

She took a step away from me and I fell backward some, but she caught my neck, stopping me from smacking my head on the floor.

"Okay, bitch," she said, stepping around me. "You are into the pain. Your last dom told me you were disobedient, but now I know why. He probably wouldn't whip you unless you really forced his hand, huh?"

I gave a noncommittal shrug.

"Well, we'll just have to look for lots of ways for you to fuck up then, won't we, cunt?" I think I fell in love with her a little bit when those wonderful words fell from her lips, and a satisfied smile crossed my lips.

"First off, kneel right. Spread your thighs." She shoved the toe of her boot between my knees and kicked them apart. Once I was spread, she scraped that toe into my pussy for just a moment.

"Hands up, resting on your thighs. Jesus, Nikki, don't you know anything?" She grabbed my arms from my sides and positioned them correctly, then slapped my face. "Eyes down, unless I tell you otherwise. Just terrible."

"Fuck you." I only muttered it, but I said it nonetheless.

She huffed and stomped off. With my eyes down, I couldn't really see what she was doing, but I heard cabinets or drawers opening.

She came back with a crop. Now, her cartoon dominatrix outfit was complete. Just when I was starting to like her.

"Open your mouth, cunt. Tongue out." She grabbed my face with one hand, fingers on either side of my mouth, squeezing. She pulled a clothespin out and clamped it to my tongue.

"Now, did you wish to speak?"

"Yaa, thuck ewe." She just laughed and walked behind me.

She put her stiletto heel on my shoulder blade and pushed me down until my upper body lay across my thighs and my face was on the floor. The first faint stirrings of want started in my pussy. The crop came down on my ass quick and hard, with no warning. Ten strokes, without any words from her. The concrete was cool on my forehead. The pain in my tongue had devolved into a dull throbbing ache, and I started to drool.

She slipped her fingers into my slit, rubbing my juices around like she was savoring my slickness. She stepped away, adding ten more strokes of the crop. My breath started to come hard and fast. She repeated this routine until a final set of ten hits that she delivered to my soaking pussy.

She stepped to my side and pulled me up by my hair. With her face less than an inch from mine, she said, "Look at me."

I looked up into her beautiful blue-gray eyes, my own widening with recognition. She could be the one to master me.

"I see you, Nikki. I see what you are. I will hurt you and I won't hold back, like I've always had to. I will hurt you physically and emotionally. I see right into you." I shivered deep inside, intense satisfaction burning through me. "Lie down on your back."

I flattened myself, staring at the ceiling. She arranged my arms straight out from my shoulders. She then gingerly stepped on them, the hard soles of her boots digging into my biceps. She slipped the points of her stilettos down the insides of my arms, catching at the skin until they reached the ground.

"Uhhh." The stabbing pain of the stilettos and the pressure of her foot on my arms—it was so much to take. I felt a quick flood between my thighs and my nipples tightened. "Mmmm."

"Oh, now those are some nicer sounds." She squatted down over me and yanked the clothespin off my tongue. "Now, what do you want to say to me?"

"Please, Mistress!"

"Oh good," she said nonchalantly as she fiddled

with a zipper in her tight leggings. It zipped all the way back to her ass. As she exposed her shorn pussy to me, shifting her weight, she pushed it down on my face.

I groaned into her and started my job.

THE LOST SUITCASE

Tamsin Flowers

He said it wasn't my fault. As we watched the empty carousel turning, the other passengers disappeared through the exit. Eventually we followed them, empty-handed, and when I apologized he said no one was to blame. But we'd gone away for one reason only, and the missing case contained everything we needed. He said it wasn't my fault, but I knew he would punish me for it anyway.

At the hotel he sent me for a massage; he would phone the airport and chase the missing case. But despite the best efforts of a beautiful Norwegian girl, I couldn't relax. I kept thinking about what he had planned for me and how now none of it could happen. Back in the room, still slathered in massage oil and wrapped in the hotel robe, I paced up and down. Maybe they'd found the case and he'd gone to fetch it. Or maybe he'd gone down to the bar to take the edge off his disappointment with a gimlet. I went to the minibar and fixed myself a gin and tonic with nervous hands.

By the time he came back I had drunk two thirds of a second g&t. He arrived carrying a couple of carrier bags from Target.

"They think the suitcase went to Miami," he said.

"What's in the bags?" I said as he flung them onto the bed.

"You'll find out later."

We were down at the pool when he decided it should start. I was working on my back tan while he read Faulkner. I heard him put his Kindle down and felt his hand on my shoulder.

"Go and wait for me upstairs," he said.

"Yes, Sir."

In the room I stripped off my bikini and knelt at the end of the bed. A mixture of excitement and fear churned low in my gut. Although he had tried to hide it, I knew he'd been annoyed when the suitcase went missing and I wondered what he would do without its contents.

I didn't have to wait long. He came up to the room less than half an hour after he'd sent me up. He pulled off his robe and threw it on the bed and, with my head bent, I could just see that his trunks and leg hairs were wet; he must have taken a swim after he sent me up. I heard a rustling noise as he pulled something out of one of the shopping bags. I wondered what it might be.

"Stand up."

I stood and he came up behind me.

"Close your eyes."

Soft, silky fabric slid across my eyelids as he tied the mystery item at the back of my head. Our blindfold had been in the case but, of course, he could easily replace it with a new scarf. I wondered about the rest of the paraphernalia. But I couldn't ask him. Now that the game had started I could only speak when spoken to.

He left me standing in position and I heard a clatter as he emptied the carrier bags onto the small table by the window. He seemed to be sorting through multiple items. After a minute or so he came back to me. Again he stood behind me but this time his hands went to my neck. He pulled my hair to one side and slipped a collar around my neck. It felt rough and hard compared to the soft leather collar I normally wore. He caressed my neck as he fastened it, and his touch sent a flutter to my loins. Had Target started selling bondage gear?

"It's from the pet department," he said, reading my mind.

One of his hands cupped my right breast, and he sucked my nipple into his mouth. I tried not to sigh or fidget but his kiss sent a shimmy of desire through me and my legs trembled.

"No reaction," he said, and something bit down hard on my nipple.

At first I thought it was his teeth but then he took

hold of my other breast and sucked it until the nipple pebbled up hard. The combination of his soft mouth on one side and the fierce pinch on the other made me gasp.

"Clothespins. Thank you, Target," he said and then my left nipple felt the bite.

I took several deep breaths, savoring the burn at the apex of each breast.

"Hands in front," he said.

He had handcuffs as well. The clunk as they did up sounded cheap and tinny but they would do the job.

"Later you can put on the whole policewoman costume for me," he said with a dry laugh.

He seemed to be enjoying the need to improvise.

"Bend over the bed."

I knew the position he meant. I knelt beside the bed and leaned forward until my ass was bent over the edge. I loved this moment—and I hated it. He knew it, and made me wait until the anticipation of what might be coming next had me squirming. I wanted it and I didn't want it in equal measures.

A sharp shock of pain, a lingering after burn.

"There were so many things on the shelves at Target to choose from," he said. "I could have bought a leather belt. Electric cables. A table tennis paddle. A canoe paddle. A wooden spoon. A ruler. Let me count the ways I could mark your skin."

All the while he continued striking my ass, first one side, then the other, building up the intensity slowly. It was his special skill. I couldn't begin to guess the object slapping hard and flat against my flesh and after a while I couldn't even process his words. I lost myself in the physical sensation, living and breathing only for the moment when he would transform the pain into pleasure with a slick of lube and the work of a finger or two.

Finally he tossed his implement aside, and I heard a metallic clash on the tiled floor.

"What?" I gasped.

"A skillet," he said. "They had it on special and we could do with a new one."

He lifted me up onto the bed and swiftly brought me off, sliding a lubed finger into my ass and working my clit to make me moan and writhe as I came against his hand. Then he flipped me over onto my back and fucked me long and hard until he too hit the jackpot.

We lay side by side, glistening with sweat and lube, the blindfold and handcuffs discarded.

"See, babe, everything's okay. It didn't matter about the case."

I heard a knock at the door and he slipped on his robe to answer it. I pulled the sheet up to cover my naked body.

The bellhop who'd shown us to our room earlier stood in the doorway.

"Your suitcase, sir," I heard him say. "Sent from the airport with apologies."

It was going to be a good weekend.

THE RHINO

C. Margery Kempe

She knew they called her "the Rhino" but that didn't matter to Sheila. The boss had to be the boss. There wasn't room for deadwood in the organization. Deadlines were deadlines. If she didn't chew them out, she'd be the one out on her ear tomorrow.

Not that she'd ever been much of a pussycat.

Part of her enjoyed the fact that people moved a little quicker when she loped down the corridor. The bespectacled young mail clerk might refer to her as "the lesbanian on the seventh floor" but he was likely to stay in the basement. She was the one who'd turned Nofziger and Smith from a deadbeat chaser of other companies' discards into the hottest ad agency in town.

And the Rhino led the charge.

Her assistant buzzed her. "Mr. Howarth on line

three," she said before hanging up. Sheila smiled. Bridget knew she would always take his call. Her pulse quickened.

"Mr. Howarth."

"Ms. Evans. Six p.m. We're trying something new." He broke the connection and a thrill of anticipation sang through her veins. Sheila savored the echo of his words. Cryptic as always, yet he was not one to disappoint.

From the night they'd met six months ago at the social-media mixer, he'd continued to surprise and excite her, for he had recognized something within Sheila she'd had no idea lay in her heart: a need to abandon all control.

They'd begun conventionally enough with movie dates and roses. She'd enjoyed them, but she'd discovered a new thrill on a night in when he'd ordered her to obey—playfully first, then with solemn concentration. What began as telling her what to eat and when, turned into waiting to be told when she would be kissed—and *how*. The memory made her quiver.

Sheila found this need shocking, exhilarating and—initially—puzzling. She had always moved with confidence. If she didn't know the answer, she would ask. If someone doubted her, she would offer proof. If she didn't like a situation, she would pick up and leave.

Until he'd said, "Put that fork down," and she had obeyed.

There was a knock at the door. Bridget opened it and popped her head in. "A-Team is ready for you."

"Thanks, Bridget. I have Ben Faulkes penciled in for

five today; call him and shift it to tomorrow. Or whatever might be convenient for him."

"Will do." They both left, Sheila striding on ahead to the conference room while her assistant stopped at her own desk. Sheila had no idea she was smiling.

Her working team must have taken it as a good sign, for they visibly relaxed at the sight of her. Maura appeared eager to run with the new proposal. "We've taken on board your suggestions. The new drawings have really come together."

Anthony clicked through the pictures, annotating the changes, while Sheila did her best not to let the words *We're going to try something new* drown out the presentation. Her skin itched to be stroked. It took all her will not to charge out of the room; he would have made her wait until six anyway.

"Well done, well done," Sheila said at the end. "I like the fox particularly. It's just the right symbol: the spirit of the country invades the city. Perfect." Their faces shone with pleasure. "Maura, I want you to pitch it on Friday."

"Me!" The young woman showed a mixture of joy and terror.

"Absolutely. You've earned it." Sheila smiled quickly. It wasn't the same smile as earlier. "Both of you; make sure everything is spotless and seamless. The last few slides showed the haste of revision, Anthony. We want that account."

"Yes, Sheila," they all said together.

Sheila grinned at that. "Then we celebrate."

The rest of the day seemed to crawl by, but Sheila forced herself not check the time too often. Leaving at five meant struggling through the rush hour press of flesh; the tube was always packed at that hour. Sheila found the walk to his flat soothing after that madness.

But as she rang the bell her pulse quickened; she fought the urge to touch her nipples, which felt hard already.

"Ah, Ms. Evans, welcome," he said as if he had forgotten their appointment. A quick kiss on her cheek and then he guided her onto the entryway's white plush carpet. Sheila bent to remove her shoes but stopped halfway.

"Yes," he said walking on into the sitting room, "you may remove your shoes."

Sheila's heart pounded; she knew she was already wet. To look at him, you wouldn't necessarily guess how provocative he was. Mr. Howarth (he was always *mister*) looked the epitome of the middle-aged, middle-class sort of fellow. He wasn't conventionally handsome, although the warm intelligence of his eyes gave away much to a careful observer.

He returned from closing the curtains and smiled up at her. Sheila towered over most men, usually causing annoyance, but Mr. Howarth didn't measure himself against anyone. "Long day? You must be tired."

Sheila shook her head but didn't otherwise move. He took her shoulder bag and laid it on the little table, then led her into the sitting room, positioning her on the white rug. The fireplace crackled, casting warmth and light across the room.

"We'll soon have you comfortable." He slipped her jacket off and threw it over the back of the comfy chair. Then he reached up to unbutton her blouse, keeping his gaze locked on hers. They had the same smile on their faces. When he slipped off her blouse, he leaned forward to bite her nipple through her bra.

Sheila whimpered.

When she stood in only her bra and knickers, Mr. Howarth took off his tie, brought her hands together and lashed them tightly with the silk garment. Sheila felt a surge of excitement pound in her breast. *What's he going to do?*

Gently, he led her over to the leather armchair and bent her over the arm. They had discussed spanking, but Mr. Howarth had not accepted her plea—or so she'd thought. Sheila found herself quivering with anticipation despite her awkward position. Something about the way her bottom thrust upward made her feel so vulnerable.

She wasn't the Rhino now.

Mr. Howarth stood beside her, perfectly in control. Only his voice hinted at his own excitement. "I'm going to spank you. I suspect it may hurt. I don't want you moving, Ms. Evans."

She nodded her head to show she understood. Sheila's heart thudded against her rib cage.

His hand stroked the silky globes of her cheeks. Sheila smothered a moan. Silence was all. He pulled her knickers down to her knees, trapping her legs in the fabric, then sliding his hand up to her cleft. Finding it wet, he tsked. Sheila gasped as his fingers fluttered between her lips, then just as quickly withdrew.

It seemed like forever before his hand fell with surprising sharpness. The blow hurt more than she'd imagined it would, but before she had time to think, another fell and another and another. It was everything at once: the pain, the heat, the methodical timing, the care he took, the joy she knew.

Bliss.

MARNI'S WORKING AREA

Dominic Santi

The bright-pink speeding ticket was taped to the side of the nightstand. Even without turning my head on the pillow, I could see where my wife, Marni, had underlined *30 miles over the speed limit in a construction zone*. I wiggled my bare butt against the sheet. The handle of Marni's big black leather paddle extended over the edge of the nightstand, right above the ticket.

Looking at the paddle made my cock throb. Marni's clothes weren't helping my self-control. She has long, wavy brown hair and the kind of round, full curves a man can really get a grip on when he's riding his wife hard and heavy. Her long, flowing skirt swayed with her hips and her slinky button-down shirt clung to her huge, heavy breasts. Her nipples poked out stiff and long. Damn, I loved sucking Marni's tits!

I licked my lips and concentrated on her breasts, trying not to look at her right hand. It was covered with the translucent glow of a white rubber glove. My eyes darted back to the nightstand. I couldn't see the prostate milker, or the big pump bottle of lubricant, but I knew they were there. I came from being spanked, every single time—unless my balls were emptied beforehand.

Marni used to make me masturbate until I climaxed before she paddled me. Then she discovered that fucking cock-milking toy. Her new routine gave a whole new meaning to the word *dread* when I fucked up. She walked over to the side of the bed, her hips swaying and her boobs jiggling, frowning so hard my balls wanted to climb inside and hide. She picked up the lubricant and squeezed a long, slick stream over her middle finger.

"Pull your legs up and back."

Her finger was like a heat-seeking missile, zeroing in on my asshole, yet it was slick and cool. I gasped as she slid it deep. She pressed up toward my belly button, right into the hypersensitive place where my orgasms started—the place I'd learned the hard way was my traitorous, touch-hungry prostate. I groaned as a drop of precome leaked through my cocktube.

"You're exceptionally sensitive tonight." She rubbed until another small stream oozed through. "You should get an excellent milking."

Just like that, her finger was gone. Then she was holding that fucking prostate milker. The fat part glistened with lube. Marni said it was shaped like the life-sized inside of a rectum. I had no idea if she was right. I'd never looked up my ass. All I knew was that when she slid the milker in, it felt like it was made for me. I couldn't help squeezing. I gasped as it slid over my prostate, the knob beneath pressing up hard in back of my balls, massaging from the outside as well. The handle snugged into position in my crack.

I shuddered with each squeeze, trying to relax my hips in spite of the awesome fucking feeling. Precome ran down my cock, each drop getting me that much closer to Marni's paddle and a world of fire-assed, hurtin' bawling. But each squeeze felt so good, I couldn't make myself stop.

"Lower your legs and keep squeezing." Marni pulled off the glove and tossed it in the trash.

I shivered as the pressure shifted, hating how awesome it felt. Marni and I had masturbated together more times than I could remember. But cock milking was different. I was emptying my dick in front of her not so I could come—I sure as hell wasn't going to get to do that—but so I wouldn't be able to get an erection. All I'd be thinking about when she blistered my ass was how much it fucking *hurt*! Marni tapped her fingers impatiently, waiting for me to finish.

My whole body trembled as rivers of semen started streaming out of my prostate, up through my ultrasensitive cocktube. I panted and shook, clenching my ass muscles as hard as I could. I was so close to coming, but I couldn't quite get there!

Marni stroked one finger up the underside my shaft, pressing out what should have been the rest of my come. I lay back, panting.

"I'm empty." The words sounded hollow. I drew a ragged breath. "I, uh, guess I'm ready."

"I doubt you could ever be ready for the paddling you're going to get. But you certainly won't be distracted by another erection anytime soon." She picked up the paddle and smacked it sharply on her hand. "Move over."

I rolled shakily to the side of the bed, sitting quietly while Marni settled herself so the entire length of her thighs rested on the mattress. She tapped her lap firmly. I took a deep breath and slowly lay down across her lap, my cock lying quietly on her leg.

"Spread your legs and relax your bottom."

Marni's finger rested on the removal ring. My face heated as she pulled.

"Bear down."

It was so embarrassing, feeling the smooth, fat shaft of the cock milker slide through my asshole. Marni dropped it on the nightstand with a thunk. Then her arm tightened around my waist.

"You know better than to drive like that!"

I gasped as the paddle exploded across my butt. Fuck, that paddle hurt! I wasn't turned on at all anymore. Well, I was a little bit, knowing Marni had me over her lap and was paddling me. But my cock couldn't do anything about it. She paddled my ass until I could hardly breathe.

All I could think about was how much I wanted the pain to stop. I wasn't ever going to speed again!

Tears streamed down my face as Marni eased me off her lap, then onto the bed to lie down beside her. She pulled me into her arms, opening her top and unhooking the front clasp of her lacy white bra. Her warm, full breast fell against my face. I opened my mouth wide, latching on to the tip of her nipple and sucking hard.

"Oh, yes!" Marni's groan was pure pleasure as she pulled me toward her with one hand. The other was between us, yanking her skirt up, then fumbling in the nightstand drawer. I jumped at the buzz, then settled into a slow rhythmic sucking as the vibration between her legs had her arching against my mouth.

"Thank you for paddling me, Marni." I held her breast with both hands as I talked feverishly around her nipple. "Thank you for letting me suck your tit. I'm sorry I was such a jerk. I'll do better."

"See that you do," she gasped, shuddering as the first climax rolled through her. "One of these days, I'd really like to make you come with that thing up your ass while you're fucking me."

My exhausted cock twitched just the barest bit. I sucked her so hard she came again. With incentive like that, I sure as fuck was going to give good behavior a try.

LOST IN
THE FEELING

Nicole Gestalt

If you want to make me submit and give myself totally, just show me fur. Cover me, smother me, then grant me permission to writhe upon it and I'm all yours. Let me feel the warm inviting hairs brush up against my body, tickling it into complete and pure submission. It doesn't even have to be real.

I didn't tell Ian about my fetish when we got together but he soon found out. How he did I don't know, but one day he turned up with a fur blanket and a lustful look in his eyes. A day later we emerged, our relationship changed forever, with the understanding we would explore one another's desires completely. From that point on Ian became my Master, taking control of my fetish and allowing me to completely indulge in it. We decided to lock my furs away when he is not home.

So now I wait outside of what has become our play-room, naked, in a position of submission—kneeling down with my head back, looking toward the ceiling. I'm already aroused at the thought of all the fur just inches away from me. My nipples are aching, my pussy already wet with anticipation. I've been in this position for over an hour, since I got his text, and my legs are aching from the strain. Arching my back, I push my breasts higher, with my head tilted back—all to please him. I don't look to the door as I hear the key in the latch.

A dull thud suggests he's putting his bag on the floor and undressing, then total silence. In my mind I can see him staring at me, a familiar smile on his face. My body aches from exertion but I force myself to remain in position, the thought of letting him down—or worse, not getting my fur—is almost too much for me to bear. Sweat begins to bead as my muscles burn and scream to change position.

A shadow moves over me and I almost weep in plea-sure as his hand brushes up my body, starting between my legs, stopping to squeeze my breasts. When he looks down at me, I catch my first glimpse of him today. I shiver as his dark eyes drink me in; I would do anything for this man. A knowing but loving smile briefly settles on his lips before he hungrily squeezes harder, pinching my nipples until I have to squirm a little. At that he stops and with one hand reaches down, taking my wrists in his grasp and pulling me up. I've been in one position so long my muscles cry out in both relief and protest as

I move. Though I'm shaking, he easily holds me up and unlocks the playroom door, guiding me in.

With him standing behind me but holding me close, I can feel his arousal pressing against me. My body melts with the thought of him pushing his way inside me. My heart begins to pound as I tremble with delight. Whatever happens, I must get to that fur so I can get the sweet release only it can give me.

He leads me away from the rug and the throw to an area that at first appears free of fur and pulls me down onto a seat. It's an oddly shaped seat; the front part is wider than the back, meaning to sit on it comfortably you have to do so with legs open wide. Upon the sides are wide cuffs designed for my thighs whilst upon the back of the chair is a cuff large enough to hold both my wrists together firmly. With a practiced hand, he does them up so I am held helpless on the chair, spread wide, knowing full well in this position he could do absolutely anything to me. My enforced confinement from the fur-lined cuffs makes my submission that much sweeter. By wriggling and straining against the cuffs, I can get the fur to move against my skin, sending arcs of pleasure through me.

He stands back, watching me as I writhe, slowly stroking his cock. Seeing me watching, he shakes his head and picks up something from a table behind him. In one swift movement that teasingly leaves his cock dancing over my breasts, a faint trail of precome forming a strand between them, he places the object tight around my eyes and I am plunged into darkness. It takes me a moment before I realize this is a new blindfold; to my joy, I can feel more fur brushing up against my eyes.

I already know I'm wet, aroused beyond comparison, trapped upon a chair and slowly being covered in fur. When his fingers suddenly press themselves into me, I push up against them. He presses the heel of his palm against my clit and I hear him chuckle as I desperately grind against it.

My body tenses as I try to force myself down against his hand, crying out in need every time the fur brushes against me. Before I am able to climax, however, he is gone, withdrawing from me. I'm left in the dark, unsure where he is. I try to listen for any noise to hint at his whereabouts, but he is silent. My only indication he is still there is when fabric surrounds me, pulling me back against the chair and pinning me in place. Gasping with shock and need, I feel his hot breath next to my ear before his lips press against my neck, his breathing fast, his kisses urgent. It is only then that I feel a hand pushing the fur down between my legs. Straining, I find I can press myself against the material, building up friction with the fur. My nipples ache as they pucker harder with each movement, causing me to shudder with each brush of my nubs against my favorite fabric. I want to take deep breaths but I'm so confined all I can do is truly focus on the release of coming.

Acutely aware that this is all at my Master's whim, I writhe faster, desperate to climax before he removes all the beautiful things.

His lips remain pressed against my skin as the tension in my body rises. When I almost can't bear it any longer, he bites down on my shoulder. With a voice dripping with lust, he growls, "You're mine."

His words are enough to break the tension. My orgasm crashes over me. I cry out and stars flash in front of my eyes.

When I am sated and calm, he will remove everything and lovingly carry me to bed, where our roles will twist. Then I will be the one to decide if he's waited long enough, before seeing to his release. He doesn't mind, of course; in fact, giving me the chance to decide turns him on even more. He knows exactly how to make me his.

After he's sated we'll spend time together on the fur throw that covers the bed until he decides it's time to lead me from our room and lock it all away from my clutches. Until next time, that is.

CHOKER

Sean Finn

I thought I'd learned the art of giving the perfect blow job with my college boyfriend, Bruce. We were both horny freshman who'd known we were gay for years but were stuck in towns where we couldn't do anything about it. Finding each other, then being granted the gift of being able to switch rooms so we could share beds in addition to BJs was like a sign that not only was I gay, but the universe wanted to reward me for it.

We grew apart after that year, but I practiced sucking cock like I was majoring in it. I knew just where to lick and suck, how to hold my hand around the base, and when to add some spit, go for the balls or tickle or probe the other guy's asshole. I considered myself well versed in the art of oral. That is, until I met Tyler.

It's not that he wasn't appreciative of my technique,

but he was playing a whole other game altogether. He didn't want me to show him what I could do—he wanted to control every last movement of my tongue and lips, not to mention the rest of me. "What're you into?" he asked me bluntly the night we met, right after I'd added his next beer to my tab. We were at a gay bar, so there was no reason to beat around the bush. I'd just landed a new job as a manager at a gym, and was pumped from my first day—I'd had each of the trainers give me their best moves in ten minutes. I could practically hear the blood pounding through my body.

My voice trembled when I said, "Blow jobs. Giving them." It's not that I was ashamed in any way of my oral proclivity, but Tyler was staring at me like he could see into my soul, like he already knew exactly what I was into and was simply waiting to hear whether I'd tell the truth.

"You have a patented technique or something?" Again, that stare drilled into me, his tone not at all impressed. He was taunting me to prove it.

"I guess you won't know until you try it," I attempted to banter back.

"Oh, I'm going to try you out, there's no question about that." Now his tone had taken on hints of steel. "I think you knew that the minute you bought me that beer. But I have a feeling what I want you to do isn't like what any of those guys who let you go to town on them wanted."

By then I wasn't just rock hard, as turned on as I'd

ever been, but intensely curious. How different could a blow job be, especially for a connoisseur like me? "Ready?" Tyler asked. I was ready right then and there; though I probably would've balked at doing it in front of the assembled guys, he could've had me in the bathroom.

Instead, Tyler pulled me close for a rough kiss that bruised my lips, his hand on the back of my neck speaking volumes. He was in charge, and he wasn't just going to "let me do the honors." He was going to fuck my mouth, just like his tongue was probing its depths.

I whimpered when he finally pulled away, utterly shaken—in the best possible way. I was more nervous than I'd been with my very first blow job, my confidence knocked to the ground. I followed Tyler, in awe of how he'd gotten me to give up any semblance of control or confidence in mere seconds.

"We're going to my place," he told me. I didn't nod or reply, since it wasn't a question. The ten-block walk seemed to take far longer than I'd have liked, yet once we were there I had a moment of panic. Should I back out, let this be just a fantasy? Tyler sensed my hesitation. "You can stop now, go home and jerk that nice cock off," he said, running a hand up the hardness bulging against my jeans, "but if you come inside, you play by my rules. You in?"

I nodded, following him up the stairs. He didn't give me a tour. Instead he pushed me, a hand around my throat, into his room. "On the floor," he uttered. I sank down, missing the pressure of his hand the moment it was gone. I swallowed a few times, trying to make my mouth as wet as possible. His dick appeared before me, incredibly long, thick and juicy, already sporting precome. "No, you don't get to lick that," he snapped, slapping his dick across my cheek. "You're going to take the whole thing, swallow it—choke on it. If you're good, I might come in your mouth. If you're not, I'm going to come all over your face and neck and shirt, and send you on your way." That image practically had me spurting in my pants, but I didn't have time even for that. Tyler grabbed that spot on the back of my neck that seemed like a magic button and shoved half his length down my throat. I acclimated quickly, breathing deeply through my nose as he pushed a little bit more.

This was totally different from any other deep-throating I'd done. The other times, I'd heard moans of encouragement and ecstasy. I'd gotten off on those verbal cues and compliments, my head swelling along with my dick. Managing to swallow even a large dick felt like a point of pride. There was no pride in what Tyler was doing to me; there was just subservience. He pushed more, and I fought not to gag. When I started to whimper, his fingers pinched my neck. "I want you to like choking on me, Sean. That's what good slutty boys do, and I know you want to be my good slutty boy, don't you?"

His words acted like a lubricant, giving my body the will to stretch my throat even further. My jaw ached as my whole being centered on him filling my mouth. As he eased back, I pushed forward, wanting him there again. Soon we were rocking back and forth in a fast rhythm, and each time his cockhead hit the back of my throat I was overcome with the urge to cry tears of joy. When Tyler shifted his hand from the back of my neck to the front, as if massaging his dick from the outside, I lost it, coming in my pants like a teenager.

"That's a good choke slut," he said, pausing for a moment with his entire hardness buried in my mouth before pulling out and slamming it against my lips. "Now you're going to choke on my come." I looked up at him for a split second, and was rewarded with a gorgeous, filthy smile. Then he shoved his dick back inside me and gave me a giant load. I sucked and sucked until he was dry. He carried me to the bed, but didn't let me take off my jeans. "Next time, you're going to do that with a butt plug in your ass." I smiled, ready for the challenge.

REVERSE PSYCHOLOGY

Rachel Kramer Bussel

B ite my nipples harder," Sasha hissed at me, the edge of frustration making her hiss hint at true anger. I focused on the way her body trembled on the bed before me as I sank my teeth into her nub. "That's better," she said, grabbing me roughly by the hair. "I hope your cock is getting ready to fuck me the way I like it. First you need to do your job."

I pressed as hard as I dared, tugging on her nipple while I twisted the other one between my fingers. I hoped my cock was getting hard too. See, I'm not a sadist by nature—I wouldn't hurt a fly. Really—I'm the kind of guy who goes out of my way to give directions or help little old ladies across the street. I'm a service sub, the worshipping sort, but I fell madly in love with a woman who happens to be a masochistic domme. Sasha likes pain, but for her it has nothing to do with being a "bad girl" or any of that. If I dared to call her names like *slut* or *whore* during sex, she'd lock up my cock for a week.

For her, it's about the sensation, the intensity. She says getting flogged is cathartic, being spanked releases endorphins, having her nipples bitten makes her blood boil. And because I love her and want to please her, I do as she says. It's a different kind of submission from any I've ever known, but I like obeying her, and knowing how turned on she gets. It's like reverse psychology, where you tell someone to do something and hope they do the opposite. With us, though, I do the opposite of my impulses, for her. Sasha makes sure to show me appreciation—when she's not ordering me around.

"Now the other one," Sasha grunted, and I transferred my lips to her right nipple while she tugged at my hair. I dared to brush my cock against her leg to show her how hard I was. I'm grateful that she likes to get fucked; I've been with women who loved nothing more than to tease me, to have me watch them with other men's dicks in their mouths and pussies, to tie me up and let me see a vibrator do the work I longed to do. With Sasha, as long as I get her primed with her favorite kind of pain, she is more than ready for my cock.

She usually holds herself back from convulsing, but this time she didn't. "That's it, right there," she moaned as she leaned back, making my teeth tug her nipple even more. When her fingers tapped my cheek, I opened my mouth. She handed me a flogger. Yes, it's true—I flog my domme. Before her, I'd never so much as raised my hand to a woman. I'd discovered early on which way my kink went—or thought I had. Now, I actually like hitting her. Not the causing pain part, but the giving pleasure part.

"You know what to do," Sasha said with the smile that can indeed get me to do anything. She whipped her favorite little vibrator off the bedside stand and pressed it to her cunt. The buzzing was the signal that I should start beating her breasts with the red suede toy. If it were my choice, I would gently stroke the soft lashes all along her body, thud it against her back to a beautiful rhythm, drape it against her pussy. But my Sasha wanted something else entirely. Instead, I reared back and slammed it hard against her tits. How she managed to stay composed enough to keep the toy vibrating where she wanted it was beyond me, but with each strike of the flogger against her large breasts, Sasha let out a fierce exhalation of breath. She slammed the toy against her clit as I struck her.

I was breathing hard by the time she dropped the vibe on the bed. "Slap my pussy," she barked, getting on her hands and knees. If it sounds incongruous that a woman could be so controlling while she's asking for such a naughty thing, you don't know Sasha. There's nothing weak or needy about her; I'm well aware that, should I refuse her requests, she could easily find a man—or woman—to take over my duties. We've even discussed it—she loves me deeply, but she has needs, ones that aren't negotiable. I admire her for knowing what she wants and making sure she gets it.

Plus I love looking at and touching her pussy, even if that means slapping it with my hand. I still felt the wetness with each stroke. "Get the plug," she said after ten smacks. I glanced at her as I fetched the butt plug; Sasha had a pillow stuffed between her lips, lest she whimper too loudly. "You're the whimperer," she once told me.

I got the lube and, rather than gently licking her anus, then massaging her tender hole, as I would have preferred, I slicked up my thumb and shoved it into her ass. "Yeah," she grunted, shoving herself back against me. I fucked her with my thumb until I knew she was ready, then repeated the process with the red butt plug.

I didn't need any more orders. I dragged her to the edge of the bed, massaged her asscheeks for a few seconds, pulling them apart and pushing them together, then gave her clit a sharp pinch for good measure. Once she was positioned on the edge of the bed, I rammed my cock into her. This is the one time when I truly feel like the alpha male I could've been in another life. How could I not want to shove my dick inside the tight, beautiful cunt of the woman I adore?

Once in a while she lets me make love to her. Today, she dictated the pace. I slapped her ass as I pulled all the way out and rammed back in, focused entirely on giving her the hardest fuck of her life—and not coming too soon. I'd made that mistake early on and my backside had paid the price. I held on to her cheeks as Sasha said, "Don't hold back on me, slut boy, give me all of that nice fat cock." Her fingers had found their way to her clit, which made her even tighter. I speared her with my cock, drilling into her wetness as fast as I could.

"That's it, fuck me harder than you've ever fucked anyone." The faster I went, the more urgently I needed to come, but I couldn't—wouldn't—ask. Thankfully, after a few more thrusts that almost sent me flying backward, Sasha came, tightening around me. "Fill my ass," she insisted. I eased the plug out and replaced it with my cock, immediately erupting inside her.

She let me rest a few minutes before I got to run her a bath and wash her hair. "Sweet boy," she crooned. I'm not, actually—not with her—but I loved hearing her say it anyway.

AFTERMATH

Michael in Texas

When the alarm clock rings, my back is to it. I roll over to hit the snooze button and my asscheeks feel like they're on fire. I gasp in surprise. When I'm asleep, I forget I've been spanked.

I've been in much worse shape. Some mornings after I play hard, my hips feel frozen in position, and it's agony to move them. This morning I'm merely sore. If I move carefully, the pain is nothing special.

I ease my legs over the side of the bed, stand up gingerly and totter to the bathroom, where I pull up my nightshirt and twist to examine my ass in the mirror. It's completely unmarked. Even after all the times we've played, I'm still amazed how hard he can spank me and not leave a mark. The night before, after he'd used his hand, a leather paddle, and the hairbrush, both my cheeks were cherry red, and now they are their usual color, even though they're sore to the touch. He knows just how hard he can spank without bruising.

He once told me he learned to do that because some spankees need to be discreet. I said there was no need to be careful with me—for better or worse, no one sees my bare ass except him and me. He replied that someday he may tell me to show up for a date wearing nothing below the waist except a thong, or with my skirt tucked up to display my bare ass, and if he does, he'd prefer it be unmarked.

As if. He doesn't have that kind of authority. At least, I never told him he did. We never agreed on it. I mean, I don't *think* he has that authority. If he told me to do something like that, I'd just laugh at him. Wouldn't I? In any case, I certainly wouldn't do it. At least I assume I wouldn't.

He once suggested that after a spanking, whenever I'm sitting down, I pull up my skirt so my bottom—at least the part below the panties—is bare on the seat. It was a suggestion, not an order—he knows better than that. On the drive to work, I try it. The upholstery is scratchy against my thighs; it tingles and itches. I become aroused. I feel ridiculous, so at the first stoplight, I pull my skirt back down. My ass muscles burn when I raise my hips.

At work, as I squirm in my chair and hope no one will notice, my mind keeps wandering to what we did last night, and what we might do next time. I think

about what positions he'll use, and whether he'll hold
me down or require me to maintain position on my own.
I have trouble maintaining position. When I move and
he has to wait before giving the next spank, it makes
him impatient and he gives me extra. I think about what
implements he'll use, and how many of my clothes he'll
remove. He loves to spank me naked. He loves to touch
me and make me climax, but he's never fucked me. I'm
not sure whether I'm insulted or relieved by that. I guess
there's no reason it can't be both. I wonder what I'll do
if he ever does try to fuck me.

Our spankings are role-play. Not naughty schoolgirl
or lazy secretary or kidnapped by pirates; that'd make me
feel silly. But at some point, while we're together, he says
I need a spanking, and I say, "Nuh uh," and he insists,
and I sulk, and eventually he grabs me and spanks me,
and I resist, and say it's unfair, and call him every name in
the book, which makes him spank me longer and harder.
As long as I never say "red" three times in a row, he can
do whatever he wants. I've never safeworded, and sometimes when I'm squealing, and my eyes are watering, and
I'm laughing at how ridiculous it is, and trying not to cry,
I wonder why not. Am I curious how much I can take?
Am I curious how much he'll give? Do I not want to
admit he can dish out more than I can stand? Do I actually enjoy the pain? Do I enjoy it even when it becomes
so intense that it no longer arouses me?

In the middle of the afternoon he sends a text. It says
to come to his place right after work, and to arrive not

wearing panties. He wants to play again today? Does he have any idea how sore my ass still is? It's too soon. And no panties? If I do that, it'll give him the wrong idea. I want to be spanked, but I don't want to be ordered around; I'm not a submissive. Besides, how would I do it? I'm not going to take them off in the car or in some filthy public restroom. I'd have to do it here at work. I'd have to walk through the office with no panties on. What if someone found out?

I just won't do it. I'll tell him I'm busy tonight. No, I don't want to disappoint him. I'll go ahead and play, no matter how sore my ass is. We've done that before. It makes my arousal more intense, even though it hurts like hell. But I'm definitely going to show up with my panties still on, and if he spanks me for that, then fine. Maybe that's what he wants me to do.

When it's time to leave work, I go into a toilet stall, take off my panties and put them in my purse. I blush as I walk through the office; thank goodness there's no one around to see. I become aroused again. By the time I get to the car, I'm almost ready to climax. He'd better not get the wrong idea from this.

But he will; I just bet he will. Next thing I know, I'll be walking up to his place with my bare ass hanging out. And I'll hate it. And love it.

TAKEDOWN

Marievie

J ust go," he says. "I will find you."

I spin around, staring at him. Find me? This is a farm. Acres of pastures and woods. A few red barns too, turned into versatile dungeons for all kinds of kinky pleasure for this long weekend of FetFest. It could take him hours to find me, no? And what about…?

He's not even looking at me. His expression makes it clear that questions would go unanswered. Friendly enough, but firm. An expression that over the last two years I've learned to respect and defy, embrace and reject, both love and fear.

I rummage through my bag. Miniskirt and leather top? Black corset and stockings? Meaningless choices in light of his demand. I put on what my trembling hands find first—short skirt, pink lacy top, forget any panties.

I leave the tent he set up for us two days earlier—not without trying to catch his eye, but he doesn't look up from the cruel contents of his infamous Bag of Props. He pays me no attention.

My mind is racing. What did he come up with this time? As much as I love his kinky creativity, its fulfillment often means surprise, always pain. Confusion. Excitement. Curiosity. Stomach-churning fear—that too.

I head left, up the muddy little path that leads to a barn-turned-dungeon. One of my favorite couples of the weekend is playing on the prayer bench outside. The night before they'd seduced a sweet blonde together. They'd taken public advantage of her—including ropes and crops, a strap-on and his cock—with such pleasure and skill that their scene got a top listing in my repertoire of masturbation fantasies.

Sadly, they soon pack up and head off toward the bondage barn, holding hands, emanating confidence and happiness. I stroll behind them, my eyes fastened on his strong arms, her curvy figure, my mind replaying the moment they both penetrated the tied-up, suspended blonde last night. My thoughts start to wander happily through kinkyland...

Suddenly, there's a sharp whoosh right behind me. Before I can recognize it and bolt, two arms grab me from behind, hard and hurting, hoisting me onto a shoulder. I gasp for air, my heart hammering. Through the terror, somehow, I realize these are his hands restraining me.

Outrage. How dare he scare me like this? I try to kick, wriggle furiously, pound at his back with my fists. But with his arms firmly around my legs and my head dangling down his back, it's useless. I start howling in rage. Utterly unimpressed, he keeps walking across the lawn, bypassing groups of tents and kinky people looking on curiously, eventually throwing me onto the grassy center field with force, knocking the breath out of me. I howl, trying to get up, attacking him with hands and feet and teeth. He just holds me down on my back with his weight, panting, determination showing in icy eyes that finally meet mine.

A deep voice: "I think you'll need this, Sir!" Something heavy lands by my head. I turn and recognize the black leather case: his Bag of Props. Apprehension flushes through me at the realization that all this was planned, scripted, arranged beforehand. On an adrenaline high, I flip over, trying to coil my way out from under, hungry to chase down the mean conspirator.

The body above me is too heavy, the grass too slippery, his grip too tight. Instead, he turns me back over, grabs my wrists right above my head. I feel bondage tape being wrapped around first my wrists, then my legs. I struggle in horror, groaning. Both of us are covered in sweat by now, so the tape keeps slipping and my hands and legs stay free. As he leans over to reach into his bag, I grab anything within reach, clawing the grass, his shirt, his chest, until my hands get hold of his kilt and I tear it off, leaving him naked but for boots and socks.

I burst out laughing, mocking him—enraging him. His grip on my wrists tightens, his expression hardens. He pushes me down again, pinning my hands underneath his knees with all his weight, reaching over to the left. Turning, I realize what he is doing: screwing hooks into the ground! Metal hooks, the kind used to fasten wild dogs on leashes.

Panic washes over me. Immobilized on my stomach, I manage to free my right hand and start throwing the props from his bag as far as I can—rope, more hooks, whips, a crop. He cries out in frustration, forces me down hard, and in one swift motion grabs rope and both my hands, tying them tightly behind me. I gasp in pain as he ties my feet together too, making me feel utterly helpless, vulnerable.

He gets up. I can see him out of the corner of my eye collecting his scattered dom tools. Escape on my mind, and freed of his weight, I move in the only way possible: I start rolling down the hill. Laughter from the sidelines. I realize to my embarrassment that quite a crowd has gathered, seemingly enjoying the spectacle.

Of course I don't get far. Long strides come after me, catching up before I reach the bottom of the hill. Grabbing the rope tied to my wrists, he starts pulling me behind him, fury radiating from his body. My shirt is torn and my skirt pulled up, exposing breasts and legs, skin scraped from being dragged up the hill. My mind races desperately for another escape.

But there is none. Arriving back where he left his Bag

of Props, he just drops my arms and uses his foot to roll me over on my stomach. When he reaches for the bag, my body stiffens in fearful anticipation. There is no mercy in his retaliation, his use of the leather paddle on my ass, my back, and those tender spots on my thighs! Over and over again, my cries fueling his enthusiasm, his endurance.

I gasp, my body nothing but pain and resistance. Covered in dirt, mouth filling with it every time I move my head. Thoughts of escape fading, strength waning. Now he's back on top of me, heavy, tying each outstretched limb to the hooks placed in a rectangle around us. Soon I am spread out like a canvas, my pussy exposed to everyone on that lawn.

He gets up, pleased. Puts his kilt back on. Now choosing his weapons carefully—the crop, then a whip, again!—he takes his time, relishing their impact, undoubtedly enjoying his audience. When I hear the switch, followed by that familiar, rattling sound, I have already given in, my mind curled up in the pain, my body immersed in surrender. My pussy open and wet, ready for the oversized, pumping dildo at the end of his fuck saw.

HARD THINGS

Joy Faolán

You know how some people just *have something* you can taste from across the room? You can smell it on them. You can feel them coming from a mile away. I never understood how they got it. It's a *glow*, a shining light in their aura that I can't describe. It's like they know something I don't. Like they've taken a piece of Life and claimed it as their own and nobody can ever take it away from them. I've always wanted that for myself. Who hasn't?

For several weeks, I had been asking my Mistress for a Hard Thing that I could do for her. I find that doing Hard Things is important because I have an intense need to *give* of myself and show her that I love her. I wished to give of myself in a way that would please her. I wanted it to be something for her pleasure alone, even if I found it not pleasurable…or, as it turned out, even if it consumed me with fear.

We had only spoken briefly about what we wanted to do during the precious few moments we had for a scene at a local event. When she asked me, "What do you want, Joy?" I found it nearly impossible to tell her. This wasn't because I was having problems communicating. Not by any stretch of the imagination. It is just that for me, play is not about the activity. It is about *giving myself*. It is about showing my submission through my suffering. When I play, I give the person I am playing with specific lines that are not to be crossed. As long as they play within those lines, I enjoy it because I get off on the pleasure of my partner. As soon as I dictate or even request a specific activity, it becomes about *me*, and I cease to get what I need out of the scene. Ma'am was very understanding about this, and after listening to my current list of limits, which included needles, she uttered three fateful words.

"What about scalpels?

I froze. *Shit*. My heart leaped up into my throat and my stomach took a nosedive down into my lower intestines.

Fuck!

I am unsure exactly how long it took my intestines to reorganize themselves in my body, but as they did, I came to a realization. This was my opportunity. This was my Hard Thing. My chance to give back to her, for all she has given to me. To show her how much I loved her. And *god*, I loved her. So much that it hurt.

I said I've never let anyone do that before. I said I was scared. I said I didn't know what to expect. I said I knew it would make her happy. I said I knew this was my Hard Thing. And then...

Then I said yes.

I knew that this would be intense. I knew it would not be easy. I knew, actually, that it would be *the* hardest thing I have done for her...for anyone.

I spent a good portion of the week before the event trying to gear myself up for the cutting scene on Friday. "We'll start small," she assured me...and I had to stop myself from typing, *Um, Ma'am? Have you met...you?* She does nothing halfway. I knew this would be no different.

I told her every night that I was frightened. I assured her that I was trying to work through my fear and that I was excited and eager and scared to tears all at the same time. And she, in her patient and quiet way, calmly watched as I worked through my panicked emotions and arrived, inevitably, at submission.

Walking into the medical dungeon was hard for me. I was dizzy. My heart was pounding in my ears. I felt like I couldn't breathe. I just knew if I stepped the wrong way on those heels I would teeter and fall flat on my face. I remember sitting in the chair while she set up, grinning over at me every now and again, cracking jokes. Then, just before we started, she took me in her arms and hugged me tightly. She told me I was her treasure

and that if I didn't want to do this, I didn't have to. She
told me that if I didn't feel I was ready, I could back
out. That if, halfway through, I decided that I didn't
want this anymore, I was to tell her. But I had already
decided.

When I say I decided, I mean that I was determined
to do this in the way one is determined to lose weight
or finish a project by a deadline. I wanted *so very badly*
for my Mistress to be proud of me in a way she has
never been before…but the *peace* about my decision
didn't come until after I felt the cold, sharp steel dragging along my flesh. I didn't *accept* it until after I felt her
drawing it across my skin and the heat of the blood that
seeped from the wound travel through me. The sensation trickled across my flesh and shot out through the
tips of my fingers and toes, and I couldn't help but gasp
at each little jolt of warm, intoxicating pain.

I don't know how long I lay there while she carved
into my skin. I was dizzy. I was trembling. I was crying.
All I could hear was her voice every now and again,
telling me I bled for her so beautifully and how proud
she was of me. What a *good girl* I was being.

Somewhere in the midst of it all, the heat of the pain
and the blood melted my fear away and left nothing but
perfect submission, perfect trust and perfect love. There
was nobody in the entire world in those moments except
her and me, Owner and property, bound by pain.

You know how some people just *have something*
inside them that you can taste from across a room? You

can smell it on them and feel them coming from a mile away. Like they've taken a piece of Life and claimed it as their own. Now I have it, too.

I have faced one of my most intense fears. I have walked through darkness, trembling and frightened... and not only did I survive, but I found light and love to embrace me as I came out the other end.

And I wear the marks of my journey with pride.

BREATHLESS

Dorla Moorehouse

The ridges of your index fingers press against my trachea, and I know that there will be exactly ninety heartbeats until I lose consciousness. Every time we begin, there's always the knowledge that accidents do happen, that people make mistakes, that they count wrong, lose control. Every time we begin, there's always the fear that this will be the last minute of my life, that something will go wrong and I'll never wake up. And then my family and friends will find out my dirty secret.

But if I'm going to die, at least I'm going to enjoy myself.

A staticky tingle runs along my neck and around my collarbone. Then, after the first dozen beats, the rest of my body starts to register what's happening. The sparks of sensation hop down my spine and roll down my chest until my nipples perk up, and both electric paths meet in my cunt. Now my legs are twitching, and I attempt to hook them around your hips, but you widen your stance. Your hands are all I get for now.

You won't even kiss me, not like this. That's for after, to reward me.

You won't do a single thing to me except hold me there and watch me gasp, watch my face flush, watch me thrash with a mix of arousal and fear.

No touch other than the pressure against my throat.

No look but the hard control in your eyes.

No words. We have other ways to communicate.

At twenty beats, my heart rate accelerates, caught up in the lack of air and the surge of my adrenaline. If you don't notice when the speed change happens, if you miscount, I'm in danger. Before I know it, I've lost count. Now, my life really is in your hands. I let my vision wander a minute, gaze on your ever-hardening cock, then zero back in on your face before the tunnel vision sets in. Your face is my focus. Your eyes are my strength and my trust.

I focus on your hands, meditating on your skin and the pressure it provides. You'll leave a few marks on me, two purple thumbprints in the gap between my collarbones, and from the correct angle, they'll look like a heart. I love the way those marks linger, the way I get to wear the evidence, even though I'll have to spend the better part of a week being careful with my wardrobe. I don't want to deal with questions—or worse, assumptions.

Trying to zero in on the feeling of your fingertips, on the bruise forming beneath my skin, I close my eyes, yearning to become pure sensation.

But you don't let me keep my eyes closed. Eye contact turns you on; staring into my dilated pupils as my body trembles, knowing your power over me, makes your cock grow even harder, makes your biceps tense. You shake me just a little, not enough to hurt, but enough to keep me here, in reality.

Eye contact lets you know I'm still conscious.

As I get closer to my limit, instinct tries to have its way with me. My fingers fiddle with the smooth cord attached to the bell I'm supposed to ring if I need to stop, but I won't let instinct win. I won't let fear take over. I want the reward that will come from my endurance. I feel my pulse everywhere when you have me trapped like this, and it's strongest in my cunt. All that rhythm, tightening my muscles, leaving me desperate for release that might not ever come if you forget yourself, if you hold me just a little too long.

Suddenly, your hands pull away. The bell drops, muffled by the carpet as my fingers engage, grip your shoulders, and I arch my hips to welcome your cock, pull you toward my panting lips for a kiss. I've barely had a chance to draw a full breath, and already your cock is inside me.

You never go slow, and I don't blame you. I've seen you growing harder by the second, your dick straining away from your abdomen, stiffening as I struggle. I pull you deeper into my body, muscles trembling as oxygen flows back in, hooking my legs and refusing to let go this time. Even though I'm lying down, I get a head rush, and for a moment I think that now I'm going to pass out, but I breathe deep, focus on your eyes, which are now fluttering open and closed as you get closer and closer to orgasm.

My own body has been ready from the moment you circled your fingers around my throat. The energy stored up rips free, and *this*—this is worth every bit of risk I take when I let you choke me. Heat slams out of my lungs and races out of my cunt and up through my chest, down through my legs, leaving me quaking against the pillows. When it's done, I'm swept right back up into your body, still rocking and thrusting, still absorbed in your own tension. I squeeze my thighs even tighter, gripping you so deep in my body that you can barely pull back. Your quads suddenly go rock hard and you stop moving, bracing yourself against me. Your fingers clench against my shoulders; there will be more bruises there, more marks of your ferocious devotion. As you reach your apex, rough, ragged breaths spill out of your throat, and when you're finally spent, you collapse on top of me, your heart pounding so hard that I can feel it setting off my own rhythm.

When you regain your senses, you place soft kisses at the spot on my throat where you've bruised me, and then move your lips along my collarbone, brushing the other areas you've marked in your passion.

"Are you sated, love?"

These are the first words I've heard from you since the moment you walked in my door, slammed it shut and carried me upstairs.

"Yes."

Tonight, when we go to dinner, I might not wear jewelry that conceals the bruise at the base of my throat. Tonight, I might not wear a high-collared shirt, or something with sleeves. Tonight, I might let people see, let them stare. Assumptions be damned.

Perhaps some secrets should be left open.

PERFECT GENTLEMAN

Donna George Storey

It's strange to be ringing her doorbell in a suit and tie. Perversely, he feels a stirring in his groin. She made it clear he wouldn't get any tonight unless he proved himself the perfect gentleman. Not that he's exactly gentleman material. The world of fancy manners and elaborate rules is about as sexy to him as a moldy fish fork.

She, on the other hand, looks very sexy in her old-fashioned dress cinched at the waist, hair swept up like a 1950s movie star. She waits outside his car, gazing regally into the distance, until he realizes he's supposed to open the door for her.

It's not a very promising start to the evening.

At the fussy French restaurant, he finds the menu incomprehensible and the waiter a pompous ass. She watches him the whole time, a smile playing at her lips, as if she knows he's hard as a rock under the white linen tablecloth.

Back on her porch, she extends her hand. "Thank you. I had a lovely time."

Enough is enough of this stupid game. Impulsively, he pulls her in tight for a kiss. She shakes free, glancing disapprovingly at the bulge in his trousers. Obviously he's failed the test.

Then she smiles and invites him inside.

Settling beside him on the sofa, several chaste inches away, she asks if he likes being a gentleman.

"It's not exactly my style, but you were right."

"About what?"

"The pleasures of restraint."

"*Self*-restraint," she corrects him. "It's turning me on, too."

His cock twitches. Suddenly his chances are looking much brighter.

"Do you want to keep playing?" she asks.

A simple *Fuck, no,* and he'd have her naked in bed in an instant, but something dark and twisted inside him makes him shrug and say, "Sure, why not?"

She narrows her eyes, cat-like. "Aren't you going to try to kiss me again?"

"May I?"

She giggles, but opens her mouth to him easily enough. Their tongues dance. She makes mewing noises, like she always does when she's ready to go at it. Yet whenever he tries to touch her breast, she twists away. She's not wearing a bra, either, but some weird, rigid undergarment—a corset? His penis throbs in his pants, oozing precome.

"Control yourself, please. Remember that I'm a lady."

In spite of her protest, she's the one who practically pulls him down on top of her. She wiggles, as if to resist, but it's the same move she makes when they're fucking, to get more friction on her clit.

"No, please," she whimpers as she lodges her thigh between his so she's putting just the right pressure on his cock.

"Come on, let's do it," he begs.

"You know I'm saving myself for my honeymoon."

Cut the crap, he almost blurts out. Suddenly he understands those suckers in days gone by who proposed in the heat of the moment. He's so desperate he'd do anything to get inside her pants. Stealthily, he grasps the hem of her skirt and eases it up. His fingers meet bare thigh above a band of stocking. He shivers. As coy as she pretends to be, the little cocktease is soaking wet down there.

She pushes him off, straightens her clothes. "I don't think you *are* a gentleman."

He blushes, oddly ashamed of his animal urges, which doesn't make sense because this woman is no spotless virgin. She's let him fuck her ass and liked it.

She purses her lips. "The trouble is, if I send you

home now, you'll just play with *your thing* by yourself, won't you? That's bad for your character."

He smiles weakly. It wouldn't be gentlemanly to lie.

She lifts her eyebrows. "But if you follow the rules, *my* rules, there might be hope for you. Will you be good?"

Does he have a choice? Kinky game or no, the woman always has you by the balls anyway. Of course, her "rules" are more dominatrix than Miss Manners. She orders him to pull his trousers and briefs down to his ankles. Then she makes him jack off so she can see what boys do to their willies when they're being naughty.

"And don't you dare come. A gentleman doesn't make a nasty mess in front of a lady."

She stands before him, eyes fixed on his busy hand. Slowly, she removes her dress, revealing a whorish, red satin corset and matching panties.

"Come here, damn it," he breathes.

"Keep wanking, you dirty little masturbator." She starts touching herself between her legs. "It's just like when you're at your computer, jerking off to porn, isn't it?"

He stops, panting.

"Good. You're learning self-control. We'll make a gentleman out of you yet." She jerks her chin at him. "Now back to work."

A few more tugs under her gaze and he has to stop again.

"Poor baby. You're doing so well." She sits next to

him and wraps her dainty hand around his shaft. "If I rub it, do you promise not to make a mess?"

He chokes out a pleading "Yes." Why does he love this so much? The insults, the frustration, the delicious pleasure of being seen for the horny bastard he is.

She jerks him, faster and faster. "Don't you dare come," she sings. "Stop me just in time."

"Stop," he hisses.

She brushes his cheek tenderly. "How long has it been like this? You were hard when you came to pick me up, weren't you?"

He nods.

"Four hours of *expectation*. Not bad for the first time. When I'm done training you, you'll be a perfect gentleman who can stand up in a lady's presence all night long."

The thought of such sweet torture makes him groan.

"Tonight you'll get a reward for trying. But you can't touch it anymore. Keep your hands flat on the sofa like a good boy." She stands and heads for the kitchen. What he'd do to bury himself in that luscious, scarlet satin ass.

She returns with a timer and punches in one minute.

"If you don't come by the time this goes off, the next stop for you is a cold shower." Her eyes sparkle with challenge.

The numbers tick down.

His fingers tingle helplessly at his sides. "Can you, uh, do something to help?"

"I suppose I could."

Forty-five seconds to go.

At last she bends over and takes his throbbing cock in her mouth.

Hot. Liquid. Heaven.

He's so used to holding back, he instinctively steels himself against the sensation.

Thirty-eight seconds.

Her soft lips fuck him, up and down. For such a proper lady, she gives head like a pro.

His balls ache terribly from the hours of cruel teasing. Suddenly his thigh and ass muscles stiffen. His cock slides deeper into the wet softness. With a strangled cry, he shoots straight into that taunting pink mouth, flooding her with his seed in spasms of spine-shattering bliss.

She swallows it down to the buzz of the timer's bell.

"Such lovely manners," she whispers in his ear. "But I'm sure you can do better next time."

He sinks back into the sofa, floating.

Maybe there's something to being a gentleman after all?

ABOUT
THE EDITOR

RACHEL KRAMER BUSSEL (rachelkramerbussel.com) is an author, editor and blogger. She has edited over fifty books of erotica, including *Serving Him: Sexy Stories of Submission; Please, Sir; Please, Ma'am; He's on Top; She's on Top; Cheeky Spanking Stories; Bottoms Up; Spanked: Red-Cheeked Erotica; Lust in Latex; Flying High; The Big Book of Orgasms; Gotta Have It: 69 Stories of Sudden Sex; Anything for You; Baby Got Back: Anal Erotica; Suite Encounters; Going Down; Irresistible; Obsessed; Women in Lust; Surrender; Orgasmic; Fast Girls; Do Not Disturb; Going Down; Tasting Him; Tasting Her; Caught Looking; Hide and Seek; Crossdressing;* and is Best Bondage Erotica series editor. Her anthologies have won eight IPPY (Independent Publisher) Awards, and submission-themed

Surrender won the National Leather Association Samois Anthology Award. Her work has been published in over one hundred anthologies, including *Best American Erotica 2004* and *2006*. She wrote the popular "Lusty Lady" column for the *Village Voice*.

Rachel has written for *AVN, Bust,* Cleansheets.com, *Cosmopolitan, Curve,* The Daily Beast, Elle.com, TheFrisky.com, *Glamour*, Gothamist, *Harper's Bazaar*, The Hairpin, Huffington Post, *Inked*, Mediabistro, *Newsday, New York Post, New York Observer, Penthouse,* The Root, Salon, *San Francisco Chronicle, Time Out New York,* xoJane and *Zink,* among others. She has appeared on "The Gayle King Show," "The Martha Stewart Show," "The Berman and Berman Show," NY1 and Showtime's "Family Business." She speaks at colleges, conferences and sex toy stores, does readings and teaches erotic writing workshops across the country. She blogs at lustylady.blogspot.com and Tweets @raquelita.

More from Rachel Kramer Bussel

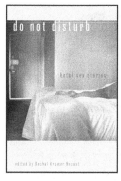

Do Not Disturb
Hotel Sex Stories
Edited by Rachel Kramer Bussel

A delicious array of hotel hookups where it seems like anything can happen—and quite often does. "If *Do Not Disturb*
were a hotel, it would be a 5-star hotel with the luxury of
24/7 entertainment available."—Erotica Revealed
978-1-57344-344-9 $14.95

Bottoms Up
Spanking Good Stories
Edited by Rachel Kramer Bussel

As sweet as it is kinky, *Bottoms Up*
will propel you to pick up a paddle
and share in both pleasure and pain,
or perhaps simply turn the other
cheek.
ISBN 978-1-57344-362-3 $15.95

Orgasmic
Erotica for Women
Edited by Rachel Kramer Bussel

What gets you off ? Let *Orgasmic*
count the ways...with 25 stories
focused on female orgasm, there is
something here for every reader.
ISBN 978-1-57344-402-6 $14.95

Please, Sir
Erotic Stories of Female Submission
Edited by Rachel Kramer Bussel

These 22 kinky stories celebrate the
thrill of submission by women who
know exactly what they want.
ISBN 978-1-57344-389-0 $14.95

Fast Girls
Erotica for Women
Edited by Rachel Kramer Bussel

Fast Girls celebrates the girl with a
reputation, the girl who goes all the
way, and the girl who doesn't know
how to say "no."
ISBN 978-1-57344-384-5 $14.95

Many More Than Fifty Shades of Erotica

Happy Endings Forever And Ever

Dark Secret Love
A Story of Submission
By Alison Tyler

Inspired by her own BDSM exploits and private diaries,
Alison Tyler draws on twenty-five years of penning sultry stories to create a scorchingly hot work of fiction, a
memoir-inspired novel with reality at its core. A modern-day
Story of O, a *9 1/2 Weeks*-style journey fueled by lust, longing
and the search for true love.
ISBN 978-1-57344-956-4 $16.95

High-Octane Heroes
Erotic Romance for Women
Edited by Delilah Devlin

One glance and your heart will melt—these
chiseled, brave men will ignite your fantasies
with their courage and charisma. Award-
winning romance writer Delilah Devlin has
gathered stories of hunky, red-blooded guys
who enter danger zones in the name of
duty, honor, country and even love.
ISBN 978-1-57344-969-4 $15.95

Duty and Desire
Military Erotic Romance
Edited by Kristina Wright

The only thing stronger than the call of
duty is the call of desire. *Duty and Desire*
enlists a team of hot-blooded men and
women from every branch of the military who serve their country and follow
their hearts.
ISBN 978-1-57344-823-9 $15.95

Smokin' Hot Firemen
Erotic Romance Stories for Women
Edited by Delilah Devlin

Delilah delivers tales of these courageous
men breaking down doors to steal readers'
hearts! *Smokin' Hot Firemen* imagines the
romantic possibilities of being held against
a massively muscled chest by a man whose
mission is to save lives and serve *every* need.
ISBN 978-1-57344-934-2 $15.95

Only You
Erotic Romance for Women
Edited by Rachel Kramer Bussel

Only You is full of tenderness, raw passion,
love, longing and the many emotions that
kindle true romance. The couples in *Only
You* test the boundaries of their love to
make their relationships stronger.
ISBN 978-1-57344-909-0 $15.95

Red Hot Erotic Romance

Obsessed
Erotic Romance for Women
Edited by Rachel Kramer Bussel

These stories sizzle with the kind of obsession that is fueled by our deepest desires, the ones that hold couples together, the ones that haunt us and don't let go. Whether just-blooming passions, rekindled sparks or reinvented relationships, these lovers put the object of their obsession first.
ISBN 978-1-57344-718-8 $14.95

Passion
Erotic Romance for Women
Edited by Rachel Kramer Bussel

Love and sex have always been intimately intertwined—and *Passion* shows just how delicious the possibilities are when they mingle in this sensual collection edited by award-winning author Rachel Kramer Bussel.
ISBN 978-1-57344-415-6 $14.95

Girls Who Bite
Lesbian Vampire Erotica
Edited by Delilah Devlin

Bestselling romance writer Delilah Devlin and her contributors add fresh girl-on-girl blood to the pantheon of the paranormal. The stories in *Girls Who Bite* are varied, unexpected, and soul-scorching.
ISBN 978-1-57344-715-7 $14.95

Irresistible
Erotic Romance for Couples
Edited by Rachel Kramer Bussel

This prolific editor has gathered the most popular fantasies and created a sizzling, no-holds-barred collection of explicit encounters in which couples turn their deepest desires into reality.
978-1-57344-762-1 $14.95

Heat Wave
Hot, Hot, Hot Erotica
Edited by Alison Tyler

What could be sexier or more seductive than bare, sun-warmed skin? Bestselling erotica author Alison Tyler gathers explicit stories of summer sex bursting with the sweet eroticism of swimsuits, sprinklers, and ripe strawberries.
ISBN 978-1-57344-710-2 $15.95

Best Erotica Series

"Gets racier every year."—*San Francisco Bay Guardian*

Best Women's Erotica 2014
Edited by Violet Blue
ISBN 978-1-62778-003-2 $15.95

Best Women's Erotica 2013
Edited by Violet Blue
ISBN 978-1-57344-898-7 $15.95

Best Women's Erotica 2012
Edited by Violet Blue
ISBN 978-1-57344-755-3 $15.95

Best Bondage Erotica 2014
Edited by Rachel Kramer Bussel
ISBN 978-1-62778-012-4 $15.95

Best Bondage Erotica 2013
Edited by Rachel Kramer Bussel
ISBN 978-1-57344-897-0 $15.95

Best Bondage Erotica 2012
Edited by Rachel Kramer Bussel
ISBN 978-1-57344-754-6 $15.95

Best Lesbian Erotica 2014
Edited by Kathleen Warnock
ISBN 978-1-62778-002-5 $15.95

Best Lesbian Erotica 2013
Edited by Kathleen Warnock
Selected and introduced by
Jewelle Gomez
ISBN 978-1-57344-896-3 $15.95

Best Lesbian Erotica 2012
Edited by Kathleen Warnock
Selected and introduced by
Sinclair Sexsmith
ISBN 978-1-57344-752-2 $15.95

Best Gay Erotica 2014
Edited by Larry Duplechan
Selected and introduced by Joe Manetti
ISBN 978-1-62778-001-8 $15.95

Best Gay Erotica 2013
Edited by Richard Labonté
Selected and introduced by Paul Russell
ISBN 978-1-57344-895-6 $15.95

Best Gay Erotica 2012
Edited by Richard Labonté
Selected and introduced by
Larry Duplechan
ISBN 978-1-57344-753-9 $15.95

Best Fetish Erotica
Edited by Cara Bruce
ISBN 978-1-57344-355-5 $15.95

Best Bisexual Women's Erotica
Edited by Cara Bruce
ISBN 978-1-57344-320-3 $15.95

Best Lesbian Bondage Erotica
Edited by Tristan Taormino
ISBN 978-1-57344-287-9 $16.95

* Free book of equal or lesser value. Shipping and applicable sales tax extra.
Cleis Press • (800) 780-2279 • orders@cleispress.com
www.cleispress.com

Ordering is easy! Call us toll free or fax us to place your MC/VISA order.
You can also mail the order form below with payment to:
Cleis Press, 2246 Sixth St., Berkeley, CA 94710.

ORDER FORM

QTY	TITLE	PRICE
___	_____	____
___	_____	____
___	_____	____
___	_____	____
___	_____	____
___	_____	____
___	_____	____
___	_____	____

SUBTOTAL _____

SHIPPING _____

SALES TAX _____

TOTAL _____

Add $3.95 postage/handling for the first book ordered and $1.00 for each additional book. Outside North America, please contact us for shipping rates. California residents add 9% sales tax. Payment in U.S. dollars only.

* Free book of equal or lesser value. Shipping and applicable sales tax extra.

Cleis Press • Phone: (800) 780-2279 • Fax: (510) 845-8001
orders@cleispress.com • www.cleispress.com
You'll find more great books on our website

Follow us on Twitter @cleispress • Friend/fan us on Facebook

Printed in the United States
By Bookmasters